The Bishop
in the
Old Neighborhood

Also by Andrew M. Greeley

Bishop Blackie Ryan Mysteries
The Bishop and the Missing L Train
The Bishop and the Beggar Girl of St. Germain
The Bishop in the West Wing
The Bishop Goes to The *University*

Nuala Anne McGrail Novels

The O'Malleys in the Twentieth Century
A Midwinter's Tale
Younger Than Springtime
A Christmas Wedding
September Song
Second Spring
Golden Years

All About Women
Angel Fire
Angel Light
Contract with an Angel
Faithful Attraction
The Final Planet
Furthermore!: Memories of a Parish Priest
God Game
Star Bright!
Summer at the Lake
White Smoke
Sacred Visions (editor with Michael Cassutt)
The Book of Love (editor with Mary G. Durkin)
Emerald Magic (editor)

The *Bishop*

in the

Old Neighborhood

• A BLACKIE RYAN STORY •

Andrew M. Greeley

A Tom Doherty Associates Book
NEW YORK

THE BISHOP IN THE OLD NEIGHBORHOOD

Copyright © 2005 by Andrew M. Greeley Enterprises, Ltd.

A Forge Book
Published by Tom Doherty Associates, LLC
175 Fifth Avenue
New York, NY 10010

Forge® is a registered trademark of Tom Doherty Associates, LLC.

ISBN 0-765-30334-5

Printed in the United States of America

Author's Note

The "neighborhood" in this story is a fictionalized and fantasy version of the neighborhood of my preschool years. I recall it to memory—more particularly the Mudhole, so that as the French fella said, remembered, it may continue to exist. Regentrification is slipping slowly towards it and even into it. Whether and when it will change dramatically is not the subject of this story, only what the change might be like. St. Lucy's parish and church—where I was baptized—disappeared in 1977, the kind of planning mistake that Bishop Ryan laments in the early pages of this story. We Chicago Irish clergy have little taste or concern for history and hence little wisdom about our future.

All the people, places, and institutions in this story are products of my perhaps hyperactive imagination or are used fictitiously. In particular the units and personnel of the Chicago Police Department presented herein are fiction, as are the various offices of prosecuting attorneys and their staffs.

The Bishop
in the
Old Neighborhood

Blackie

"Blackwood, there's trouble in the old neighborhood! Murder in the sanctuary of the church!"

I glanced away from my computer and remarked again to myself that as he grew older, Sean Cardinal Cronin had come to look like a very High Church Anglican cleric, save for the scarlet shirts the latter affected. Tall, handsome, trim, broad-shouldered, white hair, immaculately groomed, perfectly tailored, and with a large ruby ring, a bejeweled pectoral cross, and only a touch of red at the edge of his Roman collar, he was much too presentable to be one of ours. Generally our kind look like tired and corrupt old men in funny dresses. Or dumpy little men in jeans and Chicago sports jackets like me.

The Anglican illusion faded when one saw the wild Celtic blue eyes—a gallowglass mercenary warrior disguised as a prelate.

"I have heard no alarms from St. Praxides," I said, referring to my own neighborhood of origin.

"I meant the West Side, of course," he said impatiently. "A locked church murder at St. Lucy's! Three bodies!"

"Deplorable," I sighed.

And fascinating.

"Mick Woljy wants the place reconsecrated right away and I'm off to Rome to pick up some heavy markers. So you'd better see to it!"

"Markers" are part of a Chicago theory of economic exchange, though the theory originates not at *The* University but at City Hall. Suppose you ask me for a "personal favor." I respond, "Name it and you got it." Then I hold your marker, which entitles you to a similar exchange, no questions asked.

"They don't believe in markers over there."

A wicked grin crossed his face. The return of the gallowglass.

"They'll believe in mine . . . Look, do you know Mick Woljy?"

He put down his suitcase and the garment bag carrying his cardinalatial finery, shoved aside a stack of precious computer output, and sat on the edge of my easy chair, a pilgrim ready with his staff in hand and his loins girded.

"Mikal Wolodyjowski," I spoke his name with a proper Polish pronunciation, "by the length of his name and his demeanor a cultivated member of the Polish nobility. We Irish don't have any such."

As best as I can transliterate the name is pronounced *volodyovaski*.

"He's a great priest," Milord Cronin repeated the defensive clerical cliché. "He's held that parish together for years, long after we should have closed it. Now it's gentrifying he has everyone on his side, blacks, whites, Hispanics, old-timers in the parish, and the yuppie newcomers. He says that the superstitions in the neighborhood are multicultural. He wants the church reconsecrated today—as soon as the cops get out. The school opens again next week. He'll probably have to build a new and bigger one next year . . . So get out there and reconsecrate the church."

Milord did not perceive the contradiction. They should have closed the schools years ago, but now there would be yet another new school. I sighed mentally. I had not been able to exorcise those who proclaimed themselves city planners for the Archdiocese.

"I doubt that we can do that," I replied with my loudest sigh of protest. "It is after all a temporary basement church, even if it is almost a century old. It was never consecrated in the first place."

The Poles and the Germans built beautiful churches when they arrived in America. We put up parochial schools and used the basement "school hall" for a church until we could build a "new" church. In some places for reasons of hard times, poverty, or pastoral indolence, the dream of the new church faded away.

Milord Cronin frowned. He did not like liturgical rules to interfere with his plans. He leaned back in the chair, loins still girded but staff on the floor.

"Mickey and I went through the seminary, then on to Rome for graduate school. We were never exactly close friends—hard to break through that Polish formality. Still we got along all right. He's an extraordinary guy, brilliant, cultivated, knows everything. The people out in the neighborhood seem to adore his European aristocratic style . . ."

He shut his eyes as if to blot out an unhappy memory.

"Every Polish priest in the city thinks that he ought to have my job. And they're right, Blackwood. He should be in this room talking to you, not me . . . Only reason he doesn't have it is that he's Polish. In those days they were afraid to take that risk."

"I doubt that I would be in this room if Pan Mikal was in the room at the other end of the corridor."

"He's never said a word to me about it, Blackwood, nor as far as I know to anyone else. Totally loyal, though he is incapable of anything else. Yet it must bother him."

"Arguably he prefers reviving St. Lucy's to dealing with the Curia Romana."

"I owe him, Blackwood." He bounded out of the chair, metaphorical staff back in hand. "He needs help out there. I won't tolerate murders in one of my churches. See to it!"

He disappeared out the door of my office, a night train rushing through the darkness. His trip to Rome boded no good for anyone. The subject of his markers doubtless pertained to his approaching seventy-fifth birthday. He would be expected to submit his resignation. It would not be accepted, because the Curia lived in mortal fear of Sean Cronin. They knew full well over there that he did not give a damn about them and their increasingly empty power. A re-

Andrew M. Greeley

signed Sean Cronin would be an even looser cannon. He might insist, even demand that his resignation be accepted. Or he might impose conditions for staying in power that would push them into a corner.

Nor were they likely to find consolation in appearances of declining health. Nora Cronin, his foster sister and sister-in-law (and one time long ago, as he had admitted to me, his temporary lover), had participated in a makeover aided and abetted by a certain all-seeing little auxiliary bishop—one cup of coffee every morning, one small glass of Bushmills every evening, exercise every day, proper meals (of the sort I would never eat), a day off every week, a limited schedule of confirmation and anniversary appointments in the parishes, and a cap on the number of staff meetings a week. This remake had permitted the Cronin genes to reassert themselves and he would appear in Rome as indestructible.

The good Nora had not, however, been able to constrain his manic gallowglass moods. I doubt that she wanted to.

I called my friend Mike Casey—aka Mike the Cop—for the lay of the land out in St. Lucy's.

"It's the Lake Street L," Mike assured me. "Developers have finally figured out that it's twenty minutes to downtown inside Chicago just as it is across Austin Boulevard in Oak Park. So there's a boom between Central and Austin for six blocks from West End to Race. The old stock is prime for rehab, just like Ravenswood. The homes on West End are as elegant as any in the city. And the new town houses in close to the L are designed for prosperous Yuppies. Cops are cleaning up drug action against the south end of the tracks. There's St. Lucy's and St. Catherine's grade schools and Fenwick and Trinity High Schools. Too bad they closed Sienna. Anyway, Austin is ready for rebirth and as a native of Austin like Sean Cronin I say it's high time."

I wondered to myself what would happen when the poor were exiled from the city to suburbs and the city, like Paris, became a bastion of the white upper middle class. Again. Many of the neighborhoods of the city had been resegregated as blacks pushing for living space had moved into white neighborhoods and whites, panicked by real estate brokers called "blockbusters," fled farther out in the city's rings and into the suburbs. Then these neighborhoods deteriorated as the black middle class itself fled, pushed by street gangs, drug dealers, and the neighborhoods deteriorated physically. The next phase was the rediscovery of the possibility of the neighborhoods by the new urban professional class in search of good transportation routes back downtown. In a suburb like Oak Park, just across Austin Boulevard, the blockbusters had been foiled by property value insurance which protected home owners from panic. So now Austin was creeping towards emergence as a multiracial, multiclass community—a hard journey to rebirth.

"The three murders will delay that rebirth?"

"For a while maybe. The change, now that it's started, is too powerful to stop. It's dawning on people, then on developers, that transportation is the driving force in this city."

How did we ever forget that, I wondered.

"And the local cops?"

"Fifteenth Precinct—Austin. Over on Chicago Avenue near Laramie. Lieutenant Dawn Collins is the head of Homicide there. Area Five Homicide may try to take over but only if they want a fight with Dawn. She's a real stand-up cop. I'll tell her you'll be out there. She's African-American and Catholic."

"Aren't they all?"

I sighed loudly. There ought not to be violent crimes, much less in a church during the glorious fading days of August.

Declan

My trouble started on a Catholic retreat for cops.

My name is Declan O'Donnell and I'm a cop. I'm a lawyer too. And I'm studying for a Ph.D. in psychology. Overeducated, overqualified. But basically I'm a cop.

My father is a cop. My grandfather is a retired cop. I have two uncles, one on either side, who are cops. My little sister is in the Academy. My great-grandfather was also a cop for the old South Park district. Four generations of South Side Irish cops.

They are all stand-up cops, as I have been told repeatedly in my five years on the force—kind of a warning that I must live up to that tradition. I went on the force as soon as I had graduated from college. When my romantic life kind of sputtered out, I went to law school at night. Better than hanging around singles' bars.

All my family predecessors were detectives. They all worked hard on the street for many years before they made detective, earned it as they would say. Once they were detectives, and by all accounts, brilliant at their work, they had no interest in further promotion and indeed seemed to have turned it down. On the other hand I'm already a detective sergeant. What's worse I'm in a "Special Unit."

My family doesn't like these achievements. They don't like the law degree either, much less the Ph.D. Somehow these are not the kinds of things a stand-up cop should do. They hint that I shouldn't be spying on other cops. I tell them that's not what my Unit does, but I'm not sure they believe me. I don't explain, because I'm not supposed to. Actually when we find dirt about cops we turn it over to Internal Affairs and wash our hands of it. People say we're snoops. We're not. We're sniffers.

I should say that my little sister, who wrongly adores me, doesn't think I'm a poor cop. But what does she know?

Anyway, I didn't want to make this annual retreat for police officers. I feel suffocated when I'm surrounded by a lot of cops. I respect them and I admire them, well mostly; but I'm not like a lot of them. I would feel like a straight man might at a retreat for gays. However, everyone says that the retreat will be good for me. By which they meant it might "straighten me out."

I'm a good Catholic. Well, what's that? I go to church. Not every Sunday, but most of the time. I do volunteer work at my parish with elderly people. I pray, not often enough. I don't commit a lot of sins. But I'm not as good as I should be either. Maybe the retreat will do me some good. Besides, like my mother says, the retreat master will be a nun. One of my uncles says that might not be a good thing. I ask my priest about her and he says she's very good, but a bit of a feminist. I figure that I won't mind that because my boss in the Unit is a pretty thirty-six-year-old Asian woman with a mind as sharp as a bayonet.

The nun was indeed very tough, a solid woman in an ill-fitting pantsuit and not a hint of makeup who didn't smile much and didn't seem to like men and especially cops. She called herself a "facilitator" because, I suspect, "retreat master" is no longer politically correct. Yet she knew her stuff. She knew all about cops and the things they did. Most of my colleagues squirmed as she described the things that men do to women and, as she saw it, cops do to women. Since I'm relatively innocent in such matters—how can you abuse your wife if you don't have one?—I listened complacently. I thought to myself that she doesn't really know the spiritual needs of cops. We know how ugly human beings can be. We work in a world of cruelty, viciousness, absurdity. For many of us it is too much. We harden our hearts. That's why police marriages often break up, why cops become addicts—drugs, gambling, sex, whatever—and why they often blow their brains out with their service revolvers. They need a little hope. She was not about to give us any of that.

Then she hit me with a punch in the stomach.

"Many men become police officers because they're bullies. They think that because they have a badge and a gun they can push other people around—women, gays, drunks, homeless people, blacks, Hispanics, Asians, anyone they can arrest. Basically many of you are torturers at heart. You love to cause people pain. You were schoolyard bullies when you were growing up. You picked on kids smaller than you were, on kids who were a little strange, on black kids, and on little girls with glasses and braces and pigtails. You were proud of it. You were great big tough men and you could get away with cruelty. You ought to have been ashamed of yourselves. Then you became police so you could continue to be bullies. Before you face a just God who will punish you for your miserable sadism, you must find those whom you have victimized and make amends, whether you abused them last week or when you were a schoolyard sadist."

I didn't hear anything more she said. I remembered the film *Flatliners* in which Kevin Bacon had to seek forgiveness for teasing Kimberly Scott when she was a little black kid in a white school. I was twelve years old and I didn't link it to my own career as a bully in the yard of our parish school, but quickly forgot about it. Fourteen years later both the film and my career came back and guilt poured into my soul.

I considered talking to Sister in one the breaks, but couldn't find the courage to tell her that I had been a bully, not with my physical strength, which then as now is minimal, but with my mean Irish tongue, which I inherited from family discourse. We were always cutting each other up. We meant nothing by it. Or maybe we did. But it was part of life. So I would find kids in the schoolyard who would be vulnerable to ridicule and tear them apart. I was the scourge of recess time for a year or two, then grew out of it, perhaps because the family verbal culture had lost its attractiveness. I decided then that I didn't want to hurt anyone with my quick wit and sharp tongue, not even my obnoxious uncles.

Yet I had done so, particularly to a little girl, dark-skinned, cross-eyed, skinny, frizzled hair, bucktoothed, and Italian—no, Sicilian. She used to run from me at recess time as I shouted insults about her size, her teeth, and her Mafia background. "Ugly little greaser," was one of my milder insults.

Did I enjoy hurting her? I must have. Kids that age enjoy hurting one another. I was just playing the game. It didn't worry me, not till Sister kicked me in the gut.

I tried to remember her name that night in bed. She had moved away from St. Thomas More and didn't graduate with us. Where had she gone? What was her name, how could I find her? I climbed out of bed at three to hunt through our grammar-school class pictures. I found her just as the sun came up in a fifth-grade picture. Camilla Datillo. She was indeed a skinny little kid with thick glasses and dark skin. The glasses reminded me of another reason I delighted in tormenting her. She was too bright for her own good. I promised God that I would find Camilla and apologize to her.

How would I find her? Was I not a member of Annamaria Huong's sniffers? Aka the Dragon Lady?

Our Unit's task is to sniff around the city for the smell of corruption where the stench was especially rancid and no one else was looking at it. A certain proportion of the human race believes that it is possible to steal and escape without being caught—from shoplifters to corporate CEOs. Wherever one looked in society there would always be some kind of corruption. Most of the thieves are caught because they are not as smart as they think they are. But some of them are very smart—in the government, in health care, in business, in law, in the media, in the Church. We go after the smart ones. We get our hints from the press, from whistle-blowers, from disgusted employees, and especially from cops. We're not head-hunters or scalpers with political ambitions, we avoid publicity, we never give press conferences, we turn our research over to the Superintendent, who does what he thinks best with it, and retire into the background. Normally you can't find our fingerprints on what we've collected.

Oddly enough we get more credit than we deserve. The tendency these days when some new scandal blows up is for cops to say to one another, "That's Annamaria and her sniffers again." We just smile quietly.

It's hard to find that we exist. My business card merely asserts that I'm a member of the Chicago Police Department and gives a phone number at department headquarters and my e-mail address. We never meet at Fourteenth and Michigan. Our actual headquarters is in the basement of the Dragon Lady's home in the Balmoral District north of Wrigley Field (a place for yappy scum to gather, not for Sox fans from Thomas More). It's a big, high-tech room filled with computers. We have access to every important database in the world, to some of which entrance is quite illegal. The Dragon Lady herself designed it, so of course it's practically perfect. We don't drive police cars and park a couple of blocks away from her house and enter the basement through an alley door.

She even has spare rooms for us in the attic of the big old place where we can sleep when we've been working all night. The rooms are strictly segregated by gender because Annamaria is a very strict Catholic. Like me. Well usually.

So how come I work for this somewhat ethereal, not to say ectoplasmic group, presided over by a woman right out of *Terry and the Pirates*?

I wasn't a very promising rookie cop, which didn't surprise me. My problem, my first partner told me, was that I thought too much, then rushed into a situation too late. She warned me that I wouldn't be a good cop unless I learned to make instinctive decisions. I agreed with her that I had the problem.

Then in one particular investigation, I had an insight into a con that was going down and charged into the situation. The watch commander told me that I was an idiot, that the woman I tackled was not dangerous, and I would be charged with abusing a woman. Then it turned out that I was dead right about the perp and that she was very dangerous. If I had not jumped her, several cops, not excluding myself, would have died. The watch commander never apologized, nor did the cops in my family who called me as soon as it went down to tell me that I was a damn fool.

Then Captain Huong had invited me to meet her for tea and a discussion about the possibility of a transfer to her Unit. She gave me an address which I knew was not a precinct station and suggested I enter through the alley and the back door. I looked her up in the directory and she was listed as a captain at Fourteenth and Michigan.

So we had tea in her parlor, under a painting of *Mary Help of Christians*. She wore jeans and a Berkeley sweatshirt and was sweet and friendly and punctilious about the making of tea. Yet I knew even then that I was dealing with the Dragon Lady.

We discussed religion, politics, my family background, and police work in the city—with much nodding of heads and quirky little giggles. She asked a couple of casual questions about my incident. Then two of her adorable kids drifted in from school and we chatted with them. They seemed to think I was a nice man, or at least a funny one. That may have helped. However, the Dragon Lady was inscrutable.

As I was leaving—by the back door—she said casually, "I'll put in for a transfer to our Unit and a promotion to detective sergeant."

"What does our Unit do?" I asked, not being quick enough to say I'd think about it.

"We sniff," she said with a characteristic giggle.

So I became one of the sniffers.

Hence it was easy to trace down my "dirty little Sicilian bitch," as I had called her in the schoolyard, half-afraid that I might find her. I did not find encouragement in the discovery that her father owned a very successful pasta company and was not connected with the Outfit, that she had attended Trinity High School, Harvard

University, University of Chicago Law School (law review) and was an Assistant State's Attorney for the County of Cook.

I felt inferior. Loyola and John Marshall were not in the same league. Neither was River Forest. At least my barbed tongue had not ruined her life. No need to apologize.

Right?

I heard the retreat facilitator's voice say, "Wrong!"

Well, there was no hurry, was there?

Then one day I was hanging around the Criminal Court Building at Twenty-sixth and California sniffing about a link between a Mexican religious order house and a drug gang. A gorgeous young woman strode by me and turned into a courtroom. She was wearing a severely tailored black suit and looked like a young Sophia Loren with whom I had fallen in love on Turner Classic Movies.

"Who's that?" I asked the State's Attorney (male) with whom I'd been chatting innocently—as if anything we sniffers did was innocent.

"Cami Datillo," he said reverently. "Don't even think about it!"

"Why not?"

"You try to hit on her, it would be like you were run over by a Bradley Fighting Vehicle."

How do you apologize to someone like that?

I did notice her classically lovely, if immobile, face and deep, threatening brown eyes, and long, sleek black hair. For a moment she stopped in midflight to talk to another lawyer whose skin color suggested that he might be Sicilian too. She transformed herself into an Italian—dancing eyes, sweeping gestures, and quick laughs.

I could fall in love with her.

That was out of the question. I had to apologize, only not right then.

Then one pleasant mid-August morning, the Dragon Lady woke me up.

"Would you mind, Declan, if I asked you to drive out to Austin? There's been a triple murder in St. Lucy's Church. That's on Lake

Street, just east of Austin Boulevard. You take the Congress to Austin and turn north. After you go under the L tracks you turn right on Lake and go to Mayfield 5900 West. Lieutenant Dawn Collins is in charge of the investigation. She will be expecting you."

"I'm on my way."

A giggle.

"Eat your breakfast first and be sure you drink the green tea I gave you."

I knew that she would ask, so I ate my breakfast and drank the awful green tea.

I presented my card to Lieutenant Collins, who glanced at it and put it in the large bag she was carrying.

"Cami," she said to the woman in a beige summer suit that was standing next to her, "this is one of Captain Huong's sniffers."

Cami considered me for a moment, nodded, and turned away with obvious disinterest. My heart pounded and my stomach churned.

"I live in River Forest," Camilla said to Lieutenant Collins, "and I didn't even know that this poor, dilapidated old church was here. What a shame to have a crime in it!"

"Old it surely is," said a funny little man who had appeared with us, seemingly out of nowhere, "and arguably poor, but hardly dilapidated. Consider the tuck pointing outside the newly painted window frames. Also the excellent altar, statues, stations of the cross, and stained-glass window. Also ponder the freshly polished pews, floor, and candlesticks. Taken together they suggest careful and tasteful attention."

He was short and pudgy with Coke-bottle eyeglasses and deep blue eyes blinking behind the glasses. He wore black jeans, a black tee shirt, and a very old Chicago Bears windbreaker. If he had not spoken, we would not have known he was there.

"Hi, Father Ryan! I'm Dawn Collins. Superintendent Casey said you would be coming out. This is State's Attorney Camilla Datillo. And this is . . . a police officer."

"Bishop Ryan, I think!" Camilla said with a broad smile.

So she had excellent teeth. The orthodontics had done their work.

"O'Donnell, Bishop," I said, offering my hand.

"Call me Blackie!"

Blackie

I had turned off Austin Boulevard at West End, a parkway between Washington Boulevard and the Lake Street L tracks. Milord Cronin had forgotten that my late father, Ned Ryan, had grown up in Austin and that I knew all about the neighborhood. Austin had an affluent suburban community in the late nineteenth century with its own Town Hall and elegant homes and apartment hotels, only twenty minutes away from the Loop on the Northwestern Railroad. The Northwestern was gone now, but the L ran now on the Northwestern embankment. Chicago had expanded on the spokes of the railroads coming into the city from all over the country. It was doing so again.

Austin was founded by one Henry Austin in 1865 as a temperance settlement. For many years it was rural area like its next-door neighbor and perennial rival to the west—Oak Park. It grew rapidly after its separation from Cicero Township and annexation to Chicago in 1899. The neighborhood around the transportation arteries—the Northwestern and the L—was an elegant and prosperous residential district before and immediately after the war. Oak Park resisted annexation and thus remained distinct from Chicago which was its salvation in the 1970s when the tide of racial resegregation (pushed by real panic-peddling real estate "blockbusters") washed up against the wall of Austin Boulevard—the boundary between Chicago and Oak Park—and stopped.

The years between 1920 and 1950 were a golden age for Austin. The core of the old village remained in the area around the L tracks from Race Street to West End—parkways, expensive Queen Anne homes, mansions on West End and Midway Park, the so-called Austin Town Hall modeled after Independence Hall in Philadelphia. Irish and Italians and Greeks moved into the neighborhood and the areas both north and south of the core expanded with dense populations living in apartments and two flats—always weak in the face of resegregation. Beginning in the 1960s the neighborhood changed, at first slowly, then rapidly. Houses were abandoned, others were demolished. Crime increased. St. Lucy's parish, founded in 1907, reported 1,300 families in 1968 and 170 families in 1971. Most of the white flight occurred on "moving day" (May 1, 1970). The Archdiocese almost closed it in 1980 when Monsignor Wolodyjowski begged for a chance to save the school and the parish. Miraculously he turned it around. He became the most important figure in central Austin, winning the confidence of African-Americans and the few remaining whites.

The old homes on West End were comparable with mansions from Evanston or Hyde Park or Oak Park in the same era but there had been no legal boundary or urban-renewal project to protect them from the wave of resegregation. Like Evanston, Oak Park had been able to cope with racial integration more slowly and with greater stability. However, that was then. The rehabilitation of the big Victorian homes along West End was already under way behind the arches of thick green trees and the friendly glow of August sunlight. New construction was appearing on some of the vacant lots. In a few years, these homes, a couple of minutes' walk from the Washington Boulevard bus or the Lake Street L, would be worth numbers in seven figures and notably improve the city's tax base. Only the vagaries of racial change had prevented this transformation from happening earlier. West End would reemerge as a multicultural street with whites, blacks, Hispanics, a few Asians. The only ones missing would be the poor.

Where would they go? Farther west into the more distant suburbs. Chicago would be like Paris, a white city surrounded by suburban enclaves of poor people with darker skins. What could be done about this change? No one was quite sure, indeed no one had anticipated it, though the transportation maps certainly pointed to it. Milord Cronin should be thankful that St. Lucy's had been protected from his own city planners.

I had sighed nosily, protesting to the deity if no one else was listening and returned to Austin. Beyond the L viaduct I took a left onto Lake Street where the shops and boutiques of the affluent were already appearing and the marquee of an old theater was advertising films made in India and Iran. Across, a swath of green hugged the L tracks. Under the supervision of lifeguards and cops and vigilant moms, small kids—black, brown, and white—frolicked in the tiny pool called, according to my Old Fella (also from the neighborhood), the "Mudhole." Dating from the days before Austin was annexed by Chicago, it had long since enjoyed a cement bottom. Less than a year ago the Park had been a haven for drug dealers, who had now moved their operations two blocks north, according to Mike Casey, to Race Avenue. Crime and chaos had been eased back a bit, but darkness still impinged on the edges of the redeveloping community. Were the murders in one of the bastions of the neighborhood an attack on change?

Not only the drug lords but even the ordinary poor people might not want to see racial change in what had for a long time been their neighborhood. Who would want to buy one of the expensive and chic town houses along Lake Street when crime had violated their own parish church and its attached school? The new colonialists would rely on Chicago's equivalent of the Bengal Lancers.

I parked on Menard Avenue, a block west of Mayfield, where St. Lucy's stood as a bulwark against evil and change, which often may have been in the neighborhood the same thing. It was a very old

Andrew M. Greeley

brownish brick building dating perhaps to 1907 (there is little data on the emergence of St. Lucy's) with two floors of schoolrooms over a "school hall" which had served as a church for almost a century. "New churches"—frequently big Gothic piles—replaced most of the one-building parish "plants" from those years eventually, often only a decade or two before racial resegregation.

The scene in front of the church is one you see on television every night in the big cities—police cars, vans for technicians, ambulances, yellow tapes blocking access to the church and the schoolyard parking lot, and hordes of media folk with their cameras and their microphones and their recorders. On the fringes of this usual crowd were people who were clearly parishioners, young mothers in shorts carrying a baby, older mothers with a child in either hand, elderly couples, bemused teenagers—all silent and grave, whatever their skin color. The fierce loyalty of Catholics to their parish church, so poorly understood by Chancery Office bureaucrats, had been violated.

"Bishop"—my friend Mary Alice Quinn pushed her way to the head of the media line—"what's going on! Does the Church condone murders in its churches?"

"No," I said as blandly as I could.

"Why did Cardinal Cronin leave town as soon as he heard of this terrible crime?"

"The trip has been planned for some time. He was called to Rome for consultation."

Some equivocation in that formal response. Sean Cronin was not one to plan a trip till about twelve hours before flight time.

"Are you in charge in his absence?"

"The Cardinal is in charge wherever he might be."

"Will these victims receive a Catholic burial?" Another reporter shoved Mary Alice aside.

"If they are Catholics."

"Even though they were killed inside a Catholic church?"

"I presume that was not their fault."

"Will you exorcise the church, Bishop?" Mary Alice shoved back into her position.

"We will bless it again and pray for those who died in it."

I had then pushed my way into the building and descended into the basement, congratulating myself on the restraint of my responses. Thereupon I encountered the ineffable Dawn Collins and the mysterious Camilla Datillo.

The blood-spattered sanctuary of St. Lucy's Church looked like the scene of a firefight on a television news program. As I watched, police technicians wrapped the bodies in white, lifted them to stretchers, and carried them down the main aisle of the little church and out the front door, almost in a liturgical procession.

The gorgeous young State's Attorney suddenly began the ancient mariners' hymn to Santa Lucia in a lyrical alto voice. Some of us joined in, the diffident and quiet cop—almost as invisible as I— joined in a powerful baritone. It was a strange song for a funeral recessional, but given the place and the time, utterly appropriate.

"A Sicilian could get in trouble for singing that Neapolitan song, couldn't she, Bishop?"

"Not in this Archdiocese, Camilla."

"Do you know what medals these are, Father?" Dawn Collins held up three disks attached to pieces of string. On the front of each disk was a blurred picture of a holy person.

"I believe," I said cautiously, "that they represent St. Malverde."

"Who the hell is St. Malverde?" Lieutenant Collins demanded. She was a tall, striking woman in a navy pantsuit with small touches of white. "There is some reason to think that he is the patron saint of the *narcotrafficantes*."

"These scum have a patron saint! What kind of Catholics are they!"

"My ancestors in Sicily," State's Attorney Datillo said thoughtfully, "had patron saints for pickpockets and prostitutes."

"That's not the Catholicism the nuns taught us in grammar school!"

Lieutenant Collins spoke a version of English that was innocent of any of the delightful intonations of black English. Like TV anchorpersons she must have labored mightily to suppress her dialect. Pity.

"There are many different kinds of Catholicism, Lieutenant," I said softly.

"Criminals may need saints to protect them as much as anyone else," the State's Attorney murmured.

"Well, these three kids," Dawn Collins snapped, "sure could have used some protection. They were bound and shot somewhere else. Dragged into the church, then stripped and mutilated in the sanctuary!"

"Both the Blessed Mother and St. Joseph are smeared with blood," Camilla Datillo observed. "Solemn high sacrilege . . . Will we have a case, Dawn?"

She spoke without emotion, a trait I had noticed. No gestures either. Had she learned to suppress her Italian vivacity in such situations? Well, perhaps I was indulging in stereotypes. I enjoyed Italian emotional style just as I enjoyed African English. The world was often very unfair.

"I doubt it. It looks like a professional job. Execution-style shooting. Heavy-caliber bullets in the back of the head. The forensic people as you can see are going over every inch of the church and the school upstairs too. The pastor, Father Wodjywhateverhisname, seems very cooperative. We may want to do the rectory too."

"Msgr. Mikal Wolodyjowski," I suggested.

"Whatever! Why do they have such long names?"

"In Poland," I explained, "the nobility all have long names."

"Well, he sure is a cool customer."

"Any other priests?" the State's Attorney asked.

"An obese and pompous young one and a Nigerian. We'll interview them all and look into their records. Also the parish staff, the nuns, everyone . . . Why would professional killers want to desecrate a church?"

"Because they had been told to do so," I offered softly.

I noticed that the quiet cop who had been standing silently with us had drifted away and was talking to one of the cops with a camera.

"Doesn't Patrol Officer O'Donnell work for you, Lieutenant Collins?"

She looked around, unaware that he had slipped away.

"No, he's one of Captain Huong's people."

"The ineffable Dragon Lady?"

"Yes. He certainly seems harmless."

"If he didn't," I commented, "he wouldn't be working for her."

"I wonder why the priest isn't here in the church," the lieutenant asked. "Shouldn't he be here?"

"I would imagine Msgr. Wolodyjowski wishes to be alone with his emotions for a time," I suggested. "Presumably he discovered the bodies this morning when he came to say Mass?"

"So he says. He claims to have given them the last rites, then called 911. He wouldn't let the people in for Mass and waited for us out in front. He was calm and cool, as though he was reporting a theft from the candle box."

"I don't imagine," Ms. Datillo said, "that he's a suspect, is he, Dawn?"

"I don't see how," the cop admitted, as though reluctantly, "but he was so damn cool."

"And the church was locked, Dawn?"

"He said it was. He has some kind of high-tech system in the rectory. Video cameras"—she gestured to a camera on one of the pillars—"which scan the church. Light beams which set off warnings whenever anyone crosses them. Automatic locks which go on whenever he throws the switch in the rectory. Whenever someone tries to open a door from the inside or the outside, an alarm sounds . . ."

"Four doors?" I asked.

"The front doors are on the same system, two side doors and

one in the back into the sacristy from the rectory. Same system up-stairs in the school. Every classroom door is locked down at night. During the day, the church is open, but when the school isn't in session, like now, it is locked down too. He has a guard in the rectory who keeps an eye on the TV screens all day. Seven o'clock at night, the guard locks everything down and goes home."

"Classic locked room," Camilla murmured, her face as expressionless as ever.

"You have someone talking to the guard, I presume?"

"Sure, Bishop. He's a Hispanic kid who is saving money to go to law school. Obviously he is a suspect."

Locked-room mysteries are not usually difficult to figure out. There were any number of ways it could have been done. The real issue was why leave the bodies in the church. It was doubtless a rebuke to Msgr. Wolodyjowski.

I would have to talk to him. And inspect his security system, a subject on which I am perforce an expert. I drifted away to check out the sacristy and the school. The former was the headquarters of the cop technicians who, hopefully, had finished their searching and dusting in there. Nothing to be accomplished till they left.

"Who are you?" a young woman cop, hopelessly Irish-American, demanded, as she glanced at me from her computer screen.

"Father Ryan," I replied meekly.

"What parish are you from?"

"Cathedral of the Holy Name."

"Yeah? You got an ID?"

"That's Bishop Blackie Ryan, Dodo," an older male cop said. "He's legit."

"As far as any bishop can be legit," I agreed. "Has there been any damage to the vestments?"

"Dorothy McArdle, Bishop. Sorry, but you don't look like a bishop."

"That is a fairly common opinion."

She laughed and smiled. So little respect do we get these days.

"The perps wrapped the naked victims in those great big things you guys wear. . . ."

"Copes?"

"I guess that's it. They looked very old and very expensive. Nothing else seems to have been touched around here. We're dusting everything."

"Dodo," the other cop informed me, "is e-mailing the prints we harvested from the victims to Twelfth and Michigan. We'll check them against our databases, then send them on to the Bureau."

"They were so young," Dodo observed. "Kids my little sister's age."

"God be good to them," I said.

"Yeah, well he'd better be . . . no one else has . . . Why do they have such expensive vestments in this poor parish, Bishop?"

"It wasn't always poor, Dorothy."

She looked up at me in surprise—the reaction of the young to the suggestion that once upon a time things were different.

"Really?"

"Really. However, before you leave take a look at the school upstairs. That's where most of the money goes."

"Yeah, I will."

I went back into the church, walked over to one of the side doors, and climbed the stairs to the school. As expected I encountered freshly painted walls, recently scrubbed stairs, polished floors, bright lights, outlets for sprinklers, and bright posters. One would not have thought that the school was almost a hundred years old. Peering through the windows into a classroom I saw more bright colors, computer workstations, walls lined with books, and excellent religious art.

No surprise. Pan Wolodyjowski would tolerate nothing but the best for his pupils. I examined the lock on the door carefully. Ingenious. So were the TV cameras along the corridor—the kind that followed you as you walked by. They were still working.

"Checking the security system, Bishop Blackie?" the young man from the Dragon Lady's unit said in a mild, inoffensive voice.

The rules were that Blackie Ryan caught others by surprise, not vice versa.

"It seems to be high-quality, Sergeant," I replied. "I leave it to your greater expertise to render a more professional judgment."

"How did you know I was a sergeant?"

"If you work for my ineffable friend the Dragon Lady, that's the lowest possible rank."

His face lit up in an impish grin and his quite ordinary features became special. As in the case of the ineffable Dodo, the Irish grin is a powerful weapon. Still this one was unusual, filled with merriment, mischief, trouble, and insight. There was much more to this young man than I had expected. It was never wise to underestimate the taste of the Dragon Lady.

"You know herself?"

"We consult each other occasionally."

"She should be Pope."

"I'll not dispute the point . . . I assume you are here because this incident emits something more than the terrible smell of death?"

"Austin is a gold mine, Bishop. Lots of people stand to make lots of money. You look at that crowd of worried parishioners outside and you realize that St. Lucy's is a key piece of the action. Someone wants it out of the picture. Someone big and powerful. That sort of deal makes us start sniffing."

"Your colleagues in the department did not seem to mind your presence?"

"Some would. Lieutenant Collins doesn't. Captain Huong has clout, especially with women on the force. The lieutenant knows that we're not about to take credit from her. That's against the captain's rules."

"And this security system?"

"State of the art for the situation. Nothing can guarantee complete security, but this is about as good as you can get for a church and school."

"It is tied into a central computer?"

"They all are. If something goes off anywhere in this system, it registers in the central unit. The Monsignor or whoever has to turn it off with a special code.

"I presume, however, that in that fiendish basement up on Magnolia Street, there is the wherewithal to incapacitate it temporarily."

He considered me with his gentle blue eyes.

"Probably, if we wanted to work at it."

"Then someone else might do the same thing?"

"I had thought of that."

"So you called the valiant Madame Huong and suggested . . ."

He not only grinned this time, he laughed, a rich appealing laugh.

"Sure. And I told her you were in the picture . . ."

"And she giggled?"

"What else?"

"Will you be able to determine whether anyone took down the security system last night when the bodies were dragged into the church and mutilated?"

"With any luck, yes."

"And who did it?"

He hesitated. "With a lot more luck."

"And if someone in the rectory should have awakened and looked at the monitors over there?"

"Depends. Theoretically you might be able to keep the monitors on while the cameras were not recording what was happening in the church. It would be very tricky. More likely you would take the risk of turning them off for a few minutes. How long does it take to drag three bodies through the sacristy door and into the church, then mutilate them? If the Monsignor should see the blank monitors, he might have fooled around with the controls, then called the central security system and perhaps the police. Is he the kind of man who would have dashed over into the church?"

"I'm not sure."

"Besides," Declan said, "we don't know that anyone was hacking into the security system. It would require a high degree of sophistication."

"Yet hackers are for sale, I take it?"

"Yeah, but it would also require some sophistication to realize that a hacker might be able to do the job, then find an ingenious operative who could and would do it."

I sighed.

"Such technology could ruin locked-door mystery puzzles. Still, it would be convenient if we could sustain such an explanation."

"Then," Declan said, "the remaining mystery would be even more complex. Why bother?"

"Arguably."

"Now what exactly do you two think you are doing!"

An irate womanly voice filled the corridor. It came from a small, white-haired woman who was charging towards us, the wrath of the Lord (as it is often depicted) in her eyes.

"Sister Superior," I whispered.

"I'm Sergeant Declan O'Donnell of the Chicago Police Department," my companion said with enough charm to sink several Irish counties back into the bogs. He flashed his warrant card. "This gentleman is the legendary Bishop Blackie Ryan in his usual disguise . . . We were admiring your school and the ingenuity of your security system."

A smooth one, your Declan O'Donnell. Doubtless the Dragon Lady had noted this quality.

"Well, Bishop, I'm sorry I didn't recognize you. We're all delighted that you will reconsecrate the church for us. It is a pleasure to meet you. I'm Sister Mary Anne McCarthy."

I regained some of my lost aplomb, brushing away a lifelong terror in the face of angry Mothers Superior. "I must congratulate you, Sister, on the way in which you have kept this very old school brand-new."

"I may be prejudiced, Bishop," she replied tartly, "but I don't think there's anything wrong with being old."

"Point taken," I murmured, thoroughly reproved.

"Come down to my office and I will show you how the system works."

So like two schoolboys caught in the act of some serious mischief we followed her to her office. An entire wall was lined with monitors and control panels.

"I don't know for the life of me why it didn't work last night," she said. "Monsignor believes in the very best of equipment for St. Lucy's . . . anyway, you can see that there are cameras in every room of the school and in every corridor—which is how I saw you gentlemen, ah, pursuing your investigations. Also we have monitors covering the schoolyard, the space between the church and the rectory, and the inside and outside of the church. I can glance into any of these, turn up the volume, and see what's happening. Naturally I don't spy on my teachers. I turn off the classrooms during school,"—she flipped off a switch—"but I can still see what's going on in the corridors and stairwells."

"Impressive," I said, thinking to myself that Mother Superior could now be everywhere, a terrifying possibility.

"I'll never forget the night when he saw a drug addict try to assault a young Latino girl who was praying to the statue of Our Lady of Guadalupe. The Monsignor charged over from the rectory with a Polish cavalry saber in his hand."

Naturally it would be a cavalry saber.

"Have you experienced many glitches in the system, Sister?" Declan asked.

"Well, we've had the fire department here once on a false alarm and there's always the odd ruffian who will deliberately set the whole system on by forcing the front door."

I felt compassion for the ruffians whose grinning faces would have been forever preserved on the system's hard disks.

"I don't think we've ever had a breakdown like last night," she mused. Those poor, poor children. . . . The people from Combined Control have been working on it all morning. I suppose the police will be talking to them?"

"I'm sure they have, Sister," Declan said soothingly.

"Look, Bishop, Monsignor is coming out of the rectory to talk to the people."

She turned up the volume.

Pan Mikal Wolodyjowski, in clerical suit and Roman collar, advanced down the steps of the rectory, an old-fashioned gray Victorian edifice with turrets and gables, attics—and barred widows. He was slender and sternly upright, with a confident walk and a sense of personal dignity that most of us clerics could not command. His hair was white, as was his neatly trimmed beard. His face was solemn, indeed melancholy as befits a Slav. I imagined his frosty eyes grim and determined. The Monsignor was not a man with whom one would wisely trifle.

His people applauded enthusiastically as he mounted the three steps leading to the door of their parish church. He gently raised his left hand for silence. The media vultures descended upon him. He raised his right hand in an equally gentle dismissive motion, waving them off.

Wisely he did not tell them to turn off their cameras.

"My dear people," he began in a deep bass voice, "this is a tragic day for St. Lucy's parish. The bodies of three young people, as far as we know innocent of any crimes, have been dragged into our church and brutally mutilated in the sanctuary . . ."

A cry of rage from the parishioners. He raised his hand again.

"We do not know who the criminals are that performed these outrages. I have every confidence that the Chicago Police Department will solve the crime and that the State's Attorneys of Cook County will see that justice is done. We must pray that the victims are already with our loving God in the world to come. We must be ready to forgive those who have performed the crime and not demand in our hearts vengeance which is not appropriate for Catholics.

"We will not forget the horror which happened last night. Yet we must not permit it to interfere with our faith in God's impassioned love and in our hope for St. Lucy's. We will survive the evil that was done to us last night. Surely we must wonder if it was not the result of the rebirth of our parish, an attempt to restore the jun-

gle which once surrounded us. We must stand fast. We must pray
and trust God.

"When the police are finished with their necessary work inside
the church, we will clean it and restore it to its dignity. Then tomorrow evening Bishop Ryan, who is here today to express the
Cardinal's unity with us, will renew the blessing of the church, we
will offer the Eucharist for the three victims and sing a Te Deum in
gratitude for the return of the church of St. Lucy to the parish of
St. Lucy."

Sister was weeping. So was the astonishing Declan.

Then Pan Mikal repeated his remarks in Spanish.

I watched with great admiration and some anxiety. I would have
to preach tomorrow night. It would not be easy to follow him. Yet
he would be on all the Chicago TV stations, including the Spanish-
speaking. Not your typical Chicago Polish pastor of his generation,
nor your typical Chicago pastor of the present. He was a man of
overpowering presence.

"I must go down and congratulate him," Sister said as she fled
the office, tissue in hand.

"Is he really nobility, Bishop Blackie?" Declan asked me as he
watched the people walk up to shake their pastor's hand. No informal hugs. Hardly.

"His father was a general in the Polish Army who left in 1922
after the Poles failed to capture Moscow."

"Really!"

"Whenever Russia is weak, the Poles march into Russia. They
think that Belarus, Lithuania, and Ukraine are rightly theirs. They
didn't make it to Moscow this time and fell back in defeat. History
might have been very different . . . Anyway, I gather the general felt
he had to leave. The Monsignor was born six years later. His father
became very successful in a savings and loan company."

As we watched, Dawn Collins and Camilla Datillo joined the
end of the line. The lieutenant introduced the State's Attorney. Pan
Mikal kissed her hand.

"Would you look at that!" Declan O'Donnell protested. "I bet that's never happened to her before."

"You might try it sometime," I suggested.

"She'd think I was hitting on her. I'm not Polish nobility. I'm just a South Side Irish cop."

"Ah."

"One doesn't hit on her, I'm told. You feel you've been hit by a Bradley Fighting Vehicle."

The Monsignor waved off the media and walked slowly back to the rectory. I should pay my respects. He knew I was there doubtless because he had seen me on the monitors in the rectory.

"I have to apologize to her."

"To the fair Camilla?"

"Yeah, we were in the same grade at St. Thomas More, before she moved to River Forest. I was kind of a playground bully in those days. I said some nasty things to her about being a dirty wop."

"You would have been in deep trouble."

"Maybe she doesn't remember," he said hopefully.

"Perhaps."

"Sicilians have long memories, Bishop."

"So does everyone . . . why must you apologize?"

"To seek forgiveness, why else?"

"And why is that?"

"Because that's what the nun said at the police retreat this year."

I would not have bet against the granting of forgiveness.

Declan

"Beats me," said the tech from Combined Control. "We're absolutely certain there was no alarm from this place last night. Someone might have turned off the alarm system, but even that would have registered in our computer."

"How does that work?" I asked.

"There are three separate systems at St. Lucy's—the TV cameras, the light lines, and the door locks. In our system this means three green lights on the board. If there is a disconnect of any of the systems, the light turns yellow. If there is a violation, the light turns red and our alarms go off. We make a phone call. If there's not an answer we confirm with the Austin Police Station that there is a situation. Of course there are loud alarms on the premises, enough to wake up much of the neighborhood."

"What's a violation of the TV cameras?"

"When one of them stops working, we get a yellow light. More than one it turns red and the alarms go off. We have to be good at this, Officer O'Donnell. One blunder and we lose all our clients. We're already getting calls about this mess."

"And how are you replying?"

"That we're doing a careful investigation . . . What else can we say?"

So if someone was hacking into the system, they would have

done it without affecting the alarm mechanisms at Combined Control. Surely the tech's superiors were wondering about a hacker. We should be wondering too. I flipped open my cell phone and called herself.

"Ah," she giggled. "It will be very difficult."

"That's your problem, boss."

"There is very serious evil at work here, Declan," she said, now very serious. "Mad, ingenious, ruthless. Take great care."

"Yes, ma'am."

Then she hung up.

I tried to digest that exchange and couldn't do it. I ambled over to Lieutenant Collins and State's Attorney Datillo, who were standing in the back of the church and watching the forensic people probe around every corner. They didn't notice that I was there.

"I'm guessing," Ms. Collins said, "that we won't have their prints."

"Illegals picked up and murdered so the killers would have bodies to desecrate the church?"

"Something like that."

"It could get messy, Dawn. There'll be a lot of pressure for arrests."

"I know. That priest will be on every TV station tonight and they'll be back tomorrow to cover whatever the priests do to purify the place . . . what the hell is a tedium anyhow? Nuns never taught us that one."

"Beats me."

"It's Latin," I interrupted. "First words of a hymn called the *Te Deum Laudamus*—an ancient hymn of thanksgiving. Like when the Allies liberate Paris, they sing it in Notre Dame."

I sang softly the first couple of lines in the Gregorian chant version. Both women stared at me like I was some kind of freak.

"That's the version in Gregorian chant. There's many others. I think Verdi wrote one."

"You a choir boy, Officer?"

"I sing at my parish sometimes."

"You gonna give them a hand tomorrow night?"

"I imagine they have an excellent choir here. They won't need me."

The two of them returned to discussing the case. I tried to figure out whether Camilla was studying me carefully or was merely bored by my intrusion into their discussion of the case. Either way it wasn't good.

"There are four questions here," Lieutenant Collins recapitulated. "The first is who are these poor kids. Like I say, we may never find that out. The second is how the perps disarmed the alarm system. The third is why someone would want to drag naked and mutilated bodies into a church. The fourth is who were the perps. I figure that the answer to the last one is that they were professionals and we'll never find out who they were."

"The third is crucial," Camilla said. "Someone wants to destroy the influence of St. Lucy in the neighborhood. Despite that show of solidarity outside, I suspect they've succeeded . . . How will you proceed, Dawn?"

"We'll get the autopsy and forensic reports tomorrow or the next day. I expect they won't tell us anything. We've already begun to interview the people on the staff. Maybe we can find out who disarmed the security system. It would have to have been someone who knew the code, wouldn't it, Officer?"

For a moment I didn't answer because I didn't think I was still there. I was also, to my shame be it said, preoccupied by the shape of the State's Attorney's breasts.

"Yes, but a lot of people would have to know it. The principal of the school, the Monsignor, the guard or guards who watched the monitors, the engineer, probably the housekeeper . . ."

"We'll talk to them all . . . By the way, I suppose you've reported to Captain Huong. What did she have to say?"

"There is very serious evil at work out there, mad, ingenious, ruthless."

"What did she mean by that?"

I shrugged.

"I don't know. Captain Huong tends to be inscrutable some of the time."

"Next"—Lieutenant Collins turned back to the State's Attorney—"we'll question Alderman Crawford, who—they tell me—is opposed to new construction because whites would replace blacks and dilute his power in the ward. Then we'll try to get something out of the Mexican gang leaders and O'Boyle and Sons, who are the contractors, and Abbey Kincaid, who heads the local environmental protest group."

"She wants more low-cost housing in the redevelopment?"

"Yep. Developers don't because they say no middle-class people will buy in if they do that and there's already enough low-cost housing in the neighborhood."

"The usual suspects?"

"And from what I know about them, none of them are likely to think up something quite this bizarre . . . I figure I have a day, maybe tops a day and a half before Fifth District Homicide takes over. You under any pressure like that?"

Camilla lifted her lovely shoulders slightly.

"Not yet, but my boss hasn't seen the TV yet."

At that point, three suits, waving warrant cards, rammed their way through the cops at the door of the church.

"Who's in charge here?" the head suit shouted. "We're Federal agents and we're taking over this investigation."

"I'm Lieutenant Dawn Collins, Fifteenth Precinct, and the hell you are!"

"You're working for us from now on, Collins. This is a Federal case," Big Suit snapped. "I want all the facts on this crime immediately."

My Camilla, as I had begun to think about her, pulled a mobile phone out of her purse and punched in a number.

"No phone calls!" Little Suit demanded. "What is your name and rank?"

"Camilla Datillo, State's Attorney of the County of Cook."

"We're superseding your jurisdiction!"

"Only if my boss says you are."

"Give me that phone!"

He tried to wrestle it out of her hand. She pushed him away with a solid shove.

I wondered if I should ride to the rescue like the Seventh Cavalry. Alas, it was not at all clear what I might do.

"Dawn, will you arrest this man for assault, please?"

Lieutenant Collins whistled. Five cops appeared from outside the church.

"Officers, will you take these gentlemen into custody. All three are to be charged with disorderly conduct and trespassing on a crime scene, and charge the little guy also with assault on a law enforcement official."

"You can't do this to us! We're Federal agents! We're in charge here!"

"Only when my boss says you are."

My Camilla was speaking to a boss, a wicked grin making her look even more lovely.

"Dawn just arrested the guy who tried to take my phone away, charged him with assault on a law enforcement official . . . I agree it's pretty funny . . . So you haven't ceded jurisdiction . . . and won't . . . It's a terrible mess . . . Tell your friend over at the Dirksen Building that we'll let them cooperate with us if they are polite and respectful and that I will file a civil action against his bullyboy tomorrow . . . Yeah, I know I'm a hellion. Always have been. It's the Sicilian blood."

"I talked to Fourteenth and Michigan." Dawn snapped her phone shut. "They say we're still in charge. . . . Officer, shouldn't you call Captain Huong and get her support?"

"Good idea."

The Dragon Lady did not seem surprised, but then she never did.

"Were these suits from the Bureau?"

"More likely someone from the Homeland Security crowd, second-, maybe third-rate. Pretty dumb to think that the CPD and the State's Attorney would roll over and play dead."

"Out-of-towners."

"Maybe Immigration . . . yet why would they be interested?"

"I thought you might tell me."

She giggled and hung up.

Lieutenant Collins had gone outside, doubtless to make sure that the three suits were properly incarcerated in a patrol car. Camilla was sitting in a back pew of the church, scribbling furiously in her notebook.

It's now or never, I told myself.

So it's never.

However, she was so beautiful and I was already half in love with her.

"Miss Datillo," I croaked in a high-pitched voice, "I wonder, uh, well, I'd like . . . might I have a word with you . . . It will only take . . . I mean . . ."

My heart was pounding, my stomach grumbling, my face burning.

"All right."

She closed the notebook and stood up. The smile and the laughter of the phone call to her boss existed in another world. She considered me with cool dispassion.

"Well?"

"I'm . . . ah, Declan O'Donnell . . . from St. Thomas More, you know and I . . ." I struggled for words.

She waited patiently but without expression.

"This is very hard," I managed to mumble, "but . . . well, we were in school together and I . . . I was a bully and a boor . . . and, you know, I like kind of want to apologize . . ."

Her deep brown eyes, almost black, were unreadable. Her lips, barely outlined by makeup, did not move.

"I was a bully and said terrible things to you," the words poured out now, "and I made you cry and I'm very sorry and I want to beg your forgiveness . . ."

Where was that hole in the floor of St. Lucy's Church that was supposed to open up and swallow me?

She nodded ever so slightly.

"Of course I forgive you, Declan, if any forgiveness is necessary. Maybe you did make me cry sometimes, though I cried a lot in those days, still do. I don't remember you as a bully, though maybe you were mean occasionally. I remember you as a cute little boy who said funny things and made us laugh. I missed you when we moved away. . . . Tell you what, why don't I buy you a cup of coffee later?"

Tears stung the back of my eyes. I thought I saw hints of moisture in her black pools. I wanted to hug her. That would have to wait till later, if ever.

"That sounds like a great idea."

I turned away, she sat down and wrote in her notebook. Drained, exhausted, and relieved, I went out to the tiny porch of the old church to breathe the fresh air, to delight in the warmth of the sunlight, and to bask in the grace of forgiveness.

She had absolved me, sympathetically, generously. And for my penance I would drink a cup of coffee with the most beautiful woman in the world.

Blackie

"Pan Wolodyjowski," I said with a formal bow to the pastor of St. Lucy's.

"Pan Ryan," he said with a nod, just a touch of a hint in his frosty blue eyes that he was amused. "Please sit down. In honor of the bishop's presence I was so bold as to purchase some Irish whiskey. Might I offer the bishop a small glass?"

The third person serves often as a polite and formal second person in the Polish language.

"The bishop is grateful for your hospitality," I said gravely. "Alas, however, the bishop must drive home on the Congress Expressway in the rush hour. Let us reserve the Irish for another occasion."

"As the bishop wishes . . . Perhaps the bishop will sip a small glass of Polish wine. Excellent."

The bishop did and resisted a pained expression at the wine's vinegar taste.

The pastor of St. Lucy's was still wearing his clerical shirt and collar, both neatly tailored. "Permit me to say, Pan Wolodyjowski, that Pan Lomniki was well suited to playing your seventeenth-century namesake."

He was silent for a moment.

"Blackie, there may be a half dozen Irish priests in this city who are aware that Henryk Sienkiewicz wrote other books besides *Quo Vadis*. At the most half of these have read the trilogy, not including Sean Cronin. You are, I am sure, the only one who has watched the film."

"One must be loyal to a Nobel Prize winner who lived in this city for a time. If he had given but a single lecture at The University, his name would be on the tee shirts and sweatshirts that The University so proudly markets. We must honor him in the Archdiocese."

"I do not know whether we are descendents of Lord Michael and his beloved Krystia. We would like to think so of course. But we can trace no direct links."

"If the current Pan Wolodyjowski would permit himself to be influenced by his Irish confreres, he would of course claim it."

He permitted himself a little laugh and changed the subject.

"It is good of the bishop to visit in our time of pain."

"Do we know anything about the tragic victims?" I asked. "Are they parishioners?"

"Sad, wandering children—a husband, a wife, an unborn child, a brother, hardly in his teens, adventurers, heroes, brave pilgrims seeking a better life . . ."

Tears formed in his eyes.

"I did not recognize them nor did any of the people who saw them—*pollos* brought to Chicago by a *coyote* for a big price, then murdered and mutilated . . ."

Illegal immigrants led to Chicago for a large payment, then killed. Why, however, would the coyote kill them?

I had walked over to the rectory and was greeted promptly at the door by a tall, powerful woman.

"Priest not in!" she informed me.

"Tell him that Priest Ryan is here."

She considered with obvious disbelief.

"Priest?"

"Priest."

"I tell him."

Inside, the rectory was a mix of old Victorian and sleek modern.

The high ceilings, the recently painted walls with ornate moldings, the antique furniture, and the deep carpets spoke of the very early years of the parish while the air conditioners, the bright lighting, the fire sprinklers, and the computers and microchip readers introduced the twenty-first century. Who, I wondered, paid for the upkeep of the church, rectory, and school? The Wolodyjowski tribe had money—and so did the Cronin clan.

The rectory was permeated by what I call the rectory smell, not unpleasant perhaps, something like but not the same as the aroma of a Catholic hospital, particularly a Polish one, a blend of furniture polish, antiseptic, and what I call the stench of celibacy, which perhaps is no more than the absence of the smell of women.

The housekeeper had not invited me to sit in one of the offices. But, mostly invisible person that I am, I had wandered into the office with a wall of monitors and control panels. There were monitors everywhere in this parish. Perhaps we needed more at the Cathedral. It should never be said that Blackie Ryan had fallen behind in the technology race.

I enjoyed the contretemps between the G and the city of Chicago and the County of Cook and turned up the volume so I could hear it. The G had messed with the wrong people, especially the eejit who tried to take her cell phone away from the valiant Signorina Datillo.

Then I had watched the scene between the two young people as in a silent film. It was obvious that Declan had begged for pardon and Camilla had granted it with tender affection. Just then for the young man she was God, a God who had rediscovered Italian gestures. Perhaps she always would be his God.

He could do worse.

I turned away from the monitors to observe a very tall, very black man, dressed in African clothes and carrying an enormous spear.

"Bwana Blackie," he said, bowing from the waist and doffing his dashiki cap. "You are most welcome to the community of the people of God under the protection of St. Lucy."

He spoke in flawless English and his splendid white teeth gleamed in a broad smile—Nelson Ironman, a refugee Nigerian priest.

"Nelson," I said. "It is good to see you again. What are you doing with that spear?"

"It is my family spear, a royal spear, if I may say so, Bwana. I have been sharpening this spear in case it should be needed to defend the parish from another onslaught of the barbarians. He has his ancestral cavalry saber, I have my family spear. With these we will be able to defend the fort until relief forces arrive."

"Do you wear those clothes when you go down to the street to West Suburban Medical Center, Nelson?"

"Naturally, Bwana. With a Roman collar of course. The sick people are fascinated. I do not carry this weapon, however."

He tapped the floor with the butt end of his spear.

"Does it not make a sound like that of the Zulus attacking Roark's Drift?" he asked.

"In point of fact, Nelson, it does not. And you are an Ibo not a Zulu and the neighborhood is West Austin, not Roark's Drift. Nonetheless, it is a formidable weapon."

His smile faded.

"There is deep evil lurking, Bwana. I feel it in my jungle-sensitive bones. We must be ready."

If Nelson Ironman said he sensed evil, that made two of us. However, his madcap wit could not be deterred by serious threat.

"There is no jungle in Port Harcourt."

"Neither is there in your Ireland, Bwana, but you sense great evil too. Some of us simply know. What do you Irish call them? The dark ones?"

"Ah."

I am not in fact a dark one, though my colleague Ms. Nuala Anne McGrail certainly is.

The Polish housekeeper reappeared to lead me to Pan Mikal's rooms.

"Priest, put spear away. You hurt someone with it."

"Only bad ones, good woman." He bowed again.

In his office, Monsignor Wolodyjowski wore a white shirt with French cuffs and Polish eagle cuff links, a clerical vest, but no jacket—Polish casual. I was not in the least embarrassed by my own less formal attire. The bishop has an image to maintain. Outside the high—and barred—windows the leaves of huge oak trees filtered in summer sunlight and permitted glimpses of the Park across the street. Every available space was packed with books—in his office, in his bedroom, in the corridor outside, and in the empty room next to his suite. The books were in English, Polish, French, Spanish, and German.

He sat behind an ornate old desk with a polished and empty top. He gestured to a painting of a fierce warrior holding a sword and patently ready to kill someone—me perhaps. His violin and bow rested on its own table.

"That is the first Mikal Wolodyjowski," he gestured at the warrior on the wall. "Some see a family resemblance. I don't."

"I do."

"If I were Irish, I would say that is blarney, but welcome blarney . . . The film, as you know, was made under the socialist government. They thought that if they appealed to Polish nationalism, the Polish nation would like them. Folly!"

A big black-and-white cat with a large tail jumped up on the couch next to me, turned around in a circle, and curled up comfortably, his yellow eyes focused on me.

"He is Jan Kazimir," the pastor said, "of a breed called the Maine coon. They are very friendly and welcome petting. Also very intelligent. You see, we have Pan Mikal and Jan Kazimir in the same old house."

"And a century after those two routed the Turks at Vienna and saved Europe, Europe split up Poland and it disappeared."

Jan Kazimir snuggled up to me and welcomed my scratching of his head. Cats, dogs, and little children trust me.

"You know too much history, Pan Blackie. Now at least we are part of NATO and the EU and have taken Pomerania and Prussia and much of Brandenburg back from the Germans. Please God a thousand years of wars are over . . . I often thought that the film was a Polish Western. The Poles are the Americans and the Cossacks and Turks and Swedes are the Indians. A lot of men ride around on horses, burn down villages, kill one another, and terrorize women. Entertaining, no?"

"Who did this horror to the church?" I changed the subject abruptly.

He opened his hands in a gesture of bafflement.

"We Poles are suspicious people, some would even call us paranoid. We believe that when the sun rises in the morning it has an agenda against us. It could be the alderman or the mayor or the drug gangs or the O'Boyles or some other developers. Professor Dogherty, who believes he owns this part of Austin, has hated me since I came to St. Lucy's. If I support the redevelopment, he perforce must oppose it. I am sure, however, that the outrage was aimed at the parish and our support for the New Austin."

"The school is especially critical for the project, is it not?"

"Certainly! I have already told Pan Cronin personally that I will have to build a second school, perhaps with an underground parking lot which will serve for Green Line commuters during the week, who will help to pay for it."

"There are no other schools except the public?"

"To which our young parishioners will not send their children. There is St. Catherine four blocks to the north and St. Paul's Lutheran three blocks north of us. However, we already have a waiting list. We must build immediately."

"Downtown won't like it?"

"Sean has already approved the plan personally. He has been very good to St. Lucy's and to me personally. I fear I make him feel guilty because I am not sitting on his throne as he believes I deserve."

He had spoken quietly and with little emotion. If he was an envious man, he didn't show it. I kept my mouth shut.

"However, as I have told him often, I am more suited for St. Lucy's Rectory than the Cathedral. I never wanted to be a bishop.

He tried to make me one and I refused. So then he chose you. Surely a wise choice, no?"

"Many would have serious doubts," I said.

"They would be wrong." He dismissed that embarrassed comment with a wave of his hand. "If Pope Paul had made me Archbishop of Chicago, I believe Sean might have run off with Nora. That would have been a loss for all three of us. It is much better this way. Her love is much different now and more important."

I wasn't sure I wanted to hear these reminiscences. Yet I was fascinated by them.

"I know the Lady Nora quite well," I said. "At the end of the day, she would not have run with him."

He raised an eyebrow.

"I suspect you are right, Blackie. Sean says you are always right . . ."

"What he actually says is seldom in error and never in doubt."

"He also adds that he is damn happy that you are on his side . . . I cannot hide from myself that both our lives are running down. A new St. Lucy will be my last effort. My final tribute to our curious paths, my parish and his neighborhood."

"My Old Fella grew up on West End."

"Even more irony . . . I do not know, Blackie, about celibacy. If the Lady Nora, as you aptly call her, was the Cardinal's wife, might it not be a better Church? More human more humane? I have firmly believed in celibacy. I have loved many good women, almost always from a safe distance. If I had a wife and family, I surely would not be here at St. Lucy's creating a new neighborhood in the old neighborhood. Yet I wonder about the sweetness that might have been . . . What might I have lost?"

"In life choices," I said, "there are no discount stores."

He actually laughed.

"You understand, Blackie, that we Poles are a sad and melancholy people. All the time."

"So are we Irish, but only half the time . . . Do you think the Latin West gang might be responsible for the horror?"

"They would be the lowest on my list. It is the kind of violence that they would do routinely. They see themselves as a nation at war with other nations, survival or death. But they would not do violence in a church. Their Catholicism is different from ours, but it is deep and serious. The parish church is even more sacred to them than us. Don Pablo called me this morning. He was weeping. He begged me to believe that his people had nothing to do with it. He swore—I believe on the grave of his mother—that he would do terrible things to those who had desecrated his holy church and the school which his children attend."

"The *Jefe* of the West Lords sends his kids to St. Lucy's?"

"Two very sweet little children. They use different names for their own protection. Sister knows, of course, but none of the teachers or the children or the parents. Do not such small ones deserve our charity and our protection?"

"Certainly!" I said.

"If I had to choose someone who might be insane enough to work this horror it would be Brian Dogherty. His hates are many and his angers oceanic. Yet I do not believe him capable of breaking through our alarm system. He was once a brilliant Catholic thinker, open-minded and progressive. He is still, however, living in the world of Newman and Chesterton and Belloc. He believes that Pius XII was the last validly elected Pope. That kind of mind is capable of imagining conspiracies but not of carrying them out."

At that point our conversation was interrupted by another priest—a young man a few inches taller than I (which is not very tall) and almost as wide as he was tall. He wore a cassock, a biretta, and a light cape—as if he were a curial bureaucrat of an earlier day. He carried a large breviary in both hands.

"Very Reverend Monsignor"—he bowed over the breviary—"will we not do an exorcism of our violated church today? Must we not drive out the demons who are responsible for the obscenity? Ought we not summon the Archdiocese's exorcist?"

"The police are still working in the church, Father McDonald."

The enormous priest raised a finger, like a medieval inquisitor.

"We must order them out."

"We must wait till they finish, then clean the church, and to-morrow we will have a Mass and renew the church and sing the Te Deum."

"As you wish, Very Reverend Monsignor."

He bowed again and left us.

"He is worthless. Sean is warehousing him here. He sits in his room and reads the breviary. He says the first Mass on Sunday, but I can't let him preach. Or hear Confessions. Or teach in the school. The staff at West Suburban Medical Center down the street on Austin requested that we not let him visit the sick. Fortunately, he is lazy. His only serious activity is eating. Fortunately, Father Nelson, our Nigerian, has the energy of four priests."

"You are kind and patient with him, Mickey."

"What else would you have me do . . . Now as to the alderman. He is not an appealing man. Opposes a new school because he be-lieves it will attract white people—which it will—and dilute his power in the ward. However, we provide quality education for many of his black constituents . . . Rumor has it that the O'Boyles are threatened with bankruptcy and would like a hiatus in their construction plans."

"Could be anyone, then?"

"Or none of them. The brutality suggests a madman."

"And how did they break through your alarm system? I know something about these matters. It seems of the highest quality."

"Let me show you my alarm."

He rose slowly, wearily I thought, from his chair and led me to a spartan bedroom—a single bed, a prie-dieu, an elaborate Mexican crucifix, and a reproduction of the Black Madonna of Yasna Gora—Our Lady of Czeschtowa—the patroness of Poland. A polished saber rested alongside one of the bookcases. Above the prie-dieu hung a very large alarm bell and a panel with three lights.

"Before I go to bed every night I check the panel and monitors down in the office. The lights are all on next to the alarm. If one goes off, the alarm rings, loud enough to be heard as far as Race Avenue. It did not ring last night. I do not understand. The lights were on last night. In the office the screens were on. I turned the system off so I could enter the church for the Eucharist. I saw nothing, but I looked for nothing. I do not awaken easily. I found the horror in the sanctuary. Immediately I anointed the bodies and called the police."

"The copes were over the bodies?"

"Yes, as though to hide their nakedness. I understand none of this. I will dream of those poor young people for the rest of my life."

"I'm sure you will."

"Sean says you are good at these mysteries."

"Sometimes."

Well, every time so far.

"I hope you solve it because I am sure the police will not be able to do so. Nonetheless, we shall survive."

He ought not to rule out the Dragon Lady's bunch, but then he did not know about them.

I promised I would arrive in midafternoon to prepare for the services. He thanked me solemnly. As he walked down the stairs with me, accompanied by the redoubtable Jan Kazimir, his shoulders sloped much more than they had when he had preached to his people earlier in the day. We must keep him alive.

A line of rain clouds were creeping in on the western sky, doubtless sent from DuPaige County to torment us. The coming rain predicted the end of summer and the usual long bitter Chicago winter.

I elected to drive back to the Cathedral on Augusta Boulevard to avoid the rain-induced traffic jams on the Congress Expressway (as we Irish Democrats still call it).

I reflected that I had encountered in one day a Polish aristocrat who used a cavalry saber to protect a young woman in his church, an African-American police lieutenant who spoke better English than I did, a newly ordained reactionary a couple of hundred pounds overweight, a Nigerian prince in a dashiki and equipped with a huge spear, a Sicilian State's Attorney who sang "Santa Lucia" as bodies were carried out of church named in that saint's honor, and an Irish cop who worked for a captain whose tribal origins were in the mountains of Laos. I was the only normal one in the lot.

Declan

"Two chocolate malts," my Camilla said to the waitress at Petersen's ice-cream parlor. "With whipped cream."

"Coming right up, Cami," the young woman responded. I had the impression that she had exchanged a sign of approval over my head. I wasn't ready for this quite yet.

"I thought it was a cup of coffee."

"We should celebrate a reconciliation with something more than a cup of coffee. You don't seem to be the kind of boy I'd take into a bar. And I'm entitled to break training once in the summer."

"Training?"

"I'm in a real close beach volleyball scene at North Avenue Beach—two-person team with Amy Cline from the Feds. It's a league of women lawyers who work for the various governments."

"Dangerous people."

My Camilla in beach volleyball array. I felt even dizzier than I had during the ride down Chicago Avenue in her Lancia Fulvia Sports Coupe. Camilla, who kept her Italian gestures under control at the crime scene, made up for this crime against nature by waving her hands as she drove the car.

"I was thinking about it after we talked and I said to myself this is the best come-on I've ever heard. How did he plan it fourteen years ahead of time? Then I said, so what? Even if it is a come-on, it sure is interesting."

"It wasn't a come-on, Camilla."

"I know THAT! But tell me about it."

I was on the witness stand being cross-examined by a tough and lovely prosecuting attorney.

So I told her about the cops' retreat and Sister and my guilt. She seemed to think my narration was hilariously funny.

Then as we pulled into the parking lot at Petersen's she squeezed my arm and said, "That's a wonderful story, Declan. I know it's true. I'm glad we've met again."

Then the two malted milks came to the table and the cross-examination continued.

"Well, how did you find out where I was and what I was doing?"

"I prayed to St. Jude, the patron of lost causes."

"Come on!"

"I remembered that your family moved to River Forest, so I looked up your address in the phone book."

"We're not listed."

"Uh, I looked you up in The University Law School alumni list?"

"No way!"

"Can I take the Fifth?"

"NO!"

"Well . . . whom do I work for?"

"Captain Huong . . . You mean it was easy to find me!"

"And all the details, where you'd gone to school, law review, where you worked, your phone numbers—which I didn't keep—your bra size, everything."

"I don't believe you!"

"The Dragon Lady is watching you everywhere . . ."

"So you drove out to St. Lucy's to see what I looked like."

"I already knew what you looked like."

"How?"

"This gorgeous Mediterranean woman rushed by me at

Twenty-sixth and California. I asked some guy who you were and he warned me against hitting on you because it would be like I was run over by a Bradley Fighting Vehicle."

"He did not!"

She continued to sip her malt, gracefully of course. I was afraid to start mine.

"He did so!"

"You didn't hit on me."

"Wouldn't dare!"

"All right, tell me what you've done with your life!"

"Very little."

"Drink your malt!"

"Yes, ma'am."

"Well, where did you go to school?" She pointed an accusing finger at me.

"Where do you think?"

"Brother Rice?"

"And college?"

"Circle?"

"Loyola."

"You didn't go to law school?"

"John Marshall, way down at the bottom of the heap."

"You're a lawyer?"

"Well, I passed the bar exam, just barely."

"First time around?"

"I think so."

"I'd much sooner face a Jewish attorney from The University than one of you South Side Irish from John Marshall."

"Different culture . . . I'd not try to argue with you in court . . . Or anywhere else! Bradley Fighting Vehicle!"

She was reveling in the dialogue and I was enjoying her. Whoever married her would never have a dull moment. Too spicy for me. So what if I couldn't take my eyes off her expressive face.

"Do you have any attachments, Declan?"

A curveball. From a curvaceous woman.

"I have parents and siblings in whose house I don't live."

"You know what I mean!"

The prosecution was about to become angry at me. It was none of her business, right?

"I gave up on them when I graduated from college. Women lost interest in me when they found that they couldn't remake me."

"No one should think they have the right to do that."

Her beautiful face wrinkled in a frown.

"What about you?"

"All guys want to do is hit on me."

"I'm not hitting on you."

She considered that.

"So you drove out to Austin just to apologize to me?"

"I didn't know you'd be here. If I had, I would have asked the Dragon Lady to send someone else."

"Why would you do that?"

"Fear."

She finished her malt, dabbed her lips delicately, and asked, "Are you still afraid of me?"

"Can I come and watch you play beach volleyball?"

That stopped her cold. Good for you, Declan. You won one.

"Why would you want to do that?"

"To sketch you . . . I do a little bit of that as a hobby."

"North Avenue Beach is open to everyone . . . I have to see the sketches after the match is over."

"Maybe."

"No maybe."

"OK."

"Are you still afraid of me, Declan O'Donnell?"

"Enchanted, enthralled, enraptured, immobilized, intrigued, incoherent."

"Drink your malt."

"Yes, ma'am."

She pondered the whole exchange.

"It is strange that we meet again, isn't it, especially this way. Do you think God planned it?"

Not a fair question. We were both sinking into the delightful swamp of infatuation, from which there might not be any escape. Very dangerous.

"More likely the Blessed Mother."

My cell phone rang.

"O'Donnell."

"Annamaria. Are you earning your salary?"

"I'll call you back later."

"Hookay."

"The Dragon Lady?"

"She said I had to pay for the malts!"

"She did not!"

We drove back to St. Lucy's in silence. Rain was falling, the slow gentle rain that comes before the thunder and lightning. I was trying to absorb all that had happened—the yearnings, the needs, the chemicals, the perils, possibilities, all quite overwhelming. We could easily fall in love. Then what? The question increased my heartbeat. This was a terrifying prospect.

We were too old to be reckless.

"I'd like to see you again."

"You'll be on North Avenue Beach on Sunday to ogle me."

"Only respectfully. Well, more or less."

"I'm sure you have all my phone numbers."

She stopped by the Mudhole Park. Rain was beating against its smooth surface, warning, I thought, of aging and death.

"I wouldn't use them unless you gave them to me."

She turned and looked at me, a piercing stare of risk analysis. Then she took a business card from her purse and scribbled on the back.

"Home and personal cell phone on the back," she said as she handed the card to me.

"One more crime I didn't mention on the witness stand,

Counsel. I have most of the courses I need for a Ph.D. in psychology."

"A cop, a lawyer, and a shrink," she said with her wild Sicilian grin. "Declan O'Donnell, you're overqualified!"

"That's what they all say."

"I didn't say that you're weird," she said as she opened the door of the car.

I might have kissed her then. She wouldn't have minded. It was too soon. We both had much to digest. Instead I touched her cheek.

"I will call you, Camilla, that I promise."

She went back into the church. I phoned Annamaria from my own car.

"Captain, my captain."

"You with girl, Declan?"

"Not anymore."

"You in a bar with her?"

She was affecting her Asian accent.

"Ice-cream parlor."

"Nice girl?"

"Very nice."

"Nice CATHOLIC girl?"

"What else?"

"IRISH Catholic girl?"

"Sicilian."

"Pretty?"

"Like a young Sophia Loren on Turner Classic Movies."

"Declan, you in deep shit . . . Come to work tomorrow morning early. Much work to do."

Less than respectful images of a naked Camilla flooded my imagination. Yes, Declan, you in deep shit.

Blackie

"Father Ryan," I said into the telephone. The clock said it was three o'clock.

In the morning.

"What's happening in the old neighborhood?"

"Your friend Mickey has a Maine coon cat name Jan Kazimir . . . What's happening in the Eternal City?"

"I have them on the run, Blackwood. I told you that it's locked in. Don't worry about it. What is going on at St. Lucy's other than a cat that thinks you're cool?"

"A Maine coon cat . . . This afternoon we will rededicate the church, celebrate the Eucharist, and sing a Te Deum. Tomorrow or the next day, Pan Mikal will offer a Requiem Mass for the three victims, for whom he has bought plots at Queen of Heaven Cemetery. As you well know one of his curates is a useless slug and the other is the ineffable Nelson Ironman who calls you Bwana Sean and sharpens his spear over against another assault. The police are struggling for a solution, which I do not think they will find. The G is involved for reasons which escape and worry me. Soon it will be dismissed as a drug-war killing, an explanation which I do not for a moment accept. The parish rallies around its noble count. For the present the New Austin project seems to prosper. Finally, we have not by any means seen the last of the troubles."

Andrew M. Greeley

"Umm."

"You're staying on the case?"

"Patently."

"Any clues?"

"The interesting problem of the alarm system at night."

"Don't tell me. It didn't go off?"

"But the perps, as we in the work call them, were nonetheless able to enter the church with the bodies. This suggests considerable planning, a high degree of intelligence, and serious malice."

"Sounds bad. . . . There will be more trouble?"

"Arguably."

"Don't let any happen to Mickey! See to it, Blackwood."

I made two decisions. I would ask Mike Casey to put some of his off-duty cops to work guarding St. Lucy's and inquire of Captain Annamaria Huong about the possibility of collaboration with her gnomes. I thereupon returned to my virtuous rest, which was unfortunately troubled by thousands of Nigerians chasing me with their large spears.

After bringing Communion to Northwestern University Hospital, presiding over the Eucharist to a presentable congregation, and consuming my usual modest breakfast of bacon, pancakes, raisin bran, toast, orange juice, and tea, I called first of all the resilient Annamaria.

"Blackie! You call to brighten my day!"

"Looking out the window, Madam Captain, I note that it is already acceptably bright."

"Hookay! What you want?"

"I think you already know."

"You want to cooperate with us on the curious affair of the alarm system at St. Lucy's."

"And anything else related to that affair. I fear more violence."

"Me too. We make deal, you get rid of hot Sicilian girl who distract my number one boy, and we cooperate."

"Only God and the two principals could accomplish that. I suspect the former may be on their side."

"She nice girl?"

"Patently."

"Hookay. We leave them to heaven. You call me. I call you. Maybe number one boy come see you. Hookay?"

"Hookay."

Then I called Mike the Cop.

His wife, the valiant Annie Reilly, insisted that I must wait upon her in her gallery the next morning for my weekly ration of oatmeal raisin cookies and apple cinnamon tea. I so promised.

"What's up Blackie?"

"After consultation with Milord Cronin, I have concluded that we must ask that you provide discreet protection for St. Lucy's Church and School and the pastor of the parish."

"I'd thought about that. What about the local precinct?"

"I expect that they will be replaced by Fifth District Homicide shortly. The Feds are also lurking. In a day or two, it will be said that, while the investigation continues, the police believe that the killings were drug-related."

"Sounds like you think there'll be a cover-up?"

"The stink of that is already in the air . . . I especially don't like the G snooping around like national security is involved."

"In the Old Neighborhood?"

"It makes no sense to me either."

"How did they get into the church, Blackie?"

"Somehow the alarm system was temporarily disabled."

"That would be very difficult, wouldn't it?"

"There are several other stinks in the air."

"Yeah, well I may go out there a couple of nights myself. After all, it's my old neighborhood too."

"We will pay no extra for your presence, especially if you manage to get yourself shot!"

He laughed.

"For Sean Cronin we will give a clergy discount."

"Now about O'Boyle and Sons."

"There's only one son. The others opted out early. The old

man, Tim O'Boyle, is difficult. He came up the hard way, poor family in Galewood, north of the tracks out on the West Side. Did chemical engineering in college on the GI Bill after the war. Tough, aggressive, even if he is in his eighties. The surviving son Marshal O'Boyle is tough enough to take care of himself. He fancies himself a great architect and is waiting to inherit the firm, which will give a platform to display his skills. He's made a lot of money in the commodities markets. He could probably set up his own firm but he's determined to inherit—or buy out—his father. He's not a happy camper in any segment of his life. He's driven away his own wife and kids. Doesn't speak to his brothers or sisters and has had a long series of mistresses in his mansion on Dearborn Street. But he has no reason to want the New Austin project to fail."

"It would seem not."

"Both are gombeen men, Blackie, not to be fully trusted. Marshal studied in Ireland for a while, where they produce really heavy gombeen men."

"Ah."

"They're not upper-level developers by a long shot, upper-middle maybe. Very shrewd and close men with a buck. They've never gone bankrupt, mind you, and no one has ever nailed them for breaking a law. Currently their financial situation is dodgy, as it usually is for firms their size. However, they do not seem to be in deep trouble. A sudden decline in the market for New Austin would probably be a severe blow to them but they could soldier on."

"So they would have no motive for the murders and the desecration of the old parish."

"None obvious anyway. Like I say, they are gombeen men. Layers and layers of scheming. It might be interesting to find out who might want them to fail . . . People tell me that the relationship between father and son is strange, a love-hate sort of thing."

"Not unusual among the Irish?"

He laughed.

"As the grandchildren would say, tell me about it! Still there's layers and layers of mystery there even for two Irishmen. The other brothers got out of the firm because they couldn't stand the old man. Marshal hangs in there, though he has more than enough money and, I am told, talent to break away and start his own firm.

"Indeed . . . The project is in good order at City Hall?"

"At the top, sure. It will be a major order in the growth of the city. Again, however, there are layers and layers. However, if push comes to shove, you can certainly count on City Hall."

"I'll advise my brother Packy, who is not without some clout there, of our interest in the case."

"And tell him of my interest too . . . Anything else?"

"Your very good friend Annie Huong is interested in the case. She sent her number one boy out there yesterday."

"Best instincts in the city, saving your reverence. Let me speculate—number one boy is Irish, Catholic, from the South Side, mild and seemingly ineffectual."

"What other kind are there?"

"Don't let her phony pidgin English fool you. It's part of the persona."

"I can't imagine why anyone would do that."

As I was leaving the rectory with intent to take the subway downtown to visit the O'Boyle redoubt in the Sears Tower, I came upon Crystal Lane, our resident mystic and youth minister in her office. She was busy with posters announcing a retreat.

"Ms. Lane, good morning. The youth are no more difficult than usual, I trust?"

"Hi, Bishop Blackie. The kids are wonderful."

When they fell under the influence of her charm and goodness, the kids indeed became wonderful.

Then the smile faded from her face.

"You're involved with the St. Lucy violence, aren't you, Bishop?"

"Unfortunately, yes."

"It is very bad, very bad. You must be careful."

"This afternoon we will rededicate the church and sing a hymn of thanksgiving. That will dissipate the evil."

I didn't think it would, but I wanted to hear what Crystal's highly sensitive instincts told her.

"It's like a black cloud hovers over the whole neighborhood."

"Then it is the responsibility of the Church to banish the darkness—as best we can."

"Yes, but you must be careful. I will pray for you."

"Please do, Crystal, and for the good people in St. Lucy's."

"Oh, yes . . . All day."

Despite the warm August sunshine, I shivered as I walked around the corner to the Red Line subway station.

The office suite of O'Boyle and Sons did not at all suggest that they were in the middle ranks of Chicago developers. Done tastefully in what I could call chrome-and-glass modern, they looked out on the West Side of Chicago through large windows which disclosed under the sunlight the straight lines of the Congress Expressway, the railroad and L tracks, and the side streets all rushing straight out to the city limits and beyond, even to such inappropriate places as Oakbrook, Elmhurst, Lagrange, and, heaven save us all, Naperville and Lisle. I often thought that the vast sheet-metal wings of the Pritzker orchestra shell in Millennium Park, caught in a powerful Lake wind, would someday overfly Oak Park and River Forest and wipe out the Oakbrook Center Shopping Mall.

A lot of money had gone into the computers, the workstations, the thin television screens, the ceramic art, the large offices, and the handsome staff who were working busily as we spoke in Tim O'Boyle's vast southwest corner office. Plans for the New Austin were spread on his glass desk and artists' drawings of town houses, homes, and the new St. Lucy's were prominently displayed. A transparent blind had been drawn against the sunlight from the south. By midday the office would be shrouded in eclipselike darkness.

Since I was dressed like a real bishop because of the services that afternoon, I was given a solemn high welcome into the O'Boyle offices—and the women staff members were fascinated by the silver Brigid pectoral cross and New Grange episcopal ring, both of which my cousin Catherine Collins had created for me. God help me if I ever permanently lost either of them.

"We are proud of the New Austin project." Tim "Big Tim" O'Boyle began spreading out his arms as if to embrace the whole neighborhood. "It's the first of its kind in this country—a whole neighborhood re-created with rehabbed homes, new town houses, new and rehabbed apartments, new shops and theaters and community centers. It's not been easy, but we think it's one of the finest things we've done, do you understand?"

He doth protest too much, I thought—either a salesman or a gombeen man. "Big Tim" was not all that big; still, he was bigger than I am, which doesn't prove anything. His white hair was thin, his face pale, his body heavy with a paunch, his pale, shrewd eyes obscured by rimless trifocal lenses. He was somewhere in his early eighties yet his voice was alert and his gestures enthusiastic.

"St. Lucy's is the center of it all, isn't it, Marshal?"

Marshal O'Boyle nodded solemnly. He had not bothered to kiss my ring or even to greet me. Sleek and saturnine with a pencil-thin mustache and receding glossy hairline, he rarely looked up from the drawings, which I suspected were mostly his. Both men wore shirts and ties, Big Tim a blue shirt with a white collar, Marshal a plain white shirt and a Notre Dame tie.

There was a chemistry between them that unnerved me, as if I had walked into a family quarrel which had gone for decades without the argument ever rising to the surface in words. We Irishmen tend to be that way.

"There's a lot of money involved," Big Tim went on. "We're proud as Catholics that we are rebuilding a neighborhood which was once mostly Catholic. We may make some money, though not at first. We may lose some money, we hope not too much. But this is not a project in which anyone is going to get rich in a hurry, do you understand?"

"Not at first anyway," I said.

"We have some Federal money, thanks be to God, and some

Andrew M. Greeley

speculative investments and of course some payment for the actual construction work. Still, do you understand, we're under constant pressure from clients, contractors, building inspectors, the zoning board, the local groups, each of which wants something more than we can give, no matter how much we give, isn't that true, Marshal?"

Marshal nodded again and gave me a drawing of the new St. Lucy's School—with a parking garage beneath it and condo apartments above it. Take your children to school by riding down the elevator, then walk a block to the L tracks. Couldn't beat it.

Marshal O'Boyle, however, did not seem to be a very happy man. His eyes shifted from me to his father and back.

"Monsignor Mike, the pastor, is our strongest supporter, absolutely a hundred percent behind us. Yet even he leans on us sometimes. He knows what we're trying to do, yet he insists on some low-cost housing. We'll give them that, sure. And we'll have a completely integrated neighborhood, much better than it is now with mostly one race, Bishop, do you understand?"

"Some poor people will lose their homes?"

"They'll make a lot more money on them than they would otherwise. They can buy nice little bungalows or even two flats down in Berwyn or out in Brookfield and get away from the drug gangs too. Most of them don't go to St. Lucy's or send their children to the parish school. Still the Monsignor wants us to keep more of them in the community. I tell him that if he does that, the whites and the affluent coloreds simply won't move in. You can't make a new omelet without breaking eggs, can you, Marshal?"

He did not reply. Rather he continued to pore over his drawings.

"Have to use fresh eggs," I said.

"It will be an environment-friendly neighborhood, do you understand? I majored in chemical engineering in college. Became a developer later on. I know all about the environment."

I wasn't particularly sure that he did.

"That should be very helpful."

"So these killings, just a week before school opens, are a terrible

76

blow. Our real estate partners tell me that people have already taken offers off the table." He waved his hands as the captain of a sinking ship might have. "What can we do? I don't trust the local cops. They've been slow cleaning up the drug trade down on Waller Street, where we're trying to build a line of *very* upscale town houses. The Mexicans want their piece of the action too. That damn Pablo Sanchez with his mansion over on West End almost blackmails us for 'Mexican community work,' which means into his bank accounts down in the Caymans. The Negro clergy are on the take too. I want to spit every time the alderman whispers in my ear. We've done our best to placate everyone and now this happens, doesn't it, Marshal?"

"It's a setback all right, Bishop," Marshal agreed, without looking up from his drawings. "Everything seems to get closer to the edge. We can make it as long as there isn't more trouble."

"It's not like we had to take on the project. We're doing this because it's a good work. Almost every day now I want to pull the plug on everything, do you understand?"

"Can you guess who the murderers are?"

"Druggies, of course. That's what I told the mayor this morning when I called his office. He's solidly behind us. He knows how important the New Austin is for the city of Chicago. But even he can't stop all the inspectors who hassle us every day. Nobody understands how hard it is to push a project like this through. If we wanted to make money, we'd go out to Geneva or someplace like that and build a project in a cornfield, isn't that true, Marshal?"

"The craziest people are not the *narcotrafficantes*, Bishop, but the do-gooders like Joe Tuohey of the OBA."

He still didn't look up at me.

"Organization for a Better Austin. An umbrella pressure group for all the other local pressure groups. They say they want change, hell, everyone says that except the alderman. But they want it so slow that no one will notice it. They don't grasp that renewal doesn't work that way."

"Do you think they might have done the killing?" I asked.

Andrew M. Greeley

"I'm not saying that."

Big Tim took back the conversation.

"There's a lot of loose cannons in that bunch, free-floating nuts. They think that whatever they want God wants. Nineteen sixties all over again. They have picket lines up somewhere every day."

"What would it take to force you to end the project?"

"Close it all down? . . . Right now we couldn't afford to do that. And we don't want to. We'll fight them all the way. I only wish that Monsignor Mike could understand more about how tough our business is . . . Could I ask you a question, Bishop?"

"Sure."

Which didn't mean that I'd give him a straight answer. Irish people generally avoid straight answers, even more so if they are bishops.

"Is the Cardinal behind our project?"

"Certainly he is. He grew up in Austin. He wants the neighborhood to be prosperous and healthy again. He knows it will be good for the whole city and the whole Archdiocese. As you can imagine, we would not want to be involved in specific decisions which are beyond our technical competence."

"And is he behind Monsignor Mike?" Marshal asked as he finally looked up and presented me with an artist's drawing of the new school, very neat, very modern, very cool.

"They've been friends since their school days. He has great confidence in the Monsignor. That doesn't necessarily mean that he would personally support every decision—though I know, Marshal, that he's delighted with that picture and has signed off on it at least in principle."

All of what I had said was true, not necessarily the whole truth. In principle a bishop never tells the whole truth unless he absolutely has to. If Milord Cronin wanted a way out, I had given him plenty of room.

"Well, I'm relieved to hear that . . ." Big Tim interrupted his comment with a cough that wracked his whole body. "It was very good of you to stop by. We'll be there in the afternoon for the services of course."

Too many cigarettes, I thought.

"Thank you," I said.

Marshal showed me to the doors of the suite.

"One more question," I said to the younger O'Boyle at the door, à la Lieutenant Columbo. "What are the newest threats you're getting?"

He nodded solemnly.

"We get them almost every day. They threaten to kill the Monsignor and to blow up the school with the children in it. They claim to be Islamic terrorists. We don't take them seriously."

Why, I wondered, would Al-Quaida worry about St. Lucy's?

As I walked over to Quincy and Wells to board the Green Line as the Lake Street L was now called, I called Mike Casey.

"The O'Boyles tell me that they have received threats from what claims to be an Islamic group that they will kill Msgr. Wolodyjowski and blow up the school with all the children in it."

"Do you think the threats are real?"

"They may not even exist. The O'Boyles are patently under great stress. Yet . . ."

"I'll increase our guards and call Fourteenth and Michigan and give them a heads-up."

I then called the Chancery Office and asked whether we had received any threats. We had not.

I purchased a Chicago hot dog with everything on it from a vendor at Randolph and Wabash and, having stretched two napkins across my (only) good suit, I consumed it with great delight on the platform while waiting for the Green Line train to appear. I even remembered to bring the bag with my episcopal robes when I boarded the train. I hoped that I would also remember how to put them on.

The ride west above Lake Street was fascinating. The city was expanding west for the second time in its history, the first time through prairies, the second time through slums. Gentrification of one kind or another had reached as far as Garfield Lawn. From Pulaski Road (still Crawford Avenue to most Chicago Irish bigots) on there were signs of new construction, though the abandoned houses and storefronts still blighted the street. Then around Laramie Avenue there was more construction, finally at Central, the boundary of the first phase of the New Austin cranes and trucks and hard-hat workers were everywhere.

I had no trouble leaving the train at Austin Boulevard, though I did have to rush back to my seat to recapture my clothes bag, which a leprechaun had temporarily hidden. Now on to Pablo Sanchez of the West Lords.

Blackie

A beautiful young Mexican woman opened the door of the rehabilitated mansion on West End Lawnway.

"Good afternoon, Bishop Ryan, Pablo is expecting you. We're honored that you would come to our house. Let me take your bag. I am Luisa."

"You must promise not to let me walk out without it."

"Of course."

Her clothes were simple and elegant—and very expensive: white blouse, black trousers, lots of jewelry, careful and costly makeup. She wore a gold medallion of San Malverde. She could not be more than twenty-three or twenty-four years old. I wondered whether she realized that the shadow of death hung over her and her family. The *narcotrafficantes* now have a law among themselves that, when you kill a leader, you also killed his wife and children and his parents if they are still alive. Luisa might die before she was thirty. Queen for a day or a little longer. A large statue of Guadalupe with a burning votive candle in it dominated the room.

Trendy new shops had appeared on Austin South of the L stop. The developers had converted the rooms of the old Servile Hotel into an expensive, art-deco condominium building. A sign informed me that a few choice condos were still available.

Construction and rehabilitation stretched for several blocks, down to Washington Boulevard. Most of the work was both solid and tasteful. The O'Boyles had certainly done their best. I wondered how many of the new condos were put up on spec. Many of them doubtless, maybe most. No wonder they felt on the edge. Was some of Pablo's money, skillfully laundered, invested in the project? Better that I not ask.

Pablo Sanchez entered the room, fell to his knee, and kissed my ring. That doesn't happen very often because I don't wear it very often, lest I lose it.

"Please give your blessing, Padre."

In his culture "Padre" is about as high as you can go in ecclesiastical titles.

"May the Lord God bless you and keep you, Pablo, and grant you and your family a long and happy life."

He laughed.

"It will take a miracle, Padre, for that to happen."

He wore jeans and a white sport shirt. He was unbelievably young, almost as though he were just out of college, with bright eyes, a quick smile, and curly brown hair. He did not seem like a man who entered the narco traffic at nine and had become, because of his hard work, intelligence, and ruthlessness, a major player. His was an American dream—an immigrant, doubtless illegal, who had become a success, albeit in the sale of drugs and murder.

"On my mother's grave, Padre, I swear it was not my people who desecrated the church."

"How old was your mother when she was buried, Pablo?"

"I don't know exactly, around thirty we think."

"How old will Luisa be when she dies?"

A spasm of pain crossed his face.

"You sound like Don Miguel, Padre. We live in our cause as long as we can. Then"—he lifted his shoulders—"we hope God takes us home."

That is the way mercenaries had lived for at least a couple of millennia.

"We are only taking back what is rightfully ours," he continued. "What can we do? Gringos have exploited us for three centuries. We are at war."

The same old argument, not, perhaps, without a certain grain of truth.

"About St. Lucy's?"

He spread his hands.

"My very own children go there. I want them to grow up and be good Catholics like Luisa and I are. I want them to be good American Catholics who know all the rules and"—he grinned ruefully—"and keep them most of the time."

"They have good godparents who will take care of them?"

He sighed, not as effectively as we West of Ireland folk sigh, but with a good deal more feeling.

"Of course. They will live far away from the traffic."

"You do not know the identity of those children whose naked bodies were found in the church?"

"No, Padre! No! They were not my people. My people did not kill them and know nothing about who did. Our hands are clean."

He extended his hands as if I wanted to inspect them.

"Ah."

"You ask me what I think? I tell you I think they are *undocumentados* who came to Chicago and were killed by someone who needed bodies to put in the church. There are people who do that kind of thing. But I don't think a *Mexicano* would kill to desecrate a church. We are good Catholics. We would never do that. We would be afraid that we would be handed over to the devil."

He made the sign of the cross against such a fate.

"A Mexican might provide bodies for someone else who needed them, without asking too many questions?"

"*¿Quien sabe?*"

"You are suggesting, are you not, Don Pablo, that the desecration itself was done by professionals? Men who might kill under contract or might desecrate a church on contract?"

"Who else?" He lifted his eyebrows.

Donna Luisa appeared with a bowl of gazpacho and a cup of

wine. I did not decline. She even provided me with a napkin. Then she slipped away to permit the men to do business.

"There are many such men, Padre, some of them organized into tiny armies. Our people would not do that. Killing may be part of our business, but our business is not killing."

I left that rationalization alone.

"Puerto Ricans, perhaps. Maybe Italians, maybe Russians, maybe Vietnamese. Who knows? If I find out who did this, I swear by our Lady of Guadalupe I will kill them all. I must defend my children and my parish."

"Better we let the police arrest them."

"They never will. They pay the police. Some of them ARE the police."

I doubted this, but among the areas of corruption in our society there might be an occasional one for an organization of professional killers—so long as they were careful about whom they killed. Indeed just as some cops moonlight for Mike the Cop, so others might moonlight for Brand X. I would inquire.

"You realize that this trouble will be a big setback for Padre Mike?"

"How is this possible?"

"The renewal of the neighborhood could slow down, even stop. Parents might think the school is too dangerous. He himself might be at risk."

"I swear by the Blood of the Savior, by the Holy Virgin, and by St. Malverde that I will not permit this to happen."

West End was for a moment the Rhine River and Don Pablo was a robber baron who enforced the law within his fief. In a lawless world, he would enforce honor and peace. Austin was a land of terror in which only men of respect could protect the innocent.

Brr! This was how the Mafia began in eighteenth-century Sicily.

Pablo was Judge Roy Bean west of the Pecos.

I didn't like it.

"If you find out, let me know. I'll see that the problem is dealt with."

"They would kill you too, Padre. They have no honor."

OK, he DID know who they were or at least who they were likely to be.

Donna Luisa appeared with Sergio and Maria and asked me to bless all the family before I left. The little kids were shy darlings, who readily exchanged high fives with me. Again I asked God to bless them all, grant them long and happy lives, and grant the kids high grades and good teachers in school. Outside the house, the day, clear and clean in the morning, had become heavy. Thick curtains of haze and humidity had descended on the West Side of Chicago. Certainly, Pan Mikal would not have installed air-conditioning in the rectory or the school, of that I was certain. My purple robes would be a prison around me. I sighed. Before air-conditioning people must not have realized how uncomfortable they were. On the other hand there was no need for the deity to reinstitute the ice age because of my complaints.

Walking back up Austin Boulevard and under the L tracks, I called Mike Casey.

"Does the CPD have death squads, Mike?"

"What makes you ask that?'

"There is a hint that a band of professional killers might be involved in this situation."

Silence.

"Mike?"

"If you are asking whether there are shadowy hit groups around Chicago and suburbs, I will say yes. If you ask whether the CPD is watching them and will pounce whenever there is a hint of evidence against them, the answer is still yes."

"And?"

"And are there hints that certain cops might have shady relationships with such shadow groups?"

I waited for an answer.

"I never saw evidence of that when I was superintendent. I don't think there's any hard evidence. There are rumors that certain officers may be shady. Most other officers avoid them. If you press, the typical cop would say that someone is innocent until proven guilty. If we had real proof . . . For our own good we'd probably go to the State's Attorney. Most of us wouldn't want someone like that on the force."

"You sniff around?"

"Sure . . . You might ask your good friend Annamaria to sniff around too."

I found her number one boy, now dressed up in a dark gray suit and a Loyola tie, aimlessly ambling about in front of St. Lucy's, as if pondering the deep problems of life or at least of the Unit. Most likely he was awaiting the appearance of the fair Camilla. I also noted with some interest a bulge under his jacket.

"You're carrying your weapon into Mass."

"Normally the Dragon Lady exempts us from that rule. Today she said, Declan, you wear gun . . ."

With his easy smile, his relaxed manner, and his bright, responsive Irish eyes, Declan was certainly every mother's ideal son-in-law. The Sicilians out in River Forest would quickly dispose of their residual anti-Irish biases (which might not have been completely inappropriate) and sign him up, should the admirable Camilla drag him into the house for a family dinner. I wondered whether that young woman was aware of the fire that burned inside him, a fire the absence of which would have disqualified him to work for the Unit.

"And you said?"

"Yes, ma'am, right away, ma'am! . . . I hear you're coming on board."

"I may not unless I can replace you as number one boy."

"There are no number two boys, Blackie. Captain Huong is an egalitarian, if an authoritarian."

"I hear that there are organized hit squads in this city, some of whom may have police as members. Death squads, American style, except they don't kill for ideology."

"We are aware of them," he said softly, his eyes narrowing.

"That is reassuring."

"Some cops, my father and uncles for example, refuse to believe in that possibility. Cops are rarely if ever bent, but if they are, they must have good reasons."

"So even if convicted, let us say, of torturing suspects . . ."

"They're stand-up cops and not really guilty."

"Does your family think of you as a stand-up cop?"

"Not at all . . . Where did you hear about the death squads?"

"From Don Pablo. He points out that Mexican Americans would never desecrate a church . . . Which suggests a revisionist reading of twentieth-century Mexican history."

"What does he propose to do about them?"

"He pledged, if I remember correctly, on the Blood of the Savior, the Holy Virgin, and St. Malverde that he would kill them all."

"Do you think he might, Bishop Blackie?"

"His worldview is not the same as ours, Declan. I don't pretend to know what he might do. I suggested he talk to the Chicago police if he has evidence that a particular group of professionals was responsible. He said the police were the killers. That is instinct and hunch talking, which for him might be enough."

"I'll call Captain Huong and ask for instructions . . . By the way, it would appear that neither the autopsy nor forensics turned up any evidence. Tomorrow morning District Five will take over. They will continue to search, of course, but without any sense of urgency. They will leak the word to the press that it looks like drug-gang killings."

"But that's patently not true!"

"They want to get it out of the media, so they can work on the case at their own pace. They're a little afraid of Dawn Collins too."

"Not without reason," I noted.

"The Feds are back in the game. In the background to make sure the Chicago cops don't do anything they don't like."

"What are they covering up, Declan O'Donnell?"

"Sounds crazy, doesn't it?"

"Indeed . . . Now I must go to the rectory to find out what Pan Mikal expects of me."

"I'll call the captain."

"Give my regards to the valiant State's Attorney."

"I'm sure she won't be here."

"Count on it."

He grinned happily.

The young woman better show up, I thought.

Before I turned to walk up the rectory stairs and enter what I was sure would be a Victorian late-summer furnace, I turned back to him.

"You might also tell the beloved Captain Huong that O'Boyle and O'Boyle report threatening calls from a purported Islamic terrorist group which threatens to kill the pastor and blow up the school with the children in it."

"It's crazy . . . But so is everything else in this case . . . You came out on the L?"

I admitted that I had.

"I'll drive you back. We can't have a bishop washed away in a thunderstorm."

He would want to talk about his day-old infatuation with the Assistant State's Attorney. The best advice would be "go for it" but a priest should be more cautious, lest he be identified with parents.

"The loss of one such," I said by way of acceptance, "would barely be noticed."

Inside the rectory, I discovered that I had underestimated Pan Mikal. I was enveloped by the blessed cool air. Among the priests gathered round for the rededication ceremony—Mickey must have called his neighbors—bright, in his dashiki with Roman collar but without spear, was the ineffable Nelson Ironman.

"No spear today, Nelson?"

"Out of respect for Bwana Wolodyjowski," he said with a deep bow. The other associate, Thomas McDonald, was not in evidence. However, the good feline Jan Kazimir jumped up on a table next to the chair where I was striving to sort out my purple garments and settled in to guard me during my efforts. I reached out to scratch his neck and he purred contentedly.

The clerical conversation focused on the matter of the Lord Cardinal's "sudden" trip to Rome. All present, save the useless auxiliary bishop, had heard a number of facts on good authority. Milord had been summoned to Rome to submit his retirement. A nincompoop from another state was already packing for translation to Chicago. My destiny would be a small diocese in the Rocky Mountains. It would be nice, they opined, finally to have a place of my own. I tried to look owlish as if I knew the real story but could not talk about it.

I did, however, know that as long as Sean Cronin breathed, the nincompoop would not come to Chicago and I would leave the city only when summoned to go home to the Father in heaven. The latter point I had made clear to the Nuncio on several occasions when he hinted at future preferment. He might have heard such assertions from others before. However, he believed me.

As the rectory clock edged down towards five-thirty, I wandered into the office which contained the TV monitors. There was already a large crowd in the church and more people filing in from the parking lot. A choir in Anglican-like vestments waited in the sanctuary. Outside, several police cars were visible on Lake Street. Doubtless some of Mike Casey's folks were among the worshippers. I noted that State's Attorney Datilla entered the church on the arm of Declan O'Donnell, an arm which she had clearly claimed. Dawn Collins and several of her officers were present too.

Media trucks were parked at the entrance to the church and camera platforms blocked Lake Street. Schoolchildren and teachers filled the "Mudhole Park" across the street to watch the rededication on the large screen which Mickey Wolodyjowski had found for the occasion. I would suggest that we process across the street to pass among them.

Might there be an assassin on the L embankment? Or a bomb thrower in the congregation? Perhaps there was. We would have to take our chances.

A priest of my generation approached me, one Jeremy Dillon (born Jeremiah, if my memory serves me right).

"There's one thing Sean should do before he retires, Blackie. He ought to remove the Polack from this place before he destroys it completely. What's the point in all the expense of these security cameras? When someone wants to break into a church, they'll do it, no matter how elaborate the security. He's offended everyone in the parish, the blacks, the few Irish that are still around, the Hispanics. He's tied up with the O'Boyles, who are crooks and frauds, and this Organization for a Better Austin which is a bunch of radical pinkos. He's persuaded the poor people that there's going to be a new school here and maybe even the new church that was promised a century ago. None of that's going to happen. The alderman doesn't want it, the mayor doesn't want it, the people don't want it, especially the African-American community. They're the people who are already being driven out by all the promises. It's a bubble, Blackie, and the Polack is responsible for it."

"Ah," I said, remembering that Father Dillon had been the pastor here before he assumed a large suburban parish. These were in some sense his people. That everyone hates his successor is a clerical culture dictum that seems all too true.

"Don't get me wrong, Blackie. He's a wonderful old man, but he's still a Polack, a blockhead and now one who is losing some of his marbles. It's time for him to go, even if he's a classmate of Sean."

"Arguably."

"Bwana Ryan"—Nelson bowed respectfully—"everything is now in order."

The bishop had better not forget his carefully prepared homily.

Blackie

"I am here in this historic church only because Cardinal Sean Cronin is in Rome advising the Pope and the Roman Curia how to properly administer the Church. We can rely on him to make his instructions clear and succinct. He is, as you know, a product of this neighborhood. When he says, 'the old neighborhood' even a poor South Sider like me knows he means St. Lucy. He asked me in a phone call this morning at 3:00 A.M. Chicago time—just because you are a Cardinal it does not follow that you understand matters like time change—to assure you that he will visit St. Lucy's as soon as he returns.

"Having grown weary of His Eminence's praise of St. Lucy's, I will now be able to insist that the community represented in the church this evening is better than it ever was. It stood up to horrible violence and responded with faith and hope, with trust in God and enthusiasm for its pastor.

(Applause.)

"Evil was done in this old but beautiful building, evil which staggers the human imagination, gratuitous evil designed to shake the resolve of the people of the parish, to divide priest and people, to stir up hatred, to create fear to shatter the community that is emerging here in the New Austin.

"I myself wondered how the men and women, boys and girls of

St. Lucy's would respond. It would have been understandable if you stayed away from a place haunted by violent death, if you feared the demons which might lurk here, if you wanted to wait a few days till the TV cameras went away and police cars disappeared. If your pastor had asked me for my advice—a serious mistake—I would have said, cool it for a while till everything settles down. I would have been wrong.

"There is no doubt why this community of men and women with multihued skins from every nation under heaven have assembled inside and outside the church and across Lake Street in the Park. They are responding to evil with a triumphant ceremony of rededication and thanksgiving. In a couple of days there will be a Requiem liturgy for the three unfortunate innocents who were murdered to shake your confidence. Both services are an act of defiance against the powers of evil. You are saying, in effect, this is our parish, this is our church, and no one, no one is going to take it away from us.

"God bless you all. Do not give up the fight."

(More applause.)

There was no applause from the clergy. Priests never applaud for other priests. It's against the rules. Father McDonald, sitting in the far corner of the sacristy with his biretta firmly in place on his head, slept through my remarks, but then he slept through everything else. Was there any way this poor young man might be salvaged? Nelson Ironman, on the other hand, stared fixedly at the audience, ready to resist any assault, even in the absence of his treasured royal spear.

As I was speaking, I noted Sergeant Declan O'Donnell slip out of the pew and walk rapidly to the back of the church. Something was happening and it was not good. Again I wondered if the number one boy of the valiant Annamaria Huong might be one of the dark ones after all.

At Communion time the choir struggled with the sound of a helicopter whirling overhead. However, preceded by his State's Attorney, the virtuous Camilla, Declan approached me for the Eucharist. She was very reverent, he winked at me—a sign that all was well outside.

The copter came and went all through the singing of the Te Deum, not exactly the right accompaniment. The other clergy processed up the steps of the church, out into the humidity of Lake Street, and back to the rectory for the dinner they had been promised. As the first shadows of day's end filtered over the Park and across Lake Street, the pastor and the Ironman and I waited on the sidewalk to talk to the people as they emerged. I noted out of the corner of my eye considerable activity among the police and the media. Something had happened or was happening.

A lanky man with disorderly gray hair and a haggard face shook my hand and drew me away from the crowd.

"Joe Tuohey—with an 'e' of the OBA, Bishop," he said, still clutching my hand. "Organization for a Better Austin."

"Ah," I said.

"We're an umbrella organization of concerned community groups around here. I'm delighted that you alluded to the interracial composition of this community. It is very important that we remind people of that."

"I would have thought it patent. The parishioners are a mosaic of variety."

"We have to keep it that way. I tried for a long time to prevent white flight here in Austin. Now I'm fighting to contain black flight. New Austin is causing that. Our black people are selling their homes and running from white encroachment."

"Selling their homes at considerable profit, I am told, which was not the case when the original white residents fled."

"We're trying to talk them out of deserting the community just for money . . ."

"And for a nice bungalow in Brookfield . . . I can't imagine that this neighborhood will ever be anything but multiracial."

"That's not the point."

"Which is?"

"To preserve some of the community ties of the African-

Americans—their churches, their organizations, their schools. We are not opposed to New Austin. Monsignor Mike is a good friend of mine. We admire the work he has done in the school through the years. We would only hope that he would see the wisdom of slowing down the process of black flight. What is the rush, anyway? The L will always be here, won't it? Cannot the Church support our efforts to fight the developers and the blockbusters? They're not concerned about Austin. All they want is their profits."

There was considerable irony in concern about black flight and profit-hungry white blockbusters. Moreover, there was merit in Joe Tuohey's concerns which were the same as Jeremy Dillon's if stated with less ethnic bias. Yet how were we to dissuade African-American home owners from grabbing windfall gains? And how to "slow down" a project which needed momentum if it were not to die?

"I'm not sure, Joe," I said, finally recovering the use of my hand, "that the Cardinal would be willing to override Msgr. Wolodyjowski's prudential judgment in these matters, especially since it seems that there will be both racial and social-class integration . . ."

"Only tokenism."

"Nonetheless, I will make your wishes known to both of them."

He rubbed his hands through his hair.

"It's always the same, Bishop. The Church never listens."

I had thought I was listening.

"The leadership of the Church is made up of weak human beings who are often insensitive and not infrequently idiots."

"Tell me about it," Joe Tuohey with an "e" snarled as he stormed away.

If they expected so much from us, the reason doubtless was that we had taught them to expect that we would never be anything less than perfect.

Back in the rectory, where Ironman had reclaimed his spear, I chatted briefly with the assembled clerics and listened once again patiently to Jeremy Dillon.

"Blackie, Sean has to dump this guy. What's the point in an elaborate dinner in a poor neighborhood like this?"

"I'm sure he paid for it himself."

"That's not the point!"

"And the point is?"

"It looks bad. The community is about to throw him out if Sean doesn't."

"The community in the church and out on Lake Street and over in the Park seemed supportive of the good monsignor."

"You're as bad as he is, Blackie. You don't get it. Those people are not THE community."

Patently I did not get it.

Just then Ironman saved me.

"Your driver is here, Bwana."

"Driver?"

"Sergeant O'Donnell."

"Oh, yes . . . Jeremy, I will relay your concerns to the Cardinal when he returns."

His snort of disbelief was the functional equivalent of a vulgar word.

"Ah, Sergeant," I said. "Traveling alone."

"She went home. The Dragon Lady wants me to work all night. We're going to try to break into the Combined Control computer system to see if we can turn off the alarms here."

Without warning, Mary Alice Quinn, with lights and camera crew, appeared out of the dusk. The worthy woman thrust out her hand, which contained two spent cartridges.

Channel 3 News

Speaking for Cardinal Sean Cronin who is in Rome, auxiliary bishop John Ryan cast down the gauntlet to those who are blaming the desecration of St. Lucy's on the urban-renewal project in West Austin.

Cut to Blackie in pulpit of St. Lucy's:

There is no doubt why this community of men and women with multihued skins from every nation under heaven have assembled inside and outside the church and across Lake Street in the Park. They are responding to evil with a triumphant ceremony of rededication and thanksgiving. In a couple of days there will be a Requiem liturgy for the three unfortunate innocents who were murdered to shake your confidence. Both services are an act of defiance against the powers of evil. You are saying, in effect, this is our parish, this is our church, and no one, no one is going to take it away from us.

Yet, as Mary Alice Quinn reports from Austin, St. Lucy's is still troubled.

MAQ: That's right, Samantha. While Bishop Ryan was preaching, an alert police officer spotted a man with a rifle on the L embankment. He asked us to turn our lights back on. As you can see from this clip there was indeed a shadow figure up there. The police charged the embankment, as you see, and the man disappeared. A police copter arrived too late. The gunman was not apprehended.

SAM: You have heard, Mary Alice, that a spokesman at District Five Homicide said that the Austin Precinct police must have panicked and that the killings in the church were related to drug-gang conflict?

MAQ: Our technicians reported that they heard the whine of bullets. Subsequently we found these two spent cartridges.

SAM: How scary!

MAQ: We asked Bishop John Ryan to comment on the bullets.

JBR: Ah.

MAQ: There was a probably a silencer on the rifle.

JBR: Indeed.

MAQ: Who would try to do such a thing?

JBR: It is safe to say that they are not good people.

MAQ: Do you think you might have been a potential target, Bishop?

JBR: I am too unimportant to be killed.

MAQ: Do you think that the Cardinal should order that the opening of St. Lucy's School next week be delayed?

JBR: I'm sure the Cardinal would support whatever decision Msgr. Wolodyjowski and the St. Lucy's school board might make.

MAQ: So there you have it, Samantha. The chaos and the danger here at St. Lucy's are worse than ever.

Declan

"A dark one, Declan Patrick O'Donnell, you surely are."

"Only sometimes, Bishop, and never as strong as tonight."

"You saw the man on the embankment before you left the church?"

"Yes."

"And this had an impact on your, uh, companion?"

"Only when the chopper came over. Then she looked at me and rolled her eyes. She's very reverent in church, I guess. When I told her after Mass that I had seen the sniper on the L tracks, she said that her great-grandfather had the second sight, too."

"I would assume that there is a certain amount of dismay in the Chicago Police Department now."

"Believe it! Dawn Collins is back in charge with a bigger staff. District Five has been reprimanded. Some questions were asked of the Austin Station about why the cops charged the embankment, to which the response was that they wouldn't have had to charge it if they had been stationed up there in the first place. To make matters worse, an off-duty cop saw the sniper on the tracks and called Fourteenth and Michigan on his cell phone. They found a record of his call only a few minutes ago."

"You called in the helicopter?"

"Certainly not! People in the Unit are supposed to be invisible. I persuaded a sarge from Austin to do it."

"But you reported to her?"

"Yeah, and she said I'd better get my Sicilian friend out of there before she was hurt."

"Considerate of her."

"Yeah . . . She says that she hears—which means probably from the superintendent—that Homeland Security is backing out, so Camilla will be on the case."

"Which reminds me, I must call Superintendent Casey."

He turned on the speakerphone so I could hear the conversation.

"Blackie," Mr. Casey complained, "what's going on out there?"

"Your department caused a major snafu!"

"I know THAT! Who tried to take a shot at you?"

"Why shoot me? I'm not the problem. Mikal Wolodyjowski is."

"So we put more guards on him."

"As should the CPD. And better surveillance of the L embankment."

"Why does someone want to kill Mickey?"

"Because they don't like the New Austin project . . . However, one should consider that the contretemps this evening may have been intended only as a warning."

"Someone crazy is behind this."

"Crazy, arguably; brilliant, for sure."

"Should we put guards in the rectory?"

"Don't even think of it. You don't mess with Polish nobility. Besides, young Father Nelson Ironman from Nigeria has a royal spear."

"This is beginning to sound crazy."

"Just contemporary Catholicism . . . so increase the guards outside, Reliable Security as well as nonduty cops—the latter in uniform—with the warning that they may be dealing with dangerous killers."

"Why, Blackie? Is someone insane?"

"That we must find out and soon."

"Real soon," I added when his conversation with Superintendent Casey was over. "Captain Huong plans to work twenty-four hours a day on hacking."

"That will involve?"

"First we'll try to enter the Combined Control computer, then see if we can gain access to the alarm system at St. Lucy's. Next we'll try to turn it off for a few moments . . ."

"How will you know for sure that you can?"

"That's no problem. We'll have one of our guys out here to do electronic testing. The next step will be to determine whether anyone else has tried the same thing and, if they have, whether they've left a port from which they can enter again."

"I suspect they will have done so." The bishop sighed. "We have not heard the last of them . . . Am I correct in assuming that you can block the port that our adversaries may have created?"

"Ideally, Bishop Blackie, we can block them and yet make them think they have gained control of the St. Lucy's system. When they try to turn it off they will think they were successful, but in fact the system will still be operational, with perhaps a five-second time lag."

"So when they try to break into St. Lucy's alarms . . ."

"We'll know it immediately on Magnolia Avenue and send out a warning. Then when someone violates the sensors at St. Lucy's the whole neighborhood will know it."

"We thereupon capture some perps?"

"If we're lucky . . . It's all problematic. There's no guarantee that we can even hack into the Combined Control computer."

"Is any of this legal?"

"Hey, Bishop, we're the police, remember. We're investigating the possibility of criminal hacking. The law is on our side."

"You don't need a court order to sneak inside Combined Control?"

"That issue has never been challenged in court, so we don't know for sure. We presume that Combined won't mind if we extirpate a hacker port from their system. They probably won't even know."

"Ah."

"So, Bishop, what's happening?"

"I think we both knew from the beginning that there is some kind of conspiracy against St. Lucy's. Those behind it do not lack for resources or ruthlessness. They wish to bring the New Austin project to a halt because they view it as a threat to themselves and their values. The problem is that those who might have the resources to do so, O'Boyle and Sons and the West Lords, seem to lack the motives; and those who might have the motives, the alderman and the community organizations, do not have the resourcefulness and indeed the ruthlessness. Surely they would not be able to fund the computer hacking."

"Hackers are strange people, Bishop. Many of them don't care about the money, only the challenge."

"It is a seductive enterprise?"

"I'm too much a straight arrow to do it for anyone except the Dragon Lady, but the temptation is there."

"St. Gabriel is, I believe, the patron of those who use the Internet."

"Captain Huong has a big statue of him in the basement at Magnolia Street."

"He carries his trumpet?"

"Lifted up close to his lips."

"Daunting."

I took a deep breath and asked him a question about another daunting subject.

"Bishop Blackie, what do you think of Camilla?"

"Only that she is an intelligent, spirited, and beautiful young woman."

"It's only a day and a half and I can't get her out of my mind."

"Those things, Declan O'Donnell, have been known to happen. Sometimes, I believe, the term 'tender trap' is used. The deity's ingenious trick to sustain the existence of the species."

"I'm not sure, but I think she kind of likes me too."

I struggled to keep my attention on the Expressway.

"That's not at all improbable, especially given your past history."

"I don't know what to do."

"You may not have to do anything besides letting hormones take their course."

"That would be wrong . . . I want to be sure."

"In matters of the heart, that is never possible. As with God, human love is a great leap of faith."

I didn't quite know what that meant, but it sounded dangerous.

"Marriage is a big risk."

I turned onto Wacker Drive.

"So, Declan O'Donnell, is life. You and the fair Camilla are at a difficult time in your lives. Not quite old enough to worry that you might end up unmarried and hence ready to take a big chance, but too old to plunge into the matrimonial waters without worry."

"Yeah, I know."

"You consider your peers who have already married and the obvious strains and stresses in their relationships, some of which are in serious jeopardy. You observe that matrimony involves constant, awkward, and frequently painful adjustments. You note the loss of independence and privacy. You worry about the insistent and irrational demands of children, adorable monsters that they are. These strangers invade your love affair, take over your lives. They have no right to do so. Who invited them anyway?

"You note all these disadvantages and you think, unrealistically, that it won't be that way in your marriage because you love one another. But you're too old and too experienced to really believe that.

"Then there are your families. Her Sicilian ancestors will likely have grave reservations about an Irishman. On the other hand, they are faced with the possibility of a spinster on their hands and, for Irish, you are not all that bad. Your family, however, may not be enthused about the prospect of dark-skinned grandchildren. They may even suspect that Sicilians are in fact Saudi Arabians, which considering the occupation of the island by Saracens for a century or two is not out of the question . . ."

I pulled up in front of the Cathedral Rectory. Bishop Blackie was a funny little man. He was making a solid case against marriage, but one which he did not really believe.

"My family will hate her and try to destroy her with ridicule. They're very good at that. The atmosphere of our family is poison. We tear one another apart all the time. We cut people down. What will people say? Who do we think we are? I moved out when I went to college and see them as little as possible, but I've never been able to play the game, much less fight back. I went to law school at night to get away from them and now use my Ph.D. work as an excuse."

"Both of which ventures led them to pass comments as they would say in the old country."

"My family calls it slagging. Mom is better than the others but she does it to survive. They pretend that it is all in good fun, but it's venomous."

"A means of social control devised by members of a colonial society to survive the injustices worked upon them. The prayer was not that I have a second cow like my neighbor but that God take my neighbor's second cow from her."

"That's probably what I was doing to Camilla in sixth grade— slagging her . . . I won't let them do it to her. They drove away my first sweetheart, though I was going to break up with her anyway . . ."

"Oh, as to that, I would be surprised if the crafty Camilla could not more than hold her own . . . Well, thank you much for the ride, Declan O'Donnell. I assume that we will interact again as this case develops. Give my very best to the aforementioned Sicilian American."

He left the car, glanced around to make sure he was on Wabash Avenue, then ambled up to the rectory door.

I had expected him to reverse his field and tell me that Camilla was worth the risk. He assumed that summing up the Camilla problem would not deter me from my pursuit of her, against my better judgment. Hence his request that I give her his best.

And *he* called *her* crafty.

Blackie

Milord Cronin called me on his cell phone at noon Chicago time, not, I'm sure, because he had learned to calculate the time differential but because he had just seen St. Lucy's on CNN.

"Blackwood, what the hell is going on back there!"

"Nothing extraordinary," I said.

"It isn't extraordinary that I see the old neighborhood on international television? People over here ask me what the hell is going on!"

"Ah, you told them that I was on the case?"

"Yeah, but . . ."

"That seemed to reassure them?"

He mumbled something that indicated that they were reassured but he wasn't.

"You are picking up the markers with some ease?"

"No problem. I see the big man tomorrow, but he's already signed off . . . What about Mickey?"

"Oh, *that!* He still has his cavalry saber and the noble savage, Nelson Ironman has polished his royal spear. In addition, Chicago's Finest, both on duty and off, are swarming about the parish plant. Furthermore, your good friend Annamaria Huong is deeply involved."

"Well . . ."

"I had words of wisdom for you from your other good friend, Father Jeremy Dillon, to wit, 'tell Sean to get that Polack out of here before he destroys the place.' I relay the message . . ."

"He's an asshole, Blackie, as you well know."

"The consensus among the clergy present for the rededication is that you will have submitted your resignation, that a certain nincompoop will replace you, and that your obedient servant will be missioned to the Rocky Mountains."

"You wouldn't survive ten minutes west of the Fox River!"

"There is substantial truth in that observation."

"Anyway, I don't want any more trouble with St. Lucy's."

"No guarantees," I said.

"What! I don't want to see it on CNN again while I'm over here. See to it, Blackwood!"

And he was gone.

It seemed to me very likely that we would be back on CNN. Our adversaries, such as they may be, were implacable. Currently they seemed to hold all the cards.

I phoned Mike Casey.

"Mike, whoever our friends are, I think the next step will be to inflict harm on Msgr. Wolodyjowski and the parish house."

"I agree, Blackie. We stay with him whenever he goes out, though he thinks it's absurd. Why would anyone want to kill him?"

"Polish aristocrat."

"As bad as an Irish peasant . . . You have any leads?"

"None. On Monday I will see the alderman and professor . . . I expect nothing much will come of either interview . . . Are there any African-American gangs in the neighborhood?"

"Nothing organized. Small-time stuff. The West Lords own the turf. A lot of my people think it has to be them."

"They may well be right . . . Or someone who is trying to bring Don Pablo down."

"I'll look into it."

Before I left for the wedding over which I was to preside—one whose chances of survival were notably less than that of the proverbial snowball in hell—I phoned the inestimable Captain Huong.

"Blackie! Why you not doing weddings?" (Giggle.)

"We have only three today and the next one is still a half hour away."

"Say, you know this Sicilian bitch who is after my number one boy?"

"I have met her."

"She good girl?"

"Very good, intelligent, pretty, stable, Assistant State's Attorney."

"He crazy about her!"

"An understandable reaction."

"She like him?"

"I believe so."

"She should. Number one boy damn good catch."

"Indeed . . . I have some reason to believe that there are one or two gangs of professional killers in this city with which some very shady police officers might be affiliated."

"We know about them. No evidence yet."

"Might be a time to get evidence."

Silence.

Then, "You think they're involved?"

"Perhaps. Some of your gnomes might look into their recent behavior."

"Hookay."

I reflected that the Dragon Lady and the alleged Sicilian bitch would get along fine. The former had become Declan O'Donnell's surrogate mother. The tender trap was closing on him.

Blackie

The wedding was even worse than I had expected. There is a tempta-tion to narcissism at every wedding. This bride, however, had a life-time of self-indulgence behind her and hence was skilled at obtaining whatever attention she wanted through the time-honored technique of pouting when anyone denied her wishes. She yawned through my homily on why God made strawberries—time-tested and proven and pleasing to the congregation and the groom—and glanced at her watch several times during its thirteen-minute dura-tion. Then she pouted through the rest of the Eucharist. We must keep on schedule for the photographers.

Well, you can't please all the people all the time.

I also presided over the five o'clock Eucharist, a crowded con-gregation, most of whom were tourists and half of them from other countries. All one can do with such a transient group is to motivate them to leave the church smiling happily after good music and good liturgy and a not intolerable homily.

Following Mass I left the rectory to drive to the Ryan family compound at Grand Beach, where I would say yet another Mass on arrival.

I was late because of repairs on the Skyway and the interstate and found the clan waiting with some impatience at the house of my eldest sibling, Mary Kate Ryan Murphy, M.D. The small ones were irritable because they had played hard all day and the older ones because they had not.

However, the barbecue after was great fun and I remembered that I had not eaten all day.

"You look like hell, Punk," Mary Kate informed me. "That St. Lucy thing getting to you?"

"And the phone calls from the Cardinal wanting to know what's happening out there."

"He should make you take a real vacation."

"You tell him that when he comes back."

"Is he going to resign? That would be a disaster. We could get some idiot."

"As to the second, we could indeed. That's what is around these days. As to the first, he has already submitted his pro forma resignation, but they won't accept it because he would be less trouble as an unretired bishop than as a retired bishop."

"They say he's going to send you to Colorado Springs."

"Not likely. It is his considered opinion that I wouldn't last more than ten minutes west of the Fox River."

"I'd say five . . . You're spilling ketchup on your shirt . . . Here, let me get it off."

I submitted to this indignity.

"I remember a long time ago when we were only kids and you hadn't arrived, something happened out in St. Lucy's that caused considerable trouble. Dad had to settle it down . . . Can't remember what it was."

"Can you dredge it up?"

"It had to do with the parish and some sort of hush-hush clerical failing."

"Indeed."

"Packy might know or might have the files . . ."

Packy is my brother Patrick Edward Ryan, a political lawyer cut from the same cloth as my late Old Fella, Ned Ryan—a man with an office, an administrative assistant, and a law clerk—who brokered problems that arose in the city. The Old Fella did it for the first Mayor Daley, and Packy for the second.

I cornered him during the dessert session at which various young members of the clan plied me with vanilla raisin ice cream, known to be my favorite. He looked like the Old Fella, slender, silver hair, red face, impish grin, a talent for indirect speech, and a pragmatic intelligence that our clan had spent several centuries building up—and of which I was only a minor recipient.

Packy never answered a question when he could respond by asking another question, never said anything when a grunt would suffice, and never communicated with a grunt when silence was enough.

As with all other Ryan family abilities, I am only moderately skilled in those talents.

"You know a certain David Crawford of the Thirty-seventh Ward?" I began.

He lifted his bottle of Guinness and tilted his head in what was a positive answer.

"Tell me about him."

"Race man. Honest but not completely."

"I went to see him in his office at City Hall on Monday morning."

He grunted.

"His opposition to the New Austin plan seems less than straightforward."

He did not comment, which meant that he wasn't at all surprised.

"I suppose the Old Fella's archives are still there, some of them secret."

"Paper saver."

"The fair Mary Kathleen tells me that there was a case long ago in which St. Lucy's was somehow involved."

His response consisted of a raised eyebrow and a lip movement which meant that he really didn't know but it wasn't impossible.

"Would you ever go through the secret files and see if there's one about St. Lucy's that you can show me?"

"Don't read them myself. No point," he said with an agnostic shrug.

Which meant that he would indeed dig out the file, if such existed, and give it to me.

When I returned to the Cathedral Rectory late Sunday afternoon, I recalled my dictum that celibacy should be abolished in empty rectories on Sunday afternoon.

I found waiting for me my Saturday mail, which included a letter addressed to me "Personal and Confidential."

I opened it to be confronted with a gibberish message.

I had no notion what it meant, but it seemed sinister.

Declan

Camilla jumped high in the air, spiked the volleyball into the face of a player on the other side of the net, and cried out in joyous triumph. I sketched the transient moment as quickly as I could. She was the kind of woman you'd want at your side when the lights went off in a bar.

I am prejudiced in favor of beach volleyball because my family ridicules it. Any human endeavor that they oppose can't be all that bad.

"They're whores exhibiting their wares."

"It's a strip joint on the beach."

"They're nothing but lesbos and exhibitionists."

"Their bodies aren't all that great. I'd be ashamed to wear a bikini if I were so flat."

"Bimbos selling themselves to the media."

"*Playboy* in the open on North Avenue Beach."

Naturally I kept my mouth shut.

And so it went, on and on as they found another target for their malice.

If young women want to dress in skimpy garments, I figure that's their business, especially since they claim that such swimsuits provide the freedom of movement they need to win. Moreover, if males have nothing better to do on a Sunday afternoon than ogle women volleyball players, that's all right too. It is disrespectful to the players to bring along a camera and snap pictures while the bikini-clad women contort their bodies, but if the players don't mind the attention, who is to complain about the clicking digital cameras of hungry males.

Hence someone like me who brings a sketching pad is hardly exploiting his model. Is he? If Camilla thought I was acting like a horny old man, I could apologize.

"Your girl play volleyball on North Avenue Beach?" Captain Huong giggled as she asked the question. "That's why you want to go watch?"

"We hack into Combined Control." The Dragon Lady poked a finger at me. "You go beach and ogle girl's body."

"Not exactly," I parried.

"You no good here. Go watch girl. Then come back and we finish hacking."

There wasn't any doubt that she would give me a couple hours off. After working all night to hack into Combined Control, I had finally found a way to access St. Lucy's Church and School. I was bleary-eyed and incoherent and the Dragon Lady knew it.

"You take picture of girl?"

"Just sketch her."

"Big deal. You leave clothes on or you be in big trouble with me. I want to see your sketches."

"We artists have privacy rights."

"Not when you work here. You bring girl back with you?"

"Not on your life!"

And so I took my leave while my Laotian mother worried about my erotic propensities. She should not have troubled herself.

Still, maybe she should have. My first glimpse of Camilla leaping around the sand in a bikini, albeit one with more coverage than that of the Olympic team, shattered me and then spun me into an altered state. Probably it lasted only a few seconds, but it seemed like forever. Looking back on it I wish it had been forever. My sneakers seemed glued to the sand, my eyes fixed wide open, my heart stopped, my throat dried up. I was acutely aware of her womanly body, especially her long, slender legs; but it was womanly grace in motion that hypnotized me. Camilla ran, leaped, twisted, jumped, contorted, pounded the sand, shouted, laughed, cried out, protested, encouraged, congratulated—all in one smooth, graceful flow of movement and sound. She was no longer law review and State's Attorney, but a primal creature of sand and water, someone who had washed up on the shores of Sicily, a Saracen princess.

That was the kind of wife and mother she would be, an irresistible, elemental force of nature. I couldn't cope with her, I told myself. Besides, I was indulging in ridiculous metaphors. Time to snap out of it. Worst way, I didn't want to.

It was a dangerously attractive fantasy. Reluctantly, I shook my head to banish it and slowly emerged from my fugue. I tried to sketch the remembered magic. She saw me after a particularly brilliant return, jabbed her finger in my direction, and grinned. I almost slipped back into my delicious altered state.

Instead I scribbled frantically on my sketchbook. I realized that I was out of place—the only one on the beach in jeans, sneakers, and a sport shirt (hung out over my jeans to hide my weapon) under a sizzling sun and dense curtains of humidity. Instead of pointing a tiny digital camera at the luscious combatants, I was wielding a pencil and sketch pad. Patently, as Bishop Blackie would say, I was some kind of pervert.

The league game, it was not a formal venue, but something like a pickup game of softball in a park on Sunday afternoon—four young women slamming a volleyball over a net with a small crowd of enthusiastic observers, almost as many women as men. Both twosomes were good, but my Camilla was clearly the star and the audience favorite. The fans cheered loudly when she scored the final point of the last game. I continued to work on my sketch.

"Hey," said a young woman who had been staring over my

shoulder, "that's like totally awesome . . . Do you know Cami?"

"We went to school together."

"Gosh."

"Yeah," I said.

The woman in question had pulled on a long sweatshirt, donned beach moccasins, and was running towards me.

"Did you see that . . . We're in the finals . . . We won't win . . . But it was great . . . Lemme see the picture . . ."

"It's totally awesome!" My uninvited companion repeated her praise.

"I know that," Camilla said loyally.

"Let me buy you a hot dog and a Coke," I offered.

"Sure, it's your turn anyway."

Perspiration had already soaked her tee shirt. She smelled of violent exercise. I adored her.

"You dressed up for the beach," she said as we sat on a bench.

"Captain Huong gave me an hour off to watch the match. She wants me to bring you back, but I told her no way we should let a State's Attorney into her lair."

"And you're carrying . . . ?"

"Magnolia Center is kind of a fort these days."

"St. Lucy case?"

"I can't comment."

She nodded as she took a huge bite out of the hot dog.

"Lemme see your sketch."

"My generation of artist," I began ponderously, "are the luckiest in history. Because of Title Nine there are lots of women athletes with solid, disciplined bodies of which they're proud. In ages past, even Diana didn't look like a huntress."

"I hope you left my clothes on."

"I wouldn't have dared not to," I said, opening my sketchbook to the drawing I had labelled "Spike!"

"Oh, wow!" She grabbed my arm. "No way that I'm that beautiful!"

"You are—a Saracen princess washed up on the sands of Sicily to take over the whole island for her satrapy."

"No way!"

A woman patrol officer, uncomfortable and irritable in her uniform, joined us.

"Nice game, Cami," she began.

"Thanks, Audrey."

"Do you think your friend here has a permit for the gun he's packing?"

I showed her my cop card.

She eased up a little.

"Sorry, Sarge . . . Just doing the job."

"No problem, Officer. A guy dressed like me with a sketch pad on the beach could well be a pervert."

"Can I see?" She peered over Camilla's shoulder. "Hey, that's really good! He's captured you perfectly, Cami!"

"Not yet," I murmured.

"Smart-ass," she informed me when the cop had drifted away.

"Actually, it should be the other way around."

She ignored that crack.

"Can I take this home . . . I'll bring it back."

"Why?"

"Show my family. I've been telling them about you. They love art."

"This isn't art. It's just a sketch."

I handed her the book.

"Did you recognize me immediately at St. Lucy's?"

"Certainly! You haven't changed all that much. Same sweet eyes."

It was my turn to protest that it wasn't so.

"And you figured it was up to me to renew our conversation."

"I didn't think you knew who I was."

Silence between us.

"I'll walk you back to the parking lot . . . Are you going to turn this into a painting?"

We walked away from the beach towards the lot where I had left my bike.

"I've got to learn how to do painting first, but I probably will."

"I want it."

"We'll see."

I wanted to take this sweaty, smelly, vibrant young woman in my arms and hold her forever.

Instead, she caressed my cheeks with both hands and thus upped the ante in our relationship.

"I'll be in touch, Camilla," I promised.

"Tell Captain Huong that I'd love to see her redoubt."

"That's the kind of word Harvard graduates use."

As I pedaled back to Magnolia I imagined what my family would say about Camilla. Declan, she's FAT! Look at those thunder thighs! She's like all Sicilian women, she's losing her figure already! By the time she's thirty, she'll be obese. You know how fat they get! She's so dark, I bet she's part Negro! She'll grow a mustache soon! Do you want kids that'll look like half-breeds? Are you sure her family is not connected to the Outfit?

None of these slags would have any relationship to Camilla's reality nor indeed to the physical characteristics of my family, many of whose women on both sides were heavily overweight and some obese. Slagging did not know the rule that the pot shouldn't call the kettle black.

Similar slags were aimed at my college girlfriend Beth, who was Polish, a worse sin than being Italian. She didn't hear them directly because they were too clever for that. However, they managed to convey the same sentiment indirectly as in, "That's a lovely skirt, dear, but I don't think it's quite made for you."

"Declan," she had said, "I hate your family."

"So do I."

The relationship was doomed anyway. My family, however, had made the ending more bitter than it had to be.

If anything stronger than instant lust developed between

Camilla and me, I would give them the ultimatum: leave her alone or we're out of here.

Then, as I turned out of Lincoln Park, I saw how we could complete our hacking into the St. Lucy alarm system.

Camilla

On Monday morning in my office, I daydreamed about Declan. Color me infatuated. He is so sweet and gentle and his eyes are so kind. Yet when I look into them I see hunger. For me. Powerful, passionate hunger. He takes my breath away. He wants me. All of me. Forever. And that blows my mind because he could have me for the asking. I've had crushes before, infatuations, obsessions. They're part of growing up. But nothing like his. Maybe it's my family telling me how my biological clock is ticking away. At twenty-seven! Or maybe the hormones are catching up. Maybe I want a man and kids and all the other stuff which I have told myself I don't want. Maybe I just want to be loved and to love. Or maybe just a permanent bed partner.

That would be nice too.

We're both adults. We're too smart to plunge into a marriage. I must be careful and cautious. I get rid of boors quickly even if they are physically attractive. A guy hits on me, he's history. Declan doesn't hit, at least in the ordinary way, and I'm putty. Neither of us needs a long-term affair. I don't want to get married next spring.

Marriage! Wedding! Baptisms!

I don't want any of that.

Well, yes I do. With the right man. Is Declan O'Donnell the right man? How can I tell when I'm so much in love with him?

This is serious business.

Then a somewhat seedy-looking man, thin salt-and-pepper hair, haggard face, and stooped shoulders appears at the door of my tiny office.

"Hi, Camilla, I'm Joe Robertson of the United States Attorney's Office. May I come in?"

"No," I said firmly, "you may not."

I press the button on the tape recorder I keep ready for action on my steel desk.

TRANSCRIPT OF CONVERSATION WITH
PURPORTED UNITED STATES ATTORNEY

10:30 A.M.

A man who claims that he is Joe Robertson from the United States Attorney's Office is at the door of my office. He has not made an appointment. He is a greasy, unprepossessing individual.

That's not necessary, Camilla.

You want an appointment, you call and ask for one. Otherwise, I assume that you're hostile and make a record. You're not going to charge me with perjury later on without my having a record. I assume that you are wired. Mr. Robertson has entered my office without my permission and sat in my only empty chair.

My name is Ms. Datillo, sir. I will note any other title hints at sexual harassment.

All I want to do is to wind up the case against Marty Staples. No need to make a big deal out of it. You know that the police have dropped their charges against all three Federal agents, including Agent Staples. We hope that you will agree to do the same, just to clear this whole matter up.

Agent Staples assaulted me, sir. I have many witnesses. I will not drop the charge. I also have here a petition I will submit to the United States Court for the Northern District of Illinois charging Agent Staples and the United States, which employs him, charging him with sexual harassment and brutality and seeking financial redress from the defendants.

You were interfering with a Federal investigation, Camilla. There can be serious costs in doing something like that.

There was no evidence then or now that the Federal agents or the Office of the United States Attorney had jurisdiction in the case. Even if there were, it was appropriate for me to try to contact the Office of the State's Attorney for the County of Cook to ask for instructions. Mr. Staples twisted my arm and forcibly tried to remove my cell phone from my hand. He did so in the presence of several police officers and a Roman Catholic bishop. It would be a great pleasure to me to argue this case in court. I might also add a charge of intimidation based on this visit from you.

I would recommend strongly that you change your attitude, Camilla. You know that the Federal government has access to various sources of information in these matters. We could, for example, explore the possibility of ties between your family and the Mafia.

Sir, that is gratuitously insulting. It could also fall under the rubric of an ethnic hate crime. It will be one more item for my petition to seek relief from a Federal court.

We have long memories over at the Dirksen Building, Camilla. You have a promising career. You wouldn't want to have a bad reputation over there.

I must ask you to leave my office. You continue to harass me by claiming a familiarity to which you are not entitled. You have threatened me once again. I will not tolerate this.

Mr. Robertson stands up now.

Marty Staples is a good man, Counselor. He has a wife and four children. We just want to protect his career. Why won't you be reasonable? We'll get you a formal apology. Can't we settle this in a way that's appropriate for us who share common goals?

I take exception to your remark that I share common goals with either you or Mr. Staples. Quite the contrary; you have interfered with my duty to function as a State's Attorney in bringing to justice the parties responsible for the atrocities at St. Lucy's Roman Catholic Church in our jurisdiction. I sympathize with his wife and children, but they are not the issue.

Why do you have to be such a hard-assed bitch about a simple problem?

Mr. Robinson, having engaged in one more act of sexual harassment, has left my office. It is now 11:05 A.M.

END OF TRANSCRIPT

My boss struggled unsuccessfully to contain his laughter as he read the transcript of my conversation with Joseph Robertson.

"Why did they ever send a jerk like that over to take you on, uh, Ms. Datillo?"

"You can call me Cami, boss."

"I will call my counterpart over at the Dirksen Building and read him some of the more choice dialogue . . . They will want to settle of course. But we'll let them sweat a while."

"I want a formal apology in writing for all the offenses and penalties for all the violations of which they're guilty."

"Financial relief."

"Of course not."

"A month's suspension for each of them?"

"Sure, but let them propose it. I want to sign off on the agreement."

"Camilla, I wouldn't dream of doing it any other way . . . Did you win the match yesterday?"

"Sure."

"And Camilla Datillo, you're just a tough lawyer, not a bitch."

"Thank you, sir."

I returned to my office, happy with the vote of confidence, unhappy about the national security state in which we were caught up. I was not sure I wanted to work for it anymore. Too many incompetent bureaucrats swaggering around like they knew what they were doing. Playing what they thought was hardball when in fact it was only slow-pitch softball. Too many good people were getting hurt. I had started life as a conservative. After watching how prosecutors worked, I'm becoming a dangerous liberal. Is Declan a liberal? He laughs too much to be a conservative.

I suppose that I'll have to marry him. I'll never find a better husband, that's for sure. Let me see . . . Ring at Christmas, marriage in the spring . . . that's an awful rush . . . Not getting any younger . . . He'll have to finish his dissertation and do his internship after we marry . . . I can support him . . . We have to get to know each other better . . . I'm out of my mind . . .

Blackie

"The alderman is very busy this morning, Bishop," the matronly secretary informed me. "It will be some time before he is able to fit you into his schedule."

"You will convey to the alderman that, as a man who is used to being punctual, I don't accept excuses like that."

The woman was visibly upset.

"The alderman works very hard, Bishop."

"Would it surprise you, ma'am, to learn that I do too?"

"I'll tell him you're upset."

"Please do."

Like most third-rate politicians, Alderman Crawford had an inflated notion of his own importance. He was teaching me a lesson about that importance which I did not appreciate. Dressed in the required black suit with pectoral cross and ring, I held in my hand a list of grievances which Pan Wolodyjowski had prepared concerning the Alderman's noncooperation with St. Lucy's School. I was not about to let him get away with it.

"We've broken into the Combined Security computer and found St. Lucy's," a weary Declan O'Donnell had informed me earlier in a cell phone call to the breakfast table.

"Impressive . . . You will test it to see if you can turn off the alarms just as it happened the night of the horror?"

"Not quite yet, Bishop Blackie. The captain wants us to hunt for traces of a port that their hacker might have left in the computer for possible reentry. That won't tell us who their hacker is, but we'll be able to trap him the next time he tries."

"If he does . . . What happens next?"

"Tonight I'll do a test. I'll hide in the Park—Mudhole Park, Camilla claims is its name, and wait till I'm told on the phone that the alarms have been disabled. Then I'll shoot a minisecond beam into the rectory. If we have disarmed the alarm, there'll be no sound in the rectory and no signal on their computer to which, of course, we now have access. So we'll know that a hacker can disable the alarm system. That may not be what happened, but there is no other logical explanation."

There were in fact several more which I did not want to consider.

"And if you've made a mistake?"

"Brief jolt to the alarm system, which hopefully no one notices."

"Will Combined Control know that you're lurking in their system?"

"Not unless we tell them they have a weakness, which we will after all this is over."

"And they'll be delighted to know?"

"Sure will! Anyway we're the law and we're looking for lawbreakers . . . I hope that doesn't get tested in the courts anytime soon."

"Keep me posted . . . And how fares the Glorious Camilla?"

"I watched her play beach volleyball yesterday. It was interesting."

"I shouldn't wonder."

I had replayed this conversation as I waited for Alderman Crawford. I was uneasy with hacking and counterhacking, mostly because I did not understand it and never would. I had to trust the Dragon Lady and her number one boy to know what they were doing. What, I wondered, would happen if the hacker told his employers that the alarm system at St. Lucy's was disabled when in fact it was still working?

A few minutes later I was conducted into the alderman's office. He did not stand or offer to shake hands. He looked up from his desk, irritated by my interruption. His skin was light and his features Caucasian. His hair was straight and combed back. A thin pencil of a mustache was another suggestion that his claim to be African-American could be challenged easily if one had the mind. He was a concerto in brown, suit, shirt, tie, socks, brightly polished shoes—all very tasteful and very expensive.

Before he could speak, I opened fire.

"Cardinal Cronin has instructed me, Alderman Crawford, to ask whether you are consciously anti-Catholic or whether it is something you do without any particular awareness. I have here a list of routine requests made by St. Lucy parish to your office which have been ignored or disregarded without even the courtesy of a reply. They are the sorts of requests that are routinely honored in other wards. It would seem that St. Lucy's School is not wanted in the Thirty-seventh Ward. In view of the current incidents there, we might consider bringing these problems to public attention."

He sputtered and tried to say something.

"We are quite capable of noting that you have reason to oppose the New Austin project because it might cost you some votes in your ward but that your neglect of minor requests for, let me see, sidewalk repair, damaged-tree removal, icy streets in front of the school, antedates proposals for New Austin. You might ponder that the adage 'don't fight City Hall' has a counterpart in 'don't mess with the Catholic Church.'"

"This is outrageous . . ." he stammered.

"Your constituents who use the Catholic schools in the ward will be delighted to know that you are hostile to such schools."

"I don't believe in them," he snarled.

"That is surely your right in our society. . . ."

"If those kids were in the public schools, that would upgrade the quality of those schools." He became sullen.

"You'd be hard put to find data to support that assertion. Again, however, you have the right to your opinion. However, when that opinion becomes your public policy, your constituents have the right to know that you want to deny them any freedom of educational choice. They will find that an interesting issue in the next election, including the members of the American Federation of Teachers who send their children to St. Catherine's and St. Lucy's and St. Angela."

Like any halfway-smart politician, he knew that he was beaten and that he'd better backtrack.

"I promise you that I will look into our relationship with St. Lucy's School. I greatly admire the Monsignor and Sister for their work. I am not opposed to the New Austin project. I merely wish that it would proceed somewhat more slowly and not destabilize the neighborhood."

"Then some of your black constituents would not enjoy a windfall."

"I hate to see communities break up."

"I grew up on the South Side, Alderman," I said softly. "One phenomenon I observed out there was that communities obliterated by racial change rapidly reconstituted themselves. Moreover, the difference in the New Austin is that the Thirty-seventh Ward will likely be permanently integrated. There is no reason why you cannot continue to be its representative. Surely you have the skill to shift your platform somewhat."

Bad bishop becomes good bishop.

David Crawford relaxed. A little.

"Someone certainly wants to stop the New Austin," I continued, shifting the course of the conversation with something less than a subtle touch.

"Do you think so? I'd say the project has enough momentum now even if Father Wolodyjowski should back off. It's bigger than St. Lucy's."

"Arguably."

"My own opinion, for whatever it's worth, Bishop, is that this gruesome event in the church was more likely to be aimed at the pastor personally. People say they like him and mean it, but they resent him too. He's too perfect. He's the sort of charismatic figure who creates a lot of love/hate, if you know what I mean."

The alderman as psychologist.

"I think I do."

"Yet I ask myself who would try to punish him that way. The Spanish gangs perhaps. Maybe not Pablo, but there are surely other gangs which would like to take over his territory, or even factions within his own West Lords. They seem disposed to blood violence. The Dark Cobras, our West Side African-American gang, prefers the quick hit. Moreover, they have never been tightly organized like the gangs on the South Side. Street corner drug sales are about the only thing they can accomplish."

"So you think the desecration of the church was not aimed at the New Austin but at the pastor of St. Lucy's?"

His large brown eyes, sad in repose, clouded.

"He seems alienated from the Chicago Polish community, an aristocrat among peasants, even peasant priests."

Chicago Poles would not like that assessment. Nonetheless, Pan Mikal was different. People might be angry at him because he had failed to become the first Polish Cardinal in Chicago, even if it wasn't his fault.

"An interesting insight."

"As I said before, I like him, even if we have our differences of opinion. Sometimes I feel like I'm a peasant and he's the noble on horseback. Maybe he doesn't think that way, but it's an impression. Still as I said he has enormous charisma, which seems to grow stronger through the years. Like the Kennedys, that kind of charisma ignites anger and hatred by those who wish they had it and don't."

"Ah."

"Sometimes I wish I had a little of his charisma. Our jobs are not unlike as you surely perceive. We must unite many different factions and feelings, all the time keeping most of our constituents happy or at least not rebelliously unhappy. It is for most of us a losing game. For the Monsignor it obviously is not. Yet when I think that I'd like to share in his charisma I realize that it would be an invitation to hate, which politicians cannot afford."

"I take your point. Still, such gifts, if they be called that, are not an option."

"Should he have been Cardinal . . . ? If that's not an embarrassing question to one who works for the present Cardinal."

"Milord Cronin insists that Mikal Wolodyjowski should be Cardinal and would be if he were not Polish."

"It is a fate that we African-Americans understand all too well."

We parted politely and promised to stay in touch, which I didn't think we would. There was more substance to him than I had expected. He did not seem to be the kind of man who would take the reckless risks of sacrilege. Rather he would do exactly what was necessary to sustain his position—shift his political orientation to fit the emerging shape of the ward.

As I turned off Washington to walk to the Green Line stop at Randolph and Wells, I considered his suggestion that the problem at St. Lucy's might not be New Austin at all, but Pan Mikal himself. In a long and controversial life, one can leave behind a trail of people who feel they have been injured, grievously so. Yet mutilated bodies in a church sanctuary were a curious kind of revenge.

On the L platform my cell phone produced its usual noxious version of Beethoven's Ninth Symphony. Cardinal Cronin, I surmised, calling for his morning demand of, "What the hell's going on over there, Blackwood!"

"Certain progress is taking place. The school board at St. Lucy's has postponed school opening for another week. The media have stopped speculating about the name of the new Archbishop once your resignation is accepted next week . . ."

The last was not altogether true, but it got a reaction—loud and happy laughter.

"No worry about that, Blackwood, as I've been saying all

along . . . By the way . . . Hey, where are you? Is there an earth-quake or something?"

"Only the sound of the Loop. I am on the Randolph and Wells platform, awaiting the Green Line train to your old neighborhood."

"Riding public transportation? The other bishops won't like that! Don't worry, I won't tell them . . . Like I was saying, the big guy sends his best to you. Says you're *très formidable* or something like that."

I found that most unlikely. However, his good humor suggested that he had picked up all his markers.

"I must ask a question about your good friend Pan Wolodyjowski."

"Yeah?"

Skepticism leaped all the way across the Atlantic.

"Someone has suggested that this whole unfortunate matter may be less an assault on the New Austin than an attempt to seek perhaps belated revenge against the count."

Dead silence at the other end of the line.

"Yeah?"

"Yeah."

More silence.

"OK, this is, what does your good friend Mary Alice call it, thick description?"

"That's in anthropology. You mean deep background?"

"Right! Why did you call him a count?"

"Guess."

"Actually that isn't high enough in the Polish nobility. He's a prince. I guess they have a lot of them or had a lot of them."

"Fascinating."

"In the seminary he acted like he was a prince. In Rome too. I think it was mostly a joke. He's brilliant, Blackwood. Knows every-thing, though not as much as you. Nobody does. He didn't keep it a secret. Constantly showing off, or that's what the guys thought. Treated the other Polish guys like they were semiliterate peasants, which a lot of them were. Absolutely charming. Quite the lady's man in the old days. Charmed them all. I don't know that anything ever came of it. Just flirtations. Still . . ."

"So what's a prince doing in a mostly black parish for twenty-five years?"

"Damned if I know, Blackwood. I told him he could have anything he wanted. He said he preferred St. Lucy."

"You don't know of any specific incidents that might have been . . ."

"Covered up? Not by me, but that doesn't mean too much . . . I kind of doubt it."

"I see."

I didn't see at all.

"Still . . ."

A patent sign that Milord was thinking.

"Still," he repeated. "He's the kind of man someone could nurse a big grudge against for years, decades."

He wasn't telling me everything he knew, perhaps because we were on a cell phone.

"Prince Wolodyjowski," I said. "It sounds appropriate."

"I think it's the wrong road, Blackwood. But maybe you should have a quick look down in the secret archives. But no scandals to greet me when I come back. See to it!"

I knew a bit more than before the conversation. Sean Cardinal Cronin would not be surprised if there was some ancient scandal coming back to haunt Prince Wolodyjowski.

The next blast from Ludwig von was a call from Crystal Lane.

"I didn't see you when I came in this morning, Bishop Blackie. Is everything all right?"

"When in the last millennium has everything been all right?"

"I mean St. Lucy's."

"More confusion."

"Be very careful, Bishop. There's a lot of hatred out there."

To anyone but our resident mystic I would have said, "Tell me about it."

However, I replied, "Keep praying for me, Crystal Lane."

"I do, Bishop Blackie, all the time."

I boarded the Green Line train with the thought that Ms. Lane's promise was the only good sign all morning.

Declan

Captain Huong stared at her twenty-three-inch computer screen. I stood behind her looking over her shoulder and sniffing her perfume which suggested mysterious groves of flowers deep in Asian jungles. The aroma was part of the act, as was the incense she frequently burned in our "war room" and the Asian screens which shaped various work areas. Lucille King, an African-American woman in the Unit, was next to me. She caught my eye and rolled hers.

"You see the image of St. Lucy's security system. Very neat. (Giggle.) Light beams on in church to keep away rapists and drug dealers. Not in school. Not in rectory. Because kids still around even if it's summer. Must like school. TV on everywhere. Alarms on in church. Cool! (Another giggle.) You do well, Declan boy. Should we turn it off?"

"Not now," I said. "Wait till the whole system is on everywhere in St. Lucy's. Then, Lucille, you can turn them off for a moment, and I'll shoot a beam in the rectory. If there's no alarm sound out there or here on the screen, we'll know we've been able to knock out every alarm system that Combined Control has at St. Lucy's."

"Good deal, much fun!" the Dragon Lady chortled. "We blackmail them and make tons of money."

"We will have done them a big favor," Lucille said, "when we tell them how to deal with a potential hacker. But that won't prove that someone has hacked into St. Lucy's before, only that they could have."

"And even if we find a port that a hacker might have left so she can get in again, that won't mean she will try again."

"Woman never hack into church! (Giggle, giggle.)"

"I just hope this isn't against the law, Annamaria," Lucille said uneasily.

"We cops. We don't break law. We catch those who do. Until courts say we can't, right, Declan?"

"Right! I just wouldn't want us to be hauled into court."

"Hookay, you have good sleep. You come in, bright and fresh like you do every morning, like you better do when you marry Sicilian woman, now you look for port all day . . . Lucille, what do you find out about local Murder Incorporated? Our rogue CIA asset out in Brighton Park."

"From what I've been able to find out about them, I wouldn't dare try to hack them. First thing is that they are not an equal opportunity employer. No blacks. No Asians either."

"Or Native Americans or Aleuts or Samoans?" I asked.

"Not a one!"

"No Huong? We not Asians!"

"I know you guys are the ten lost tribes of Israel!"

"Smart-ass!"

"No Sicilians either, you'll be happy to hear, Declan . . . Incidentally I have seen the young person in court out at Twenty-sixth and California . . . Totally gorgeous . . . Don't know what she sees in you."

"You'd have to ask her."

"We will! (Giggle.) You bring her around here and we tell her all your secrets."

"Let's get down to work," I insisted as my face flamed.

"Well," Lucille went on primly, "they fit the model of the death squad. Four of them were Green Berets and two more CIA killers. The two Chicago cops have been into some very shady stuff, sometimes in years gone by for the department. Rumored to have taken out some cop killers that the courts acquitted. Nothing recent. They're a gang which the G has probably put out to pasture—at least until they need them again—paid pasture, of course. They work security jobs here in the city too and do some work of their own on the side."

"It happens," Captain Huong said grimly.

I had never heard anything like that, but what did I know?

"The CPD, the Bureau, and some of the other Feds keep an eye on them. I think we'd pick our guys up in a minute if we had something on them, but we have nothing. We figure, or so the relevant brothers and sisters tell me, that we don't need another scandal."

"Never do," the Dragon Lady said. "I light holy candles now."

She did that whenever we encountered something that scared her. I didn't argue.

"White cops wouldn't rat them out?" I asked.

"I figured ours would be more likely to, Declan . . . Anyway, this crowd does contract work around the world, sometimes even now for the Feds. Independent contractors, as the media call them. They have a house out in Brighton Lawn where they meet, but they don't live there. Except for the two of ours they all have cover jobs around the area, mostly high-level security stuff. Not, I say with relief, for Combined Control. There is no clear record or memory of their having done anything in Chicago, but there are some rumors that they took out a couple of suspicious Muslims and a couple of crack chieftains in South Chicago. They've only settled down here recently. They are very mean people . . ."

"I light holy incense, too."

"Good idea," I said piously.

"Where is this Brighton Lawn?" Captain Huong demanded as she went around the war room lighting votive lights and incense pots.

"It's out in the Clearing Industrial District," I replied, "west and southwest of Midway Airport, between Cicero Avenue and the Canal. Outside the city limits. Towns like Summit, Stickney, Bedford Park. Mostly older factories and railroad tracks, some homes. Good place to hide. The Capones used it in their day."

"I don't know," Lieutenant King observed, "that they are particularly our problem, especially since they work for the Feds sometimes. If we take them on, we better get ourselves some heavy weapons."

"I have AK-47," Captain Huong said proudly.

She produced the Russian weapon from the table where it always rested, "just in case we need."

"I was thinking more of M1A2 tanks. These guys are real."

"Why would they take on St. Lucy's?" I asked.

"Money," Lucille replied. "They'll do almost anything for money, big money."

"Who has that kind of money in Austin?"

"I think about it," the Dragon Lady replied. "May talk to big boss. We don't want them around Chicago."

"The head of the group is a certain Roderick McCalley, former major in the Green Berets. Their motto, I am told, is, 'When in doubt kill before they kill you.'

"They're all psychopaths." Lucille finished her recital. "Very smart and very dangerous. I meant it about the tanks."

"Let me know when we are going after them," I said, "so I can resign."

"Don't be silly, Declan," the boss said. "We get someone else to do that. They come after us, we use land mines like back in the mountains."

"Real ones!"

"Metaphor!" she said, her giggle returning.

"Roddy McCalley," I said, "that was the name of an Irish patriot who was hung by the Brits on the bridge of the Tuam in 1798. Maybe the guy is IRA."

"That's all we need." Lieutenant King sighed. "I don't see how we can act on them without the Feds giving permission and they certainly wouldn't do so."

"We don't need no fucking permission," Captain Huong said fiercely. "We want to take them out, we take them out."

I was very scared when I sat down at the computer. We were not an operational group. We weren't supposed to be going around shooting up bad guys.

I had an image of a guy with a rocket-propelled grenade standing on the L embankment aiming at St. Lucy's School. I'd better pass this on to Bishop Blackie before the day was over—if I survived the smell of Huong incense.

Blackie

Thick, black clouds were canceling out the perfect late-summer day that had greeted me when I left the Cathedral Rectory. As I left the Green Line station at Lake and Austin, bereft of an umbrella, I feared for the fate of my good suit. On the final leg of the trip—from Central Avenue to Austin Boulevard, I kept an eye on both sides of the L embankment in case a gunman was lurking. Of course, no one was there. The other side, whoever and whatever they are, wouldn't try the same trick twice.

Did they really plan the assassination of someone, most likely Pan Mikal? Or was it part of the terror game? I didn't know. In fact I didn't know anything about the St. Lucy's affair. I had listened to a lot of talk, most of it not implausible. There were certain people who would like to see New Austin slow down or even stop. None of them, however, would have the resources and motivations necessary to desecrate a church so spectacularly or mount a rifleman on the L embankment as the parish rededicated. An alternative possibility remained that the target wasn't New Austin at all but Mikal Wolodyjowski. Enemies of one sort or another from his past might be lurking, but would they have the ingenuity to frustrate Prinz Mikal's security system?

There remained the Mexican gangs. My good friend Pablo seemed strongly committed to New Austin and to his padre. But there might be other gangs who wanted to take over Pablo's territory or internal rebels who thought they could do better as *il jefe*. Alliances changed rapidly in that world. They certainly had the resources and ruthlessness to commit horrible crimes. The argument that they would not desecrate a church did not apply, as I had previously reflected, to persecutions of the 1930s.

I would probably receive Packy's extract from the files— doubtless in an old and battered manila envelope—before the day was over. It might, but probably would not, open new avenues of inquiry.

I was distracted from this unhelpful analysis when I heard a familiar voice.

"Blackie, what are you doing out in the old neighborhood? Trying to solve a mystery?"

It was the voice of Mike Casey, aka Superintendent Casey (retired), aka (in the Ryan clan) Mike the Cop—though we had no other relative of the same name who was not a cop. There were some who also considered him to be Flambeau to my Father Brown. His good wife Annie Reilly, however, has suggested that I am Captain Hastings to his Poirot.

Mike the Cop is the age peer of both Milord Cronin and Prinz Wolodyjowski and indeed this was his old neighborhood too, though he lived in St. Angela's, the next parish north. He looked like, to continue the mystery story metaphor, a silver-haired Basil Rathbone playing Sherlock Holmes.

"Paying court to Professor Brian Dogherty, who is alleged to own much of the land around here and to entertain a deep hatred for the pastor."

"He's a very bright guy, Blackie, but as nutty as they come."

"I note that this affair here at St. Lucy's is also as nutty as they come . . . You have come here to supervise your off-duty cops?"

"Funny thing is, those who work for me at night work for the Austin Precinct during the day and vice versa. Lots of income but not much sleep . . . I also wanted to check out the security system, which seems to have failed. It's state of the art for a place like this, even more sophisticated than yours."

"Heaven forefend."

"The housekeeper, however, lacks the charm of the Megans who guard the doors of your place."

"Winsome young women . . . What better image can the Church offer to those coming to seek rejuvenation . . . Do the cops have any clue what went down the other night?"

"Not the slightest. They still think it was a drug-related attack, but they have no evidence. They talked to Pablo earlier this morning—with his lawyer of course. The young man does not yield easily to intimidation I'm told."

"And swore frightening oaths about the fate of those who dare to violate his padre's church."

"Indeed yes . . . The Dragon Lady is working on counterhacking and other matters . . . By the way, that kid from the South Side is first-rate. I tried to hire him as an off-duty guy on my team. He turned me down because he's going to graduate school. Nice young man."

"So basically there's nothing?"

"I have a hunch, Blackie, that our friends are going to try something else soon. Maybe this time we catch them."

"Hopefully," I said without much enthusiasm. We were dealing with very ingenious enemies.

"Be careful of Professor Dogherty. He may be crazy, but he's very clever. The letters he writes to the papers are brilliantly written but nutcake."

"He agreed to see me out of respect for the validity of my orders but pointed out that I lacked proper jurisdiction because only the Pope can grant jurisdiction to a bishop and the Holy See has been vacant since the death of Pius XII. It is the *sede vacante* theory."

"How can that be?"

"He claims that the late Cardinal Siri of Genoa was elected Pope Gregory XVII on the first ballot of the conclave in 1959. But forced to resign because of a plot conceived by the CIA and the Communists and directed by the late Cardinal Spellman. He describes the plot as a well-known fact, which no intelligent person doubts. The man subsequently elected, Angelo Roncalli, was a Communist agent."

"Could it be true?"

"There is no evidence to sustain it save in secret documents which the *sede vacante* people refuse to share with anyone else."

"Have fun . . . Is my cell phone number on yours?"

"I believe so."

"Ring me when you come out of his house and I'll pick you up. It will be raining by then."

My good suit thus would survive the day—if I could remember the magic number which would connect me with Mike.

"By the way," I turned around, again as Lieutenant Columbo would, "do you remember any scandal that might have arisen when you and Sean were growing up in the neighborhood?"

"I hardly knew Sean or his brother Paul. We grew up farther north and weren't in the same social group . . . There was some kind of big controversy a few years after Pearl Harbor . . . an auto accident on Harlem Avenue near North Avenue on the Memorial Day Weekend . . . Six kids, about our age, died under mysterious circumstances, in an auto accident."

"Any survivors?"

"I can't remember. I'll ask Annie. She paid more attention to such things in the old days."

Ah, another person from the old neighborhood. And Nora Cronin too. I might have to spin together a re-creation of that forgotten era of ration cards and gasoline shortages and working women and novenas for men in service and fear that when one graduated from high school one would in a few months be fighting in the Solomon Islands or the Apennine Mountains with only limited hope of ever seeing America again. The sudden end of the war in 1945 and the explosion of possibility in the "postwar" years blotted out all those grim memories. My Old Fella, a naval reservist who commanded a destroyer escort in the Solomon Islands and ten years older than those who were in high school during the war, never forgot those years because they were years of terrible separation from his passionately beloved Catherine Collins. He often said, "Johnny, you and I are the only sane ones in the family. But we mustn't tell the others because it would spoil their fun." And then he would add apropos of the early 1940s, "They were not good times to grow up."

Brian Dogherty was part of the same cohort, a year or two older because he was able to get into the Navy in 1944 and come home with GI bill benefits. He moved into the Vetville Quonset huts at Notre Dame. He stayed on to get a degree in philosophy, married a young woman from St. Mary's, and came back to Chicago to teach at DePaul. When his father died, rich from postwar profits in the construction business, Brian retired from teaching and moved into the huge Victorian family home on Race and Mayfield, just two blocks behind St. Lucy's. He had spent the rest of his life in reading, research, and writing increasingly irate articles for Catholic publications and bizarre letters to the Chicago papers. He also bought up homes in the neighborhood when the property values plummeted during the rapid resegregation of West Austin.

A pale, sad-eyed young woman in a black dress admitted me to the vast redbrick Victorian pile on Race and Mayfield after I had laboriously climbed the two flights of steps to the door.

"I'm Eileen, Bishop," she said to me, respectfully though she made no attempt to kiss the ring that I was still wearing. "My grandfather is very energetic some of the time, but grows weary easily, especially when he thinks about the Church."

"So do I."

She smiled wanly and led me up yet more stairways to a third-floor room which overlooked the neighborhood—St. Lucy's to the south across Midway Park and West Suburban Medical Center to the west on the other side of Austin Boulevard and firmly planted in Oak Park. Lightning crackled in the southern sky.

"Welcome, Bishop Ryan." A sprightly, bald old man, with thick white eyebrows rose painfully from a judge's chair behind a vast desk, more cluttered even than my own, and fell on his knee to kiss my ring.

I helped him up and eased him back into his chair. He was, I thought, a crippled leprechaun with the bad moods those creatures frequently display.

"Newgrange symbol," he muttered. "Pagan."

"As is the Brigid Cross," I said, displaying my pectoral cross. "And even the Celtic Cross. The last named, as I'm sure you're aware, is an Indo-European fertility symbol and the former a sun symbol distantly related to the notorious Swastika."

"Fair play to you! Well, sit down. As I told you on the phone I respect your orders but your jurisdiction, like that of all bishops for the last half century, is invalid."

"An auxiliary bishop," I said, "for all practical purposes has no jurisdiction. No power either."

"I've read your books. Well done. William James of course was not a Catholic. Pragmatist. I don't know what that fellow David Tracy is talking about. People like him don't deserve the name theologians. I don't hold with this Transcendental Thomism. I'm just a plain old Thomist—like Jacques Maritain and Ives Simon and Etienne Gilson. Giants of twentieth-century Catholicism, even if the Church ignores them today. Still, you're obviously a very smart man. I'm surprised that Cronin wants anyone intelligent working for him."

He gestured to the bookshelves which lined all the available wall space in his office. He had read a lot of books, but was frozen in the philosophical worldview of the men he had studied at Notre Dame in the late 1940s, men who were brilliant indeed and the progressive Catholics of their time. But they did not prepare their followers for the traumatic changes of the Council.

"I do my best to hide it," I said. "But I'm afraid Milord Cronin sees through me."

"I'm an Aristotlean," he went on. "That's the philosophy perennis I learned at Notre Dame. I taught it there. I haven't changed my mind. When the Church has suffered enough because of the pagan and Protestant Council mess forced on us, then it will return to the traditional teaching and elect a valid Pope."

Something of a non sequitur there, but I let it go.

"I believe they're teaching Aristotlean metaphysics at Notre Dame these days. Father McMullin . . ."

"He's not a dumb man at all, but the students don't have to take the courses. When Notre Dame dropped the compulsory philosophy and theology courses they stopped being a Catholic school . . . Would you like some tea, Bishop? I'll ask Eileen to bring up a pot. She's a nice young woman even if she is a pagan."

"Thank you . . . I'm sure you and Msgr. Wolodyjowski have much to talk about. Like you he is quite a scholar."

"He's a damn fraud! Talks about those German philosophers. Nothing good intellectually has come out of Germany since Kant . . . Eileen, sweetheart, would you ever bring up a spot of tea and a cookie or two . . . I can't stand the man. Preening fake nobility! Besides, he's ruined this neighborhood. He panders to the Negroes! He could have saved Austin if he stood up to them. Now he's got all kinds of crazy people running around—Mexican drug lords, pagan hippies, Asians. I may have to sell all the homes I own on this street the situation is so bad. New Austin be damned. It's a bad situation getting worse."

"Ah."

"I don't mind the Negroes all that much. Some of them are good family people. Keep up my houses real well. But, face it, Bishop, they're culturally inferior. Not their fault maybe. Slavery and that sort of thing. Look what that Negro coach did to Notre Dame football."

"There are those who think it started to go bad when they hired a white high-school coach twenty-five years ago."

"Damn Holy Cross Fathers, they always think they know something that other people don't know."

We were silent for a moment. Eileen served the tea and cookies (two), smiled at us uncertainly, touched her grandfather's forehead.

"Take it easy, Gramps."

"Thanks, Suzy," he said.

Eileen was the girl's name. Did she remind him that much of his wife?

He waited till she left.

"Sweet girl. She reminds me of my wife when she was that age. She's a student at Notre Dame, not St. Mary's . . . Something else the goddamned Church ruined . . . Letting women into Notre Dame . . . It's not a man's school anymore . . . The child is a pagan . . . Dates an East Indian, black as coal . . . Claims he's a Catholic . . . She's probably sleeping with him . . . Goddamned Church fucked everything up . . ."

He wound down for a minute. Then he took a deep breath.

"I hate the miserable son of a bitch," he exploded, his face turning crimson. "Do you see this woman? This is my Suzy when she was a sophomore at Notre Dame and we fell in love . . . Here she is with our first child . . . and here at our twentieth wedding anniversary . . . Isn't she beautiful?"

She was indeed.

"She's from the neighborhood. Died of cancer a few years after that picture . . . And that fucking bastard wouldn't let her be buried in the church she was baptized in . . . I hope they blow the fucking place up on him."

The woman looked very much like their granddaughter.

"Why not?"

"Because I wanted her to be buried at a valid Catholic Mass, that's why. The least I could do for her was to have a real Mass!"

"Tridentine Latin?"

"Sure, what else? You know the words of consecration are invalid in the English Mass. Everyone with any sense knows that. It's all a fucking fraud! I loved her so much!"

Tears poured down his withered cheeks.

"If she's in hell because of her funeral Mass, I hope he rots forever!"

"I'm sure she's in heaven waiting for you with a heart filled with love."

"Fuck it all . . . I got down on my knees and begged him, pleaded with him, and he just said it was against the rules. I told him that the rules were invalid. He just smiled his goddamn Polack nobility smile and said they were valid and he was surprised I wanted to break them . . . Would you have said that about my last wish for my dear Suzy?"

"No, I wouldn't . . . *sacramenta propter hominem*. The Sacraments exist for humans not vice versa."

Sean Cronin would have agreed if the request had come across his desk.

"Please leave me alone, Father Ted. I can't stand the pain. I don't know who's taking shots at him, but I hope they blow him up."

I walked down the stairs and encountered Eileen.

"He's upset," I said.

She nodded.

"Every day it gets a little worse, Bishop. He is a good and kind man. He never got over her death . . . I think the Church is better than it was when he was young."

"Much better, Eileen. More confusing, but better. So is Notre Dame, though don't tell him I said so."

"Mr. Casey is outside waiting for you in his car." She wiped away a tear of her own.

"Thank you," I said as I remarked to myself that it was the first time I had ever been confused with Father Hesburgh.

Mike Casey's driver was waiting at the door with an umbrella.

"If this kind of treatment continues," I observed as I slipped in next to Mike, "I shall begin to think I'm someone important."

"Is Mr. Dogherty a suspect?"

"If intense hatred for Msgr. W. was a sufficient motive for crimes against St. Lucy's, he certainly has it. I doubt, however, that he has the stamina and the health, and maybe even the character to act on his hatred."

I explained the story of the refused funeral mass.

"You wouldn't do that, would you?"

"No, but don't blame it on the Monsignor's Polish heritage. A lot of Irish pastors would have done the same thing in the old days and some recently. What's the point in having power unless you can use it to hurt people?"

I asked again about the suburban hit gang.

"Brighton Lawn. To be exact. Seventieth and Central. We're watching them. No reason to think they're involved. We suspect the house is an arsenal. However, we do not wish to search it until we have enough other information about the bunch. They are dangerous and scummy people. Perhaps at one time they were brave men doing their patriotic duty to serve their country. However, the kind of duty they did is corrupting. They became indistinguishable from the bad guys they're killing."

"Would they have killed the unfortunate young people in the sanctuary of St. Lucy's?"

"More likely they took the bodies on consignment from the coyote who did kill them."

"Are the local Brighton Lawn police aware of them?"

"We haven't asked."

Blackie

When I entered the Cathedral Rectory, exhausted by my morning's work and deserving of brief opportunity to rest my eyes, I uncovered Sergeant Declan O'Donnell engaged in conversation with the four Megans and Crystal Lane who, it appeared, had attended Loyola with him. The Megans, representing each of four ethnic groups (Korean, Mexican, African, and Irish-American), are the high-school porter persons who run our parish from three to ten every afternoon. Only one need be on duty, but the others periodically swarm to the rectory, allegedly to cooperate on their homework.

"Bishop Blackie," Megan Kim insisted, "this boy says he's a police officer. He really isn't, is he?"

From their viewpoint Declan seemed hardly old enough to be in college.

"In truth, he is a sergeant in the CPD and one of considerable influence."

"I told you, kids," Crystal chortled. "I agree he doesn't look like a cop. He's a lawyer too. And studying to be a psychologist."

"No way!" they shouted in chorus.

"If you don't mind," Declan said to them, "I think I'd better talk to the Bishop so he doesn't accuse me of disrupting the parish staff."

"Back to work, gang," Crystal said.

"I didn't realize she works here," Declan said when we entered my parlorlike office on the first floor—a room which violates all clerical rules for sterile rectory offices. I don't even have a computer in it.

"I didn't know Crystal worked here," Declan repeated as I sank into the easy chair which I require to deal with the problems of the human condition.

"Lives here too—in the housekeeper's quarters. She's our mystic in residence. Prays for all of us. Every cathedral should have one."

"Does she have second sight?"

"Not that I know of, but I wouldn't put it past her."

He was silent for a moment.

"I've had it again."

"Ah?"

"I saw a man on the L embankment with a rocket-propelled grenade launcher."

"Indeed!"

"I kind of sensed that the school was filled with children."

It was the time of the terrorist attack on Russian schoolchildren in North Ossetia.

"You have communicated this information to the worthy Dragon Lady."

"Reluctantly and privately. I didn't want them to think they were working with a freak."

"Are you a freak, Declan O'Donnell?"

He grinned.

"Only one of the dark ones and only occasionally."

"And the Dragon Lady's reaction?"

"She didn't giggle, Bishop. She took it very seriously. I think she'll recommend that the Austin Station put officers on the L embankment when school begins."

"Patently a prudent move. Your unit may be the only one in the whole CPD that makes a decision based on second sight."

"Cops always follow their instincts," he replied with the modest smile that had already broken the heart of the local Lady of the Camillas. "This is just another kind of instinct."

"Indeed . . . What else is happening up there on Magnolia Street?"

"We've been able to enter the computer at Combined Control and gain access to St. Lucy's security system."

Somehow I didn't like that.

"You could do the same with our system?"

"Why would we want to?"

A good point but hardly reassuring.

"So tonight," he continued, "I'm going out to Austin. When the Unit tells me that they've turned off St. Lucy's protection, I'll fire a beam into the rectory and the church. If there's no reaction, we'll know that we can turn the system off at will. Then they'll turn it on again."

"How long will this delicate operation require?"

"Fifteen seconds, unless we foul up."

"I see."

I still didn't like it.

"Then what?"

"We've also uncovered a port—a software patch—which the original hacker created so that he would have easy access to St. Lucy's whenever he wished."

"This can be done?"

"Combined Control will need to insert a blocking mechanism when this has all gone down."

"So what happens the next time our Internet pirate chooses to attack?"

"He'll enter Combined Control's master computer and send a message to St. Lucy's to shut down the security system. Only it won't work. He'll think it worked, but whoever is trying to violate the system will hear a lot of alarms and bells and maybe we can scoop them up."

"A trap?"

"Two traps actually. One for the invaders and one for the hacker. With any luck we can get both of them."

"Ah. And then?"

"Well then I'll drive out to River Forest and Camilla and I will go to a theater called The Lake and see *Hero*."

"A date this soon?"

"It's not really a date. We're only seeing a movie."

"And you're going to meet your Lady of the Camillias in the lobby of The Lake?"

"I thought of that but I didn't have the nerve to suggest it. She wants me to meet her parents."

"Are you not moving too quickly, Declan O'Donnell?"

He grinned.

"Arguably."

"May I make a suggestion?"

"Sure, I always listen to a priest. Don't always do what they say."

"You must tell the Delicious Camilla of your occasional second sight. Patently not of the rocket aimed at St. Lucy's."

"The rifleman on the embankment?"

"By way of illustration."

"Lovers, even just beginning and very cautious lovers, need to know that their tentatively beloved is just a little different."

"To prepare for a second sight experience . . . I don't have them very often, Bishop Blackie."

"Still."

He hesitated.

"It will not trouble her. I believe her ethnic group is as likely to have dark ones as we do. She'll probably refer to an uncle or a grandparent who was alleged to see things and dismiss it as an interesting and possibly attractive oddity, not worth her concern."

"They believe in the evil eye too, don't they?"

"I find it inconceivable, Declan Patrick O'Donnell, that you have the evil eye."

Later, after he had left, I encountered Crystal Lane.

"He's a nice young man, isn't he, Bishop Blackie?"

"Patently."

"He had a very rough relationship when he was in college. His family were vicious to Beth. They're terrible people. They ruined his sister's wedding. Declan and Beth wouldn't have lasted anyway, yet I think it broke his heart. But he has a new lover, doesn't he?"

"I cannot testify to that word. It's a very new relationship . . . You can tell?"

"Naturally . . . And he knows she loves him."

"The whole parish staff seems to have been taken in by that slow and patently insincere smile of his."

She laughed at my slander of the decent Declan.

"As you know, Blackie, I have another love interest, one that smiles often too. But if I were not involved in that relationship I could be mesmerized by Declan's smile and maybe feel a touch of envy towards Declan's lover."

That's the kind of thing mystics say.

Before the early evening rush of people to the rectory seeking salvation in any one of the available forms I put in a call to Nora Cronin.

"I suppose he's on the phone every day?" she said, opening the conversation, "barking out orders which you humor but take with a grain of salt."

"Only because they are meant to be taken with a grain of salt."

"He sounds like he's the cat that has devastated the whole canary population of Rome, so I guess he's got what he wants?"

"Such as that may be."

"He is greatly amused about the rumors of your moving to the mountains. Says you couldn't last ten minutes west of the Des Plaines River."

"Ah, the perimeter has moved in. Only recently it was the Fox River. In truth, he might say Bubbly Creek."

"He seems concerned about the situation with Mike Wolodyjowski."

"As well he might. It is a mess out there."

"Have you talked to Brian Dogherty yet? He's a strange, irascible old man."

"Indeed."

"Everything in his life's work would suggest that he would have supported the changes at the Council. Yet he is bitterly opposed."

"You know him then?"

"He is one of the neighborhood characters. He is quite capable of anything that would destroy Mike."

"In his state of health?"

"He is sick all right, Blackie; but he is insane and vicious. Don't cross him off your list."

"I'll take your word for that . . . I hear stories about a scandal from long ago that might figure in the case."

"The past never leaves us alone, does it?"

"Indeed not."

"I suppose it must be the accident at Harlem and North in 1944. Six kids killed. The driver was drunk as I remember."

"Tragedies like that happen all the time," I said.

"I'm not sure why this one was different, Blackie. The driver of the other car was accused of reckless homicide but acquitted. He was a German immigrant and they said he was a Nazi. There were rumors of a cover-up, though I don't think that was the word in those days. I didn't know the young people who were killed . . ."

A hint of something but not much.

"Sean might remember more. I think he knew something about it . . . But how could that all affect St. Lucy's sixty years later?"

A fair enough question.

My first visitor in the evening rectory crowd was the ineffable Joe Tuohey (with an "e") of the OBA.

"I want to continue our conversation from the other night, Bishop," he began with little ceremony.

"Please do."

"I don't like to have to say this but I think the cause of the problem out in Austin is Monsignor Mike."

"That has been suggested to me before. The community blames him for the crisis and would like to see him leave."

"What crisis?"

"The desecration of the church, of course, but also the white invasion of the community."

"Ah."

"People love their community, Bishop. They don't like it when others try to take it away from them."

"They don't want to lose the empty buildings, the vacant lots, the drug corners, the shuttered-up stores, the gangbangers?"

He shook his head patiently.

"That's what it looks like to an outsider. Even if it doesn't look like much, to the community it's still theirs—their friends, their churches, their schools, their groups. They don't like white people taking it away from them just because they want access to the Green Line."

I always wonder about who "community activists"—especially when they are of different skin color—mean by "the community." To what extent, I ask myself, is it merely a projection of the "activist's" wishes and dreams.

I did not say that, however.

"Are you suggesting that members of the community are responsible for that obscene display in the church?"

"I knew you would misinterpret me, Bishop. You guys always do."

"Please correct my misinterpretation."

"I'm saying that as the situation in the community gets worse, no one can control some of the marginal and misguided victims. They might do anything. The pressures will diminish considerably after the Monsignor is removed and replaced by an African-American priest."

"Like Father Nelson?"

"He's not an African-American. He's an African, and a stage African at that."

"Indeed."

"Look . . . It wouldn't be so bad if this white invasion hadn't been going on for years. Even before the New Austin project half the people in the church on the weekend were white."

"An integrated congregation was bad?" I asked, feigning surprise.

"It is when the white people are from outside the community and have a lot more money . . . It's the whites who paid for the improvements in the school and the church and that erratic alarm system . . . Lords and ladies bountiful coming to Austin to help the poor natives . . ."

"Who were these invaders?" I asked with some surprise.

"Rich white people from Oak Park and River Forest and Forest Park and heaven knows where else. They invaded a neighborhood where they were not wanted. They took over our parish."

"Why?"

"That's the whole point I'm trying to make. They came because of the Monsignor."

"Indeed!"

"They love his aristocratic charm, his learned homilies, his wonderful choir. So they leave the parishes where they belong and take over St. Lucy's."

"They dominate the parish council or the finance committee?"

"No, he's too smart to let them do that, but they still own the parish and everyone in the community knows it. We figure now it was just the first step in driving out Blacks and replacing them with whites."

"I understand your point."

I also understood that the same thing was being said by whites in 1970 when St. Lucy's was being resegregated the first time around. The question in both cases was how many people were saying it.

"I hope, Bishop, that you will relay my message to the Cardinal. If he wants to save St. Lucy's before he retires, he'll have to replace the Monsignor with a pastor who is acceptable to the community."

"I will certainly tell him precisely what you said."

"I hope you do," he said skeptically.

There was no chance that Milord Cronin would replace Pan Wolodyjowski because of such complaints. However, might there be a possibility that some of the discontented in the "community" might be orchestrating a campaign against New Austin? One ought not to rule out that possibility. I couldn't see a disorganized and hapless Joe Tuohey as the genius behind such a plan, but he might be capable of being an *agent provocateur* who was stirring up the masses.

The Cathedral Rectory was busy that night. When I finally stumbled out of the parlor office, I was bleary-eyed and almost incoherent. I had listened for over an hour to a couple, both lawyers, hurling insults at one another about their turbulent marriage. I didn't see how love could stand such vicious rage. However, neither seemed to want a divorce or an annulment. Nor would they consider consulting a counselor. Everything would be fine if I just told the other spouse that s/he was wrong. Their belief in the power of a parish priest to win an argument for them was touchingly old-fashioned. However, when they left they were angry at me for not taking a stand. The Lord made them, as the saying went, and the divil matched them. They would continue to fight for the rest of their lives. Would not a divorce be better? Neither one of them could survive in an intimacy without making it adversarial. Better that they ruin each other's lives than taking on another target for their neurosis.

My parting words to them were, "God did not appoint me to adjudicate between you two!"

They thereupon blamed one another for the failure of the session with me.

I found in my box in the office the expected secondhand envelope with the words "Bishop Ryan" scrawled on it. The pen seemed to have run out of ink halfway through.

I left it in the box and adjourned to the basketball game that Crystal had organized for the young people—a contest which was surely an essential part of the effort to proclaim good news in Galilee a couple of millennia ago.

Crystal had introduced an innovation in the game such that there were three boys and two girls on each team. The result seemed to be much happy laughter.

I walked back to the office, picked up the envelope from Packy, and ascended to my room. Before I opened the envelope I turned on Channel 3 for the ten o'clock news. I beheld the tireless Mary Alice Quinn talking to Alderman David Crawford of the Thirty-seventh Ward in one of the many caverns of City Hall.

"Are you saying, Alderman Crawford, that West Austin is currently a tinderbox ready to explode?"

"I wouldn't go that far, Mary Alice. I'm saying that there is a lot of tension in the community because of the New Austin development. That tension might have been responsible for the ghastly event in St. Lucy's the other night."

"And you think that the New Austin project ought to be suspended to ease the tensions."

"I certainly feel that it should be slowed down till tension in the community eases."

It had been, I reflected as I poured myself a small drop of Bushmills Green, a very difficult day. Both the alderman and the community organizer were blaming St. Lucy's for the attack. That sounded like nonsense, but there might yet be some truth in the nonsense—as there often is.

I settled back in my easy chair to read the Old Fella's document. It was written in large, clear script in faded black ink—he did not like typewriters.

On the first sheet, a warning—

Not to be read till 1995

Internal evidence seemed to indicate that it had been written before 1950. Hence the embargo was more than forty years. He had not expected to live that long—though in fact he had. He must also have assumed that the people in the story would be dead too. That was before antibiotics.

I hesitated to write this story down. I asked myself what good it would do to account for the horrible deaths of innocent young people. They are with God who loves them. Their tainted reputations cannot be cleared now. Some of those who loved them have heard the report of my investigation and are at peace with it. Already their names and stories have faded into the past. Very few remember them or care about their fate. This document is for the historical record, but will a historian ever be interested and would such an interested party seek to find an answer in my archives?

Yet I write the story on the possibility that someday someone will have good reason to be interested in the truth and smart enough to want to examine my papers in hope of learning it. As I write my two-year-old son Johnny is playing with blocks at my feet. He is an interesting and interested young man. Maybe he will be the one to read this document. If he is, I salute him.

The letter from beyond the grave, so to speak, brought tears to my sleepy eyes. They did not, however, make it easier to stay awake. Wisely I put the document aside and, having said a brief prayer to the deity in which I apologized for all the mistakes of the day, I immediately fell into a restless sleep.

Declan

"Thirty seconds!"

Lucille King's voice was sharp and precise on my cell phone.

"I thought it was fifteen?"

I was standing in the Park across Lake Street from the rectory in the expanding shadows of dusk. The thunderstorm had passed over and the air was clean and fresh. Cops, on duty and off, were loitering around St. Lucy's. They were bored, I was sure, but they were doing their best to seem alert. Their problem was that they had no idea what they should be looking for. A chopper had come over while I had chatted with the officers. It focused its beam on the L embankment. I had a dim recollection of the man with the rocket launcher, but he was certainly not there. I ambled away from the cops and stood next to one of the old oak trees in the Park. Precisely on time, Lieutenant King was on the phone.

"Madam wants to make sure . . . I will turn off the alarm system at St. Lucy's at the count of one. You will fire the electronic beam at the count of ten. You will fire it for five seconds. If the alarm sounds, we will abort the mission and you will retreat with as much dignity as you can. You will inform me both when you begin and end. Then you will count ten seconds and fire it again for another five seconds. Madam insists that this all be precise."

"Anything to keep Madam happy."

Andrew M. Greeley

I aimed the magic box at the rectory.

"One and counting. Two. Three. Four. Five. Six. Seven. Eight. Nine. Ten."

"Firing," I said, pushing the button on the beamer which was no bigger than my cell phone. "One. Two. Three. Four. Five. No alarms."

Lucille counted ten more seconds. I fired the beamer again. Nothing.

"Any activity around the site?"

"Just cops trying to stay awake."

"Well done, Declan. Now you can go on to your date."

"It's not a date!"

I was not dressed exactly for a date—black jeans, sneakers, a blue tee shirt, and my Loyola windbreaker to cover my weapon. This whole event must be low-key.

As if it could possibly be low-key.

I was scared when I crossed Harlem Avenue and entered River Forest from Oak Park. I was afraid of her parents. I was afraid of her. I was afraid of myself. Faint heart . . . ? Yeah, but I am perennially faint-hearted.

The Datillo house was one of those big Georgian brick places in River Forest which during the Christmas seasons are usually covered with thousands of lights. That frightened me even more. I had never met any rich Sicilians.

Camilla answered the door. My heart skipped every few beats. She was wearing tailored brown slacks and a brown blouse, an ad for autumn from a woman's magazine, a medal to Our Lady hung from her neck. A warning against the passions of a hungry male?

I didn't think so. She knew me well enough already to know that a conquest, should there be one, would be slow, gentle, and long-term. Dammit.

"Hi," I said tentatively.

"Hi," she replied with a mischievous grin.

Yet she was nervous too.

Her parents were not my stereotypical West Side Sicilians. They were rather slender people in their middle sixties with dark skin and silver hair, graceful gestures when they talked, and oceans of low-key Mediterranean charm. Martina, my beloved's mom, wore the required black dress, which hinted at a figure that was a good omen for Camilla's sexiness forty years hence. Tonio, her father, wore a vest over a white shirt. They had to look their best for Camilla's young man. The art in their house was expensive and tasteful, traditional (impressionist) rather than modern. Elegant, cultivated people, even if their wealth came from making pasta and they had once lived in Thomas More.

I had memorized a half dozen jokes about the Irish and the Italians from one of my joke books, which would have been in terrible taste. Instead I smiled my diffident smile and turned on all the Irish charm I could manage. It seemed to work. They told me how nice it was to see me again, how proud they were of their Camilla, especially of her skill at beach volleyball and how much they liked my drawing (which was prominently displayed on an end table).

"You can keep it," I assured them. "I've already made a copy out of my sketchbook."

"We knew you were a nice boy," her mother said, "when we saw you sketching instead of taking pictures at the match."

"You come to the matches?" I said in some surprise.

"We are very proud of her," her father said simply.

We left for the movie. It was only a short walk to The Lake. The streets of River Forest were safe at night, especially if you had an armed police sergeant as an escort.

"My parents adore you," she said proudly. "I could tell."

"Taken in by the Irish charm."

"They've seen enough to be able to separate the real from the phony."

"Your mother is gorgeous."

"I plan to be that way when I'm her age."

A promise?

"I don't doubt that you will."

"Are you good with that weapon, Declan?"

169

"Some marksmanship awards. I've never used it on the job and I never will."

The film, admission to which I paid for without protest, was all about warriors, but warriors prettied up in wonderful Chinese colors. We held hands through it, I'm not sure who the aggressor was, probably me. But she surrendered her hand quickly enough.

We were acting like a pair of teenagers in their first crush.

"You do martial arts too, Declan?"

"A little," I said. "You too?"

"Only enough to throw a rapist on the ground and then stomp on him."

"Fearsome Saracen princess."

"You bet."

She took my arm in hers, definitely she was the aggressor in this matter, but I did not resist. We drifted into Petersen's. "Last one this month," she insisted. She paid for the malts and I did not protest.

"I have two things I must tell you, Camilla," I said as we walked out on Chicago Avenue in the calm summer air, dominated by a very large moon, a night for romance.

"OK." She squeezed my arm for reassurance.

"First of all, you remember when I left church during that Mass?"

"And came back and that helicopter flew over?"

"Yes. What did you think?"

"I thought that like my great-uncle Alberto you had second sight . . . Do you?"

"I had a picture of a man with a rifle on the embankment."

"Good thing you did . . . That means that a woman must be careful with you. You'll be seeing all kinds of things about her."

She was utterly calm about the whole thing.

"I don't have such pictures very often, and never about a woman."

"Not yet!"

"Do you mind?"

"Why should I? I have nothing to hide from you, Declan Patrick O'Donnell . . . What's the second problem?"

"My family are venomous!"

"What!"

"Our family culture is dysfunctional. They drove away my college sweetheart with their nastiness. It would have ended anyway, but it was terrible. They absolutely ruined my older sister's wedding. She doesn't speak to any of them anymore."

"Not even to you?"

"I'm not like the rest of them . . . I stopped in high school because I couldn't stand it anymore and moved out of the house when I was a freshman in college. I got a job as a busboy at the Ambria and rented an apartment of my own."

"You have clout there? You can get reservations?"

"Yeah . . ."

"Good! That's our next nondate. I'll pay for it!"

"It's a thing the Irish call slagging—ridiculing people to cut them down to size, all with the pretense it is in good fun, just joking around, but it's deadly."

"You were slagging me in the schoolyard?"

"I'm so sorry, Camilla, so very sorry."

"I did give you absolution, Declan. Now forget it."

"Your parents are so nice . . . If I bring you into my parents' house, they'll try to eat you alive!"

"Not twice!" she said, squeezing my arm even more fiercely. "If we ever become enough involved that you have to bring me home, I'll tear them to pieces."

I had not the slightest doubt that she could and she would. We stopped on the sidewalk of Jackson Street. She disengaged her arm and pointed her finger at me.

"If I'm that involved with you, no one, absolutely no one, will ever take you away from me! Do you understand that?"

"Yes, ma'am. I don't doubt it for a minute."

"Good." She took my arm again and held me close. "That settles that . . . But poor Declan . . . How awful!"

I knew I would have to kiss her at the door of her house. The lights were out inside. Her parents trusted the nice Irish boy, perhaps unwisely.

Perhaps not. My kiss was confident, even firm, but gentle and brief. She leaned her head on my shoulder after it was over.

"That was very nice, Declan . . . I'm so frightened."

"That makes two of us, Camilla."

She kissed me this time, same kind of kiss. Well, maybe a little more passionate. Then she ducked into the house.

"I'll call you, Camilla," I shouted after her.

She opened the door.

"You darn well better!"

I drove home on the Expressway. I was still scared. But happy.

Until I had an impression of a big explosion.

Black-E

"Turn on Channel 3. Big show."

Thus the so-called Dragon Lady at 3:00 A.M. Or so my clock insisted. The good Gabriel with his last Judgment Day horn could not have hit me more powerfully. I stumbled into my study, turned on the TV, and witnessed the good Mary Alice Quinn interviewing Dawn Collins with Jan Kazimir curled up contentedly in the latter's arms.

This was clearly a nightmare.

Lieutenant Collins was speaking.

"At 1:55 this morning two perpetrators broke into the back door of St. Lucy's rectory, activating the alarm system. Police officers attempted to enter the front but were unable to open it. They were directed to the back door, which they found had been torn off its hinges. Upon entering the rectory they discovered two subjects trapped on the stairway to the second floor. Above them Msgr. Wolodyjowski was waving his Polish cavalry saber and pounding one of the subjects with its flat surface. At the bottom of the stairs, Father Nelson Ironman was thumping the other subject with the back of his royal spear. In addition this cute little kitty was scratching the face of one of the subjects. Police officers apprehended the two subjects. They are now in the lockup at the Austin police station."

Jan Kazimir was hardly a cute little kitty. His yellow eyes stared balefully at the TV camera but he was clearly purring as Lieutenant Collins stroked his neck.

Still a nightmare, though perhaps a comic one.

"Were the two men armed?"

"One with a baseball bat and the other with brass knuckles."

"And then the Monsignor had a heart attack?"

"He experienced a shortage of breath. He is now in intensive care at West Suburban Medical Center just down the street. We believe that his condition is described as good. You'll have to inquire over there."

"Do you think, Lieutenant, this will be the end of the disturbances at St. Lucy's?"

"Our investigations are continuing."

I turned off the television, found my wrinkled priest suit, put on my ring and pectoral cross, and descended to the offices, where I left a note. Across the street I backed my car out of its parking space, drove north a half block to Chicago Avenue, and headed for the West Side.

My siblings provide a car for me every year or two, often a vehicle discarded by one of their children. This year it was a two-door Chrysler PT Cruiser, a "retro" car that looked like it was manufactured in the nineteen thirties. My sisters thought it was "cute" and I looked "cute" driving it. To add to the cuteness the car had been painted a color that matched the purple of my episcopal robes. To complete the picture the license was BLACK-E.

I turned off Chicago Avenue at Milwaukee, then onto Augusta Boulevard. At that hour of the night I may have well set a permanent record for the eight-mile trip from the Cathedral to West Suburban Hospital. I parked in the doctors' parking lot, affixed my BISHOP RYAN sign to the dashboard, and rushed into the hospital. Only then did I notice it was raining again.

"He's OK, Father," said the young woman resident in the ICU. "Resting comfortably. We'll monitor him for a day or maybe two and let him go home . . . Father Nelson is guarding him."

"I can well imagine."

In a bright red dashiki and Roman collar, Reverend Nelson stood at the entrance to his pastor's room, arms folded implacably.

"Bwana Blackie." He bowed solemnly, then grinned. "Bwana Wolodyjowski is resting comfortably and talking in Polish to a Polish nurse."

"They wouldn't let you bring your spear into the hospital, Nelson?"

"In the spirit of holy prudence, Bwana, I did not try to bring it in."

"Shouldn't you be sleeping? You haven't had much sleep lately."

"I am on an emotional high. I have never used my family spear in combat before. I feel I have proven myself a warrior."

"I'm delighted to hear that."

I didn't think he was serious, but what did I know about African customs?

"What happened to Father McDonald during the contretemps?"

"I believe he slept through the event. He needs his sleep, Bwana."

"I would think he does . . . And the housekeeper?"

"She fell on her knees in her room and prayed to the Black Madonna of Yasna Gora, which undoubtedly helped our conquest of the invaders—though I could never understand why a black woman was in Poland. Possibly she was a Turkish slave freed by Polish warriors."

I knocked on the door. Mickey said, "Come in" in a strong voice.

"Panna Yakubowska and I were practicing our Polish, Bishop Ryan."

The nurse, a handsome woman in her midforties, bowed and kissed my ring. At least she didn't genuflect.

"I hear you're resting comfortably, Pan Mikal."

"It's a mantra they repeat frequently." He moved his lips in his usual smile. "It has been a long time since I have engaged in a saber fight."

The nurse had blushed when I entered the room, doubtless enchanted as all women are, if one was to believe Sean Cronin, by Mickey's charm—which was probably greater in his mother tongue.

"It was quite a fight according to the good Mary Alice Quinn."

"Father Ironman is a good man in a battle."

"As I gather is the good Jan Kazimir."

"A fearsome beast . . . It was good of you to rise early in the morning to visit me, Pan Ryan. Father Ironman has administered the Sacraments to me, which always helps even if it is not a matter of necessity."

"I was prepared to do so if necessary. However, if I did not rush out here, Milord Cronin would fire me."

"Is it true, as they say, that he has gone to Rome to insist that his resignation be accepted?"

"You and I know that's not going to happen. Also I am not leaving either. Milord Cardinal alleges that I would not survive ten minutes west of the Fox River."

"He is certainly wrong, though you must not tell him I said so."

"It was helpful that the alarm system was working this time."

"Strangely, they were inside the house before it rang. However, it did the job if ten seconds late."

That was interesting information that I must pass on to Captain Huong.

"The men that we kept at bay," he continued, "surely assumed that there would be no alarm . . . They were, I believe, ignorant thugs—mercenaries in the service of someone else."

"Who might be that someone else?"

"Someone who wants our school to close. Why attack me personally? I am not worth such an invasion."

"I interacted with your parishioner Brian Dogherty yesterday afternoon."

"Brian hates me, Blackie. However, he would not hire thugs to attack me, of that I'm sure . . . He was a progressive a long time ago. It was the birth control issue that turned him around. He became angry when Paul VI established the commission to examine that question. Like so many others, Brian assumed that there would be a change and that would negate his wife's courage in enduring five miscarriages. When the Pope issued his encyclical, Brian continued to be angry because, as he said, it was too late. People had made up their minds."

"An original twist," I said.

"His wife was a wonderful woman, Blackie. She had always been the center of his life. He interpreted everything in terms of its impact on her—as he personally interpreted that impact. She told me that she was glad that birth control was no longer a serious sin. She would never have said that to him, however. . . . Unless there is new information about these attacks, I will suggest to the school board that we delay the opening of the school for another week. Do you think Sean will object to that decision?"

"Hardly."

The invasion of the rectory had accomplished its goal.

"Nurse Yakubowska," I said, "would it be all right if I attempted a phone call to Rome?"

"Certainly, Bishop," she said, glancing at the monitor next to the bed. "I will leave you for a few moments of privacy and watch the monitor at the nursing station."

I noted that Mickey Wolodyjowski followed her shapely derriere with some appreciation as she left the room. Nothing wrong with that. Our species is genetically coded for such appreciation. Yet his eyes lingered on her with a lack of restraint that might be less than discreet.

"She is a very good woman, Blackie," he said with a sigh, "very reassuring to someone who finds himself suddenly in a hospital with no clear notion of what is wrong . . . Her husband is a very lucky man."

"Patently," I said as I dialed Milord's cell phone number.

"I always felt that Brian idolized his wife into someone she was not. That may have been his tragic flaw. It was certainly a tragic mistake."

Ah, I thought to myself. Was there jealousy involved in Brian's dislike for his pastor? Was the controversy about the funeral Mass the effect of such jealousy and a rationale for it? Would a woman caught in the rigid paradigm into which her husband had forced her seek consolation from friendship with a charming parish priest, platonic friendship most likely, but powerful? Did Brian Dogherty resent adultery of the soul?

My speculations were cut short by the voice on the phone.

"Cronin!"

"Ryan."

"What the hell's going on, Blackwood!"

"I am at this very moment in a room at West Suburban Medical Center with your good friend Prinz Wolodyjowski."

"What's he doing there!" he shouted, implying that it was somehow my fault.

"He and his colleague Nelson Ironman routed two rectory invaders earlier this morning. In battling said invaders with his Polish Cavalry saber, with which I am sure you are familiar, he seems to have strained some muscles, which created the impression he had a heart attack . . ."

The Prinz nodded vigorously at my interpretation.

"So he is here for observation. There seems to be universal agreement in this institution that he is resting comfortably."

"No one rests comfortably in a hospital, Blackwood, you know that."

"Arguably."

"Did the alarm work this time?"

"It did."

"Were the cops there?'

"They were indeed . . . You will be interested to know that when the CPD entered the rectory, they observed the alleged perpetrators trapped between the Polish Prince's saber and the Nigerian Prince's spear. I know this to be true because your good friend Mary Alice reported it on television."

Milord Cronin thought that was hilarious.

"Nelson is all right?"

"Oh yes. And Father McDonald was sleeping the sleep of the just man."

"Figures, poor guy."

"In any event, our side won the battle of Mudhole Park decisively."

"That's the kind of PR we need more of, Blackwood—priests fighting off the infidels!"

"Strictly speaking, I suspect that they are not infidels . . . I will put the hero of the battle of Mudhole Park on the phone."

I handed the Polish Prince the phone and slipped out of the room. Panna Yakubowski was watching the monitor closely.

"The father's heartbeat has increased somewhat."

"He is talking to the Cardinal on the phone."

Nelson Ironman joined me.

"I hope that Bwana Cronin approves of our self-defense."

"Bwana Cronin is an incorrigible romantic, Nelson. He loved the story."

The nurse returned to the room and I followed her. Mickey's eyes savored her approach as they had savored her departure.

So.

"Sean seems quite happy with his successes in Rome, Blackie. He also tells me that you wouldn't last five minutes west of Austin Boulevard."

"In which case I had better leave immediately."

I bid him and the fearsome Nelson good-bye and rode down on the elevator. Prinz Wolodyjowski would not hit on the nurse. He would, however, enjoy her presence and make a mild conquest of her soul. Nothing particularly wrong with that, I supposed. Yet her husband would not approve if he knew. Fortunately for all concerned he would not know.

It still made me uneasy. Such a soul conquest would upset a man like Brian Dogherty, even if the paradigm in which he may have imprisoned his wife forbade him to acknowledge it. He would know only that he hated the pastor. It was too late in his life now to seek revenge. Or was it? And how many other angry husbands might there be somewhere in the Archdiocese?

I have always made it a rule of thumb to be wary of a woman who is frustrated in her marital relationship—at whatever level of complaint. Such a one needed emotional support and affection. To provide the former was wise. To provide the latter was dangerous. Maybe I'm old-fashioned.

Though I think not.

Four women waited for me at the entrance of West Suburban, each with an agenda about which I could do little.

I encountered young Declan's *femme formidable* in the lobby of the hospital, wearing a trench coat over a black pantsuit and looking like a prosecuting attorney who wanted the death sentence.

"I saw your car, Bishop Blackie, and I was afraid that the poor little Monsignor had taken a turn for the worse."

"A discreet, low-key, unobtrusive vehicle."

"I think it's totally cool," she said and smiled.

A young unmarried man would be swept away by such a smile if he was unprepared for it. Poor Declan.

"Monsignor Wolodyjowski is resting comfortably as the local jargon puts it. They will probably release him later in the day or first thing in the morning."

"Good! We charged the perps with attempted murder. We'll arraign them this afternoon . . . I was afraid we might have to change the charge to murder."

"He is an elderly man in excellent physical condition, even if he has very poor taste in wine . . . Who are the perps?"

"Two young African-American gangbangers and druggies. They'll be in and out of jail for the rest of their lives. A terrible waste . . ."

"Something must be done for such young men."

"You've been out to Twenty-sixth and California, Bishop?"

"Oh, yes."

"I agree that something must be done. Once I hoped we could do something about it. Now I think our efforts are doomed . . . Anyway, I'd better drive home, then down to the office to prepare the case against them. I'm sure some public defender, as cynical as I am, will want to plead them out. No way this time."

"Did they tell you who sent them to St. Lucy's?"

"Herman or Mr. Herman, some street operator who probably has a half dozen names." She waved her graceful hands in frustration. "The cops will try to hunt him down or find out who he might be working for. My guess would be that the ultimate perps have pretty well hidden themselves."

"Doubtless."

"I'll keep you informed."

She turned to walk out into the rainstorm. Then she turned around.

"Declan and I saw *Hero* last night."

"A *DATE?*"

"Course not." She smiled again. "We went to The Lake. He stopped by to meet my parents."

"And they loved him . . . What mother wouldn't think that Declan Patrick is anything but a practically perfect possible son-in-law?"

Her dark complexion reddened, a delightful shade.

"I'm scared, Bishop Blackie. So is he. It's all happening too fast."

"Your parents would probably think not fast enough."

"So much can go wrong . . ."

"A leap in the dark."

She nodded solemnly.

"I know."

Now I was supposed to say something wise and profound and insightful.

However, all I could think of was, "You both could do a lot worse."

"That's what really scares me."

She smiled again and escaped into the rainstorm.

As the blessed Holy Woman said, "All will be well, all manner of things will be well."

The next woman entered the lobby through a hallway. She too wore a dark raincoat with a hood over her head. However, her jewelry, even at this hour of the morning, identified her as Luisa Sanchez.

"My husband would like to speak to you, Bishop, only for a moment. He means no harm. Would you come with me, please?"

Pablo, I reassured myself, would not send his wife to lead me into a trap.

At the end of the corridor we went through a swinging door and down another long corridor. The exit led to an alley behind the old wing of the hospital. Next to the refuse cans, a very large Mercedes limo awaited. Donna Luisa lifted an umbrella to protect my passage to the car. Pablo, dressed in a business suit of entrepreneurial black, jumped out to hold the door open so I could enter the back. Then he ran around to the other side and reentered the car. Luisa slipped into the front with the driver. A thick transparent plastic window provided privacy for our conversation.

"Thank you very much for coming, Padre," he said grimly. "It is most necessary that I talk to you."

"Talk," I said with equal grimness.

"First, I do not believe the television. How is it with Don Miguel?"

For a moment I wasn't sure who Don Miguel was. Then I realized he meant Pan Mikal.

"For once you may believe the television. He is doing well. Nothing serious happened to him. He may be released this afternoon. Tomorrow morning certainly."

Pablo relaxed a little.

"That is very good . . . However, they meant to kill him, did they not?"

"Presumably the goons who invaded the rectory were instructed only to beat him up with their baseball bat and brass knuckles. However, given his age, the beatings might very well have killed him."

He nodded solemnly.

"Those who sent the ones you call 'goons' would have been pleased if that had happened. Their problems would have been solved and there would be no link to them."

"I'm sure that is true," I agreed. "Did they kill the young people in St. Lucy's?"

"The *coyote* killed those poor ones. Then he and his men gave the bodies to the evil *poliza* who wanted bodies. They are all dead now."

"The coyote and his crowd?"

"I did not kill them . . . Someone else did. I would have killed them too."

"A lot of killing, Don Pablo."

"We are warriors, Padre. We have to be. There is no order in our world. No law, no protection for our wives and children . . . We must be ruthless to survive . . ."

Pablo was tired of the killing, tired of the whole life of the *narcotraffiantes*. Tired enough to survive, I wondered, to get out while he still could?

"I will kill them all," he whispered. "Every one of them. I will have no mercy."

"Don't do that, Pablo," I replied. "This is not Colombia or Mexico. You cannot take justice into your own hands."

"Who else will, if I do not? I will offer myself to the cause of justice, even if it means my life."

"And the lives of Luisa and your children?"

"I will provide for them. They will be safe."

He laughed softly.

"Luisa knows that my life will be short. She is a brave woman. She will survive . . . I do not plan to die, Padre, but I will run that risk."

"You cannot be sure that you know the men behind these crimes."

"I *know*," he insisted.

"You don't know who has hired them."

"That is of no importance. I will destroy the ones who would destroy St. Lucy's. I tell you so you will know when it goes down."

"I urge you not to kill anyone, Pablo."

His lips parted in a tight little smile.

"I know you must say this, Padre. I must defend my children. I have no choice. Pray for me, Padre, and for Luisa and my children."

"I will surely do that."

He knocked on the partition. The driver jumped out, umbrella in hand, and conducted me back to the door of the hospital. I saw briefly Luisa's agonized face in the window of the front seat.

As I walked back down the long corridors I wondered what I was supposed to do with that conversation. Tell the police? They could hardly hold Pablo for more than a few hours. Warn the shadowy figures behind the plot? I did not know who they were. Mike Casey? What could he do? Annamaria Huong? Again, what could she do?

Was Pablo engaging in preventive war? We don't do that in a civilized metropolis, do we? I could only hope that the situation would resolve itself before Pablo unleashed his furies.

Finally, I concluded that I must pass the warning on to Mike the Cop. He would know what to do. If anything.

The media were waiting for me at the door of the hospital, including the implacable Mary Alice Quinn.

"How is Msgr. Wolodyjowski, Bishop?"

"It is said by everyone that he is resting comfortably. I do not dispute this diagnosis."

"When will he leave the hospital?"

"You will have to ask the hospital spokesperson."

"Will St. Lucy's school open on time?"

"That is a matter for the Monsignor and the parish school board."

"Doesn't the Church have any theories about the violence at St. Lucy's?"

"You'd have to ask the Pope."

"Does Cardinal Cronin know about the attack on one of his rectories?"

"He spoke on the phone with Msgr. Wolodyjowski only a few minutes ago."

"What is his reaction?"

A fun question, but I must not joke just yet.

"I think it would be proper to say he was troubled by the event."

"Have you started to pack yet, Bishop Blackie?"

"For what?"

My chance was coming.

"For your trip to your new diocese out in the Rockies?"

"Milord Cronin has opined that I would not survive very long, west of the Fox River; recently he reduced my survival possibilities to west of the Des Plaines River. This morning he suggested that I would be in grave danger if I were west of Austin Boulevard. I note that I am at this moment west of Austin and have been for some time. Hence I conclude I better depart immediately."

I walked away, content with myself. Naturally, I knew at least in general terms the markers he wanted to pick up. I had a pretty good idea what would happen. In effect, nothing would change.

At my car, a thin young woman in jeans and windbreaker and shivering in the rain was waiting for me. Her red hair was frizzled and her face tight with anger.

"I'm Abbey Kincaid and I want to say at the start that your car is hopelessly vulgar."

"I agree."

"What right does a Catholic priest have to drive such a monstrosity?"

"You would rather a Cadillac or a Benz or a Lexus?"

"A bishop should be nondescript and unobtrusive."

185

"I agree with that too . . . Now if you'll excuse me I'd like to get in out of the rain, behavior that my sainted mother always said I was incapable of doing."

"I've been waiting in the rain to talk to you."

"Then talk."

"What right does the Catholic Church have to blame me and my colleagues for the attacks on St. Lucy's?"

"No right at all."

"Then why has it done so . . . I'm thinking of taking legal action against you!"

"If indeed the Church has made false accusations against you, you certainly should."

"I talked to a priest who used to be here in the parish and he said the Church was blaming us."

"Did he say who was speaking for the Church?"

"He said that everyone knew who we were . . . All we want is to slow down the change so that there will be some low-income housing here in Austin."

"A worthy cause. The Archdiocese supports it too."

"All the Monsignor cares about is attracting rich people to his parish."

"That comes dangerously close to libel, Ms. Kincaid . . . Let me say for the record that no one speaking in the name of the Church has blamed you or anyone else for the crimes committed at St. Lucy's. If you bring me direct quotes from someone, then we will repudiate them and apologize."

I almost said that I had never heard of her or her organization. That would have been unwise.

"I don't believe you. I don't care what you say. You're like all the rest. The Church does not give a fuck about the poor."

"Good morning, Ms. Kincaid." Now soaking wet, I climbed into the car and redeployed out of Oak Park, Ms. Kincaid's imprecations trailing after me. Milord Cronin was quite right. It was unwise for me to be west of Austin Boulevard.

Declan

"You have fight with girl?" the Dragon Lady demanded. "You in deep shit with her? You try to hit on her? Shame on you, Declan!"

"No, to all your questions. We had a nice time. I just didn't sleep very well."

"You have guilty conscience, Declan O'Donnell!"

"No way."

A proper swain would have fallen into bed after a successful evening of courtship with the satisfied joy of conquest. I was too old for those feelings. I knew too much about the psychology of sexual pursuit. I understood how many conflicts could arise between a man and a woman which could destroy love—whatever love might be.

My dreams were about women—my mother, who had let me down; my big sister, who had fled the family; my little sister, who was slipping into the slagging culture; my fat aunts, who were the most vicious of all of them; Camilla. Especially Camilla. Darling, wonderful, beautiful, witty, fragile, strong, gorgeous Camilla. In my dreams she was interchangeable with the others. I would hold her naked body in my arms—O glorious fantasy!—and she would change into one of the women in my family, teeth bared to consume me.

Not healthy dreams, I had told myself. Declan, you're sick! You

187

need to see a shrink! OK, I will do that. As I rode my bike in the rain up to Magnolia Avenue, I realized that in the real world, as opposed to the terrors in my dreams, the most serious problem between me and Camilla would be that I concealed my rage and she revealed hers. That would never work. She shouldn't change and I couldn't change. I had swallowed too much of my anger for too many years. I stored it up, then a small spark would set off an explosion inside of me and I would become a raging monster.

Poor risk for marriage. Another and better reason to see a shrink.

So I was in no mood for Annamaria's jokes.

"They tried again last night," she had said when I stumbled into our little fortress.

"Who tried what where?"

Then she got on me about my date.

When she realized that was not a successful response to my bad mood, she gave me the facts. Two thugs had invaded St. Lucy's Rectory and been resisted by the priests. Msgr. Wolodyjowski was in the hospital. The thugs were in jail. The alarm system had worked, with only a couple of seconds' delay.

"Our friend the hacker tried again to turn the system off. The firewall you put up frustrated him. The bad guys told their goons it was safe. They got caught. Probably the hacker managed to turn the system off for a few moments, then it went back on."

"Your firewall probably save priests' lives."

No good with women, good with firewalls.

"Now we work all day and catch hacker, right?"

"Right."

So Lucille King and I worked the rest of the day, along with two other members of the Dragon team to hunt down the hacker.

"Take fifteen," Lucille ordered me sometime after lunch. "You're out of play."

"Yes, ma'am, yes, Lieutenant, ma'am."

"You call girl," Captain Huong suggested. "Tell her you're sorry that you tried to hit on her."

"More likely," Lieutenant King commented, "that you didn't hit on her."

That was a lot closer to the truth.

"Oh, Declan," my Camilla said when she answered her phone, "I'm in a very bad mood. I was at St. Lucy's early this morning . . . You heard about what went down, didn't you?"

"Only when I came to work."

"Then I had to arraign those goons this morning and the idiot public defender wanted to plead them out on a home invasion and disorderly conduct charges. I shouted at him in most unladylike terms and the charges of attempted murder will stand. But I'm beat, in a really bad mood."

"Not angry at me, I hope?"

"Declan, darling," she said softly, "how could I ever be angry at you?"

I melted into very soft margarine.

"I must apologize for last night . . ."

"You didn't do anything wrong last night, Declan. You were a perfect gentleman."

"I didn't tell you I loved you. And I should have. When I kissed you."

Big, brave, passionate lover!

Silence from the beloved. Then tears.

Then in a shaky voice, "Declan darling, I love you too. You're so sweet to call me. It makes my day. I really do love you. Forever."

That is an awfully long time.

"And, Declan, you'd better get used to saying that you love me. All the time. Understand?"

"Yes, ma'am."

"You look happy, Declan," the Dragon Lady said, when I returned to our war room. "Girl forgive you?"

"She said she'd love me forever," I mumbled, still dazed.

"You now up shit creek, Declan, without paddle! Deep shit creek!"

Lucille King was more romantic.

"Congratulations, Declan. Now get back to work!"

We had trapped the hacker all right, but a full day's work did not give us his URL. However, we would get him and soon.

Forever is indeed a very long time, I told myself. But that was not necessarily bad.

Blackie

"We don't intervene in gang wars," Mike the Cop said to me when I recounted in strictest confidence Pablo's threat. "At least generally not. If there are killings, we try to find out who's responsible and apprehend them. It's very difficult because no one wants to talk. We have to assume that your conversation with Pablo is privileged because you are a priest. If he had told you who he was going to kill, it might be a different matter, unless it was a seal of confession issue."

"It wasn't, not exactly."

"But even if you could testify about his threat, it would be very difficult to link that vague threat to something that happened to a rival gang. We'll keep an eye on the situation."

"The group stationed out in Brighton Lawn?"

"We're watching them closely, Blackie. But we have zero evidence that they are involved in the attacks on St. Lucy's. In general we don't provide protection for citizens unless they ask for it. Moreover, Brighton Lawn is out of our jurisdiction . . ."

"The CPD wouldn't shed too many tears if that gang was taken out?"

"I didn't quite say that."

"I understand."

The message was clear—Blackie, don't mess around in things

that are too big for you and about which you cannot and should not do anything.

I was not sure, however, that the priest relationship with Pablo was quite as privileged as Mike thought. Yet Pablo obviously thought he was invoking it. I would wait and see.

After returning from my Communion calls at Northwestern Hospital, I phoned the good priest Jeremy (nee Jeremiah) at his suburban fortress.

"Blackie here, Jeremy. You are certainly within your rights to talk to the valiant Ms. Kincaid. Yet you would be less than prudent to share with her your opinions of diocesan policy. There might well be grounds for civil and even canonical action if such opinions became widespread."

Knowing no canon law, I might have been wrong. But I figured that the so-called Jeremy knew even less.

"Are you telling me to shut up?" he asked with some heat.

"Heaven forefend! I am saying that a decision on your part to avoid sharing with her your opinion of our policy might be a prudent one."

He hung up.

I had angered him. More to the point, I had frightened him.

Then I walked down the street to the Chancery Office and requested that I be admitted to the secret archives.

"You can't take anything out of there," the woman in charge of the archives warned me.

I had no intention of removing anything. However, my mother's son that I am, I do not like to be ordered around.

"It may have escaped your attention but I am a moral person with Cardinal Cronin and I will do whatever I want."

With little grace she yielded.

The system was not organized to facilitate access—perhaps deliberately. Eventually I found the file of Mikal Kasimir Wolodyjowski. There were four letters inside the file from irate husbands who complained that their wives were spending too much time with Father Wolodyjowski. The letters were spread out over the fifty years Mikal had been a priest, the most recent ten years earlier. Only one complainant had received an answer, which assured the writer that the Archdiocese had warned Father Wolodyjowski, who had given assurances that the relationship was one of a counselor but that he would cease it immediately. There were no annotations on the other letters.

I concluded, cautiously, that the relationships may have been merely flirtations, harmless flirtation—if a flirtation can ever be harmless. However, there might well be men out there who wanted to do grave bodily harm to the pastor of St. Lucy's. What had he said to me? "I have loved many women, Blackie, almost always from a safe distance."

Almost?

I left the Chancery feeling slightly unclean. So what if Mikal had erred on occasion? That was between him and God and the other party or parties. Yet that was not altogether true. Even if his love affairs were platonic (and nothing between a man and woman is ever entirely platonic), there might be men who harbored strong needs for revenge.

I did not like what I had found, yet I would hardly throw the first stone. The world was growing murkier.

When I returned to the rectory there was another envelope in my box. I opened it to discover the same kind of weird scribbling on the inside.

‖‖‖ ‖‖ ‖‖ ‖ ‖ ‖‖‖ ‖‖ ∕∕ ‖‖ ‖‖

‖ ‖‖‖ ∕ ‖ ‖‖ ‖‖ ‖ ‖‖ ‖‖ ‖ ‖‖ ∕∕∕∕ ‖‖

‖‖ ‖ ‖‖ ‖‖‖ ‖‖ ‖ ‖ ‖‖ ‖‖‖ ‖‖ ‖ ‖‖ ‖‖‖

‖‖‖ ‖‖ ‖ ‖‖ ‖‖‖ ‖‖ ‖‖‖ ‖‖‖ ‖‖‖ ‖‖ ‖ ‖ ‖‖

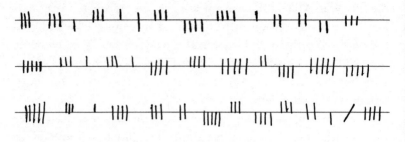

I thought I recognized it, so I made a phone call to someone who might be able to help. She said she'd come over in the afternoon.

It was time to return to the Old Fella's story.

Ned Ryan

*They were golden young people, handsome, intelligent, gifted. They were
destined for wealth and happiness. The boys might soon be in harm's way
somewhere in the world. Somehow death in combat would seem less tragic
than death in a flaming wreck on Harlem Avenue. The three girls were
strikingly beautiful, just at that age when a young woman became aware of
the bloom of beauty that was hers. When they entered the dining room at
Butterfield they stopped conversation. They knew they stopped conversation
and it did not bother them in the least. They would probably be married
now to returning servicemen, not necessarily the men with whom they dined.*

*Many people blamed God for their deaths. Catherine my wife and a
great defender of God—she believes firmly that God is a civil libertarian—
rejected such an accusation. Who are we to judge what God does and doesn't
do? I don't argue with her because I never win. She also says that I am an
incorrigible romantic and in that respect she is quite correct. On the other
hand, she doesn't know the whole story like I do.*

*The official story is simple enough—six young people attended a
formal dance at Oak Park Country Club on the Sunday night of the
Memorial Day weekend. They had been at Lake Delevan in southern
Wisconsin on Friday and Saturday. They had played tennis, swum in the
lake, and spent some time in a local roadhouse on both evenings. Some folks
at the roadhouse reported that they drank too much. They returned to the*

Burns house in Assembly Park on Lake Delevan, where they spent both nights without chaperones. It was assumed after their deaths that they had given themselves over to sexual activities. The other parents blamed the Burnses for permitting them to use the house for fornication. Msgr. McMahon the pastor of the parish in which two of the victims lived, forbade a Catholic funeral on the grounds that they had died in the state of mortal sin.

My Catherine was furious at this decision. A little necking and petting, she wrote me (I was at Pearl Harbor at the time, shaping up the crew of my DE) is not all that terrible, is it? What else are kids to do! They would not have slept together for fear that one of the crowd would tell parents and their reputations would be ruined. Besides God loved them, didn't he? I'm sure they're in heaven with him.

As I say my wife is a great defender of God.

In any event, the Chancery overruled Msgr. McMahon.

They drove into Chicago in the Burns Packard and went to their respective homes. Subsequently the parents said they were all exuberant about the great time they had at Lake Delevan and eager for the party at the Country Club. Some mumbled later that they were excited by the sex they had enjoyed. The all-knowing Catherine said that they were too young and inexperienced to enjoy sex the way it should be enjoyed.

In any event they went to Oak Park Country Club, which in fact is in Elmwood Park. They were Jack Burns, Jim Reilly, Burke Boland, Mary Dwyer, Anne Scanlon, and Elena Martinelli. They all attended Catholic high schools (of course). The girls went to Trinity, the boys to Fenwick, except Jack Burns who was in the ROTC at St. Mel's—the better to prepare for military service.

As if you can learn to be a combat infantryman in high school. Or anywhere else save on the battlefield itself.

There was much speculation afterwards about how the six had paired off—which meant who had slept with whom and hence condemned their partner to hell for all eternity. Catherine Collins Ryan protested to me that they would only have begun to pair off when they were a year older.

In any case, they left the Club at midnight, thoroughly intoxicated according to some witnesses, quite sober according to others. Everyone agreed *that they were a striking group at the dance. "Spoiled rich kids," someone had complained to the <u>Chicago Daily News</u> "they got what was coming to them."*

Jack Burns drove the Packard down Thatcher Drive and turned east on North Avenue. At the intersection of North and Harlem, the Packard collided with a large tanker truck. Some witnesses said that Jack was running a yellow light. Others said he had the green light and the tanker rammed them. In either case there was a huge explosion which blew the truck driver out of his cab and incinerated the young people instantly.

They were all dead on arrival at West Suburban Hospital an hour later. Anger, grief, guilt swept that part of the city. The newspapers railed against "uncontrolled youthful folly while our boys are dying overseas." Parents blamed one another. Everyone blamed John F. Burns, the father of the driver. Revenge was promised by one couple. Another demanded that the Elmwood Park police arrest the Burnses for the murder of their daughter. A nun at Trinity told her students that it would be a waste of time to pray for the repose of the souls of the victims because they were damned to hell for all eternity.

In fact the autopsies which were never made public but which I include in this file reveal no alcohol content in John Burns's blood and that all three young women were virgins. Catherine Collins Ryan says, "I told you so."

Indeed she had.

Presumably, therefore, her God (one which I believe in usually and try to believe in all the time) had taken these young people home to himself. I admit that I often don't know quite what that means. But I believe it nonetheless.

The driver of the tanker was badly injured in the accident but a few weeks later was dragged into the County Court at 26th and California in a wheelchair. He was a German immigrant and hence a possible enemy alien, which didn't help his cause. The State did not have much of a case because of the usual conflicting testimony of witnesses. Nonetheless he was convicted of manslaughter after a jury debate of less than an hour. The hysterical behavior of the families of the victims doubtless influenced the jury's decision. He was sentenced to twenty-five years in prison. The victims' families were furious. He should get the electric chair they claimed, even

Jimmy Martinelli who as a lawyer ought to have known better.

"You don't know how you would react in the same circumstances," my wife insists.

Right as always.

A year and a half later, the Illinois Supreme Court reversed the verdict with words of strong criticism for the judge by a four to three decision. The driver was released amid much outcry and disappeared.

John P. Burns came to me after the war and said that there was something fishy about the whole affair. He asked me to investigate the case. I discovered the true story only with great difficulty. Burns was quite right. The story I summarize above was untrue in almost every respect.

Three facts stood out as I reviewed the documents.

1) The witnesses who testified that the Packard was weaving out of control as it plunged towards its doom assumed that the driver was drunk. But we knew that there was no alcohol in his bloodstream. If Jack Burns was sober, the weaving must have been for some other reason.

2) Two witnesses testified that the tanker truck was stalled in the intersection.

3) Given the size of the conflagration, the driver of the tanker should not have survived. Not unless he had leaped out of the truck before the explosion and fled across the street.

I might have added a fourth: the reversal of the conviction by the Illinois Supreme Court smelled of fraud. Someone must have persuaded several of the judges to vote against the evidence. Who, I wondered. Mary Kathleen, my eldest daughter and unindicted coconspirator, hunted down some young people who had been with the victims at Delevan that weekend. I must note that at that time, Delevan was also called Sin Lake because of the sexual activity, especially by servicemen (from Great Lakes Naval Training Station) and their girlfriends—in desperate attempts to squeeze a little pleasure into their lives before they had to face death.

Historically, I must add, the graduates of Great Lakes had a much better chance of surviving than did either soldiers or Marines. But at that age in those days, no one calculated the odds.

Mary Kathleen, an image of her mother, reported back with several firm assertions. The six victims did not drink excessively that fateful weekend. It was highly improbable that they were promiscuous. "Maybe a little necking and light petting." They spent their time in the lake, on the tennis courts, and hiking through the nearby woods. Furthermore, they had taken under their wing a seminarian from Quigley, a cute Polish kid whose unpronounceable name began with a W.

No such person had died in the car.

I borrowed some Quigley yearbooks from a priest I knew and found a young man with the name that began with a W. I calculated that he would be at the major seminary in Mundelein now and phoned there to ask if it would be possible to interview him on an important legal matter. The rector flatly refused, no reason given. I made a few more calls and was told that I could talk to him for exactly one hour in the Aula or lecture building on Sunday afternoon at one o'clock. Because I am stubborn and contentious I insisted on two hours and won.

The seminary is a redbrick Georgian spread, a string of buildings along a stately avenue with the blue lake beyond. It's quite impressive until you take a close look at the buildings and realize that the construction is poor and that tuck pointing must drain a lot of cash from the Archdiocese.

W is a compact man, slender, medium height (which is what I am!), solid muscles, a strong presence and a magical smile. I asked him if he knew the young people who died on Memorial Day.

His face clouded. He did not know them very well. He had spent only a couple of days in their company at Lake Delevan. He wept when he heard of their death and attended two of the funeral Masses, where he also wept. We Poles are very sentimental, he explained. They were kind and attractive, the three young women incredibly beautiful. I was flattered that they wanted me in their company for a few hours. They knew I was a seminarian and respected that. I played tennis with them and lost, swam with them, hiked with them in the woods. I do not understand why God called them home so young with all the promise of their lives ahead of them. They were golden children, only children, Mr. Ryan, only children on the thin edge of adulthood.

He did not ask why I was interested in their deaths.

Why were you at the lake?

My father owns a construction company as well as a savings and loan. I wanted a few days of relaxation before I began to work. I drove up there by myself. Sometimes I find my fellow seminarians a bit . . . dull. Perhaps that is why . . . why I was attracted by these young people who were not dull. I have often thought that if they had lived they would be my friends through all the years of my priesthood. Then, I confess, I weep a little once again.

Did anything happen during your time with them that weekend?

He paused to consider very carefully.

There was one singular, I might almost say ominous, event. Or so it seemed to me. They merely laughed. They laughed so much. They were so very happy . . . we were hiking through a small wood and came out near a farm. It was Wisconsin farmland, completely different from the resort area a mile or two away. It also seemed distant from any road. There were many young men walking around the farm, stern young men. I thought it might be a military encampment. The most shocking thing were a number of dead animals stretched out on the ground.

I am Polish, as you no doubt can tell. We are very suspicious people. I wanted to leave. In fact I slipped back into the woods, but not so far away that I could not hear what was being said. One of the young men accosted them and told them they were on government property and they should leave immediately. They said they would but asked why the animals were dead. He wrote down their names and told them to leave at once. I have often wondered if that incident had anything to do with their deaths. Had they discovered something they should not have discovered? But that is impossible, is it not? They died in a tragic accident.

The man's name? I'm sorry I do not remember it. I think it was Irish.

I can assure you, Mr. Ryan, that they were not heavy drinkers as the newspapers said. An occasional bottle of beer. Nor was there any sex play. The young men talked about that among themselves, as young men do, but they knew it would not happen. I hope I have assisted you in your investigation.

I assured him that he had been a big help, shook his hand, and wished him well in his journey to the priesthood. He replied that ordination would be a very happy day but he would be very sad that his friends, so briefly known, would be with him only in spirit.

A priest stood at the door of the classroom as I left, a somber frown on his face.

This is most unusual, he told me. I thanked him.

The seminarian was, I thought, a very serious and solemn young man, mature beyond his years. For all of that, he was a sentimentalist. Tears formed often in his eyes during our conversation.

I stood in the bright winter sunlight outside the classroom building and looked up and down the elegant street. Beautiful, but not the best possible place to educate young men who would work all their priestly lives in the city.

I thought I knew what it was the young people had discovered—a government project dealing with some kind of poison. In 1944 there were many "scientific" efforts at work besides the Manhattan Project which spawned the atomic bomb. Many of them were harebrained, most of them reached dead ends. The security at some of them was absurdly weak. Yet in that week before American troops landed in Normandy the war seemed to stretch on forever. Any gimmick which might shorten it seemed worthwhile. Not all the men involved in these projects were reliable or even sane.

I decided I would fly to Washington and attempt to discover what was happening in the farm only a couple of miles off the road out of Lake Delevan. I was a reservist in the Navy and had a decoration or two, which meant that they would have to deal with me. I would never be called back, however, because of my reputation for making trouble (a reputation of which I am very proud).

The admiral with whom I had an appointment knew me from Pearl, then Leyte. He liked me—a bit unusual among the two-stripers—and was friendly but guarded. I abandoned the Irish custom of leaving the important question to the end of our meeting.

I'm interested, I told him, in the poison factory you had in southern Wisconsin in 1944.

I didn't have it, he said. In fact it never existed.

Andrew M. Greeley

It did exist and it was just crazy enough to be Navy.

What do you want to know about it, Ned?

Everything . . . I'm going to find out anyway and I'd rather hear it accurately from you.

Most of the men involved are dead now, either killed in the Pacific or by the stuff they were making.

Which was?

A "death spray." The idea was that you would spray this compound on enemy troops and they would die incidentally. Cyanide as I remember and a few other ingredients. There were a number of problems with it, not the least of which is that you had to spray it on his face from the distance of a foot or two. By the time you got that close to a Jap you'd already be dead. Also it was very unstable. It would lose its potency in a few hours . . . You remember what it was like in those days, Ned. We knew how the Japs fought to the last man. An invasion of Japan would have been a nightmare. The scheme was crackpot from day one, but it seemed worth the effort . . . Why are you interested?

Six young people from Chicago were killed, in all probability because they stumbled on the factory.

I know nothing about that. They didn't keep very good records over there. Messianic complex. They were going to save the world. If they did kill some kids, they would have justified it in the name of the war effort and not reported it. I'm sure we have no records.

Is anyone still alive from the project?

Are you going to bring charges?

I'm just collecting information for a client whose son was killed in what was set up to look like an accident. He wants to know the truth. I doubt that he would do anything. He's just too worn down. You know as well as I do that the courts wouldn't hear the case.

Blackie

"Mrs. Coyne is here to see you, Father Blackie."

"I'll be right down."

I know two women who might claim that name. One is the mother of Father Coyne, my sometime associate pastor and now pastor of his own parish, which lurks on the boundaries of the Cathedral. The other is his sister-in-law, a woman of many parts and many personae. However, "Mrs. Coyne" was a new one.

As I rode down on the rectory elevator, a relic I believe of the early seventeenth century, I pondered my Old Fella, whom I had never encountered in the role of a private eye. He was very good at it. I missed him. He never gave me any bad advice, not that advice giving was one of his things.

There was an unbecoming rumpus in the offices. So Mrs. Coyne was patently Nuala Anne, singer, actress, accountant, wife, mother, Irish-speaker, shitekicker, detective, and mystic (though of a different variety than the worthy Crystal Lane). Also one of the most important members of the North Wabash Avenue Irregulars. She had obviously brought her younger daughter, one Socra Marie, a three-year-old who had no right to be alive and celebrated life with almost uncontrollable vitality.

"I would have known from the noise that Nuala Anne and Socra Marie were here."

"Bwackie!" The pretty little kid with thick glasses rushed to me and jumped into my arms.

She was still a slight child, not much to her, a lot more, however, than when she had emerged into the world after only twenty-five weeks in Nuala Anne's womb.

"Socra Marie go to school this year," she announced proudly.

"I'm sure you'll like it."

"Don't know." She squirmed and I put her down. She was a squirming child.

"School is fun," I argued in a blatant lie.

"No." She stamped her tiny foot. "BORRING!"

In due course, the two Megans present, Kim and Jones, took charge of the child, much to her delight, and Mrs. Coyne and I adjourned. Today her persona was that of the competent business professional—dark brown suit, nylons, moderately high heels, a touch of makeup, conservative jewelry. The only hint of the West of Ireland was the manic gleam dancing in her scorching blue eyes.

Her husband often averred that she had the face and the body of an ancient Irish goddess, though he immediately qualified the comment by saying that he himself had never met one such goddess.

"So, your rivrance, you think you have a message in ogam script, which is the proper name, not druid script. Your druids were not bright enough to come up with an alphabet of their own. The early Christians did it before they took over the Latin alphabet and sure isn't ogam a more sensible alphabet altogether and itself suited perfectly to the Irish language?"

I passed her the first code.

"Well, doesn't this man know it pretty well. Let's see the first word is ailim, sail, sail uhath, or, luis, edad. Isn't it as plain as the nose on your face?"

"What does it mean!"

"Brigid, Patrick, and Colcille, isn't it a vulgarity! A terrible violation of a script designed for a pure and holy language which doesn't have any words like this at all, at all!"

"Which is why you Irish speakers use the Anglo-Saxon words with such great poetic skill!"

"Give over, your rivrance! If you pronounced the word in English it's asshole!"

"So the author is using the old Irish alphabet to communicate a message in modern American English!"

"For which, God forgive him says I. He has no respect at all, at all . . . Let me translate the rest of it for you."

She wrote English (or more properly Latin) letters over the script.

You think you know everything and you don't know anything.
I am warning you get that fuczer out of there.

"He's using that terrible word that me husband Dermot Michael Coyne forbids me to use in polite American society."

"Speaking of himself, how's he keeping these days?"

"Och, isn't he a focking saint and himself putting up with me and the kids and the dogs and all the noise confusion?"

"And herself?"

"Well, I think she's calming down a little now that she's three and going to preschool this year. Dermot thinks she's wild as ever. The doctors tell us her eyes are improving, but she'll never be much over five feet, still you could hold her in your hand when she first came into the world, so five feet isn't bad now, is it? Dermot says she'll be a point guard. . . . Let me see that other letter."

As she read the second and longer message in ogam script, Nuala's natural effervescence faded. She frowned, shook her head somberly, and said, "This is a bad man, Blackie. Bad. This is a very bad man. He's up to no good, at all, at all."

"What does he say?"

If you don't get him out of there, close down the New Austin, I'll
blow up that school with the kids in it. He won't stop me.

"Fascinating . . . Why would he write to me with that threat in ogam?"

"Isn't he one of your psychopaths? He's showing off how smart he is. Doesn't he want to prove he's a lot smarter than you are? He's fighting you."

"Ah," I whispered.

That had been tried before and it had not worked out all that well for the fighter. Still there's always a first time . . .

"Still, he's a bit of a gombeen man, isn't he now? He's not nearly as smart as you are and deep down he knows it."

How did Nuala Anne know these facts? The answer is that she *knew*.

She reached in her purse and pulled out a card.

"This explains ogam. You can translate any more letters that come . . . Your man is playing a game with you."

"That has happened before."

She smiled thinly.

"Isn't that God's truth?"

I bid good-bye to her and the tiny terrorist, as Dermot Coyne called her. The child threatened a tantrum because she had to leave the Megans, but brightened up when her mother promised ice cream. There was a time when all the ice cream in the world would not have averted a tantrum. I was willing to wager that in pre-school, canny creature that she was, she'd become a well-mannered little lady.

I carried the two missives upstairs and thought about them. Then I had an idea. I called Mike Casey and read him the two letters. Perhaps there would be a suggestive fingerprint?

"Many people may have touched the envelopes. But only Nuala and I read the message. If there is a third print. . . ."

"He couldn't be that dumb," Mike argued.

"I'd say he's pretty dumb. Most crooks are."

"Maybe . . . I think we have you and herself on file. I'll send someone over with an evidence bag to pick them up."

I returned to the Old Fella's file.

The aged folder was filled with newspaper clippings. The *Tribune* had spread photos of the six victims across the front page. They were indeed golden youth right out of an F. Scott Fitzgerald novel. Three dazzling young women in prom dresses, three young men in formal suits. Junior prom presumably. One of them looked familiar—slender face, sleek brown hair swept back from his forehead, a dangerous grin. Jacky Burns, the caption said.

I knew him. I had seen him somewhere.

That was patently impossible. John F. Burns Jr. was dead a year before I was born. Yet the face was one I knew.

Well perhaps all Irish look alike, all West Side Irish.

Maybe he wasn't dead. Maybe it wasn't his body that was incinerated in his father's Packard.

That wouldn't do. If he was still alive, he would be Sean Cronin's age. Still that was not impossible. Some men are identifiable from their youthful pictures well into their seventies. But what would be the point of such a survival? Might the bodies in the Packard all be substitutes? Most unlikely. The golden youth were long since in the ground at Mount Carmel Cemetery.

I studied their pictures closely. Did it make much difference to them whether we finally uncovered those who had killed them? Presumably they had much better things to do in the world to come. Yet if one believed with the ancient Celts that those in the many-colored lands in the west are very near us, even standing around watching us, might not these six golden children be in the room with me whispering, "See to it, Blackie!"

Had they known Sean Cronin? He was quite the famous young man in those days, just their age as was Mikal Wolodyjowski in that deeply troubled, fearsome year as the invasion of Europe was about to begin. I would discuss this matter with the Cardinal on his return.

Mike Casey's man came with the evidence bag for the envelopes.

Now I must read more of the Old Fella's story.

Ned Ryan

"Only two of them still alive," the admiral said as he returned to the office.

"Isn't that a little strange?"

"When the operation was closed down, they were all sent to the Western Pacific. You know what that was like, Ned."

"I don't think we took that many casualties."

"Some of them were on the _Indianapolis_."

That was the heavy cruiser which delivered the atomic bombs to Guam, traveling without escort because of its speed and the virtual destruction of the Imperial Japanese Navy. Unfortunately one submarine had survived and it sank the _Indianapolis_. Many of the crew were eaten by sharks.

The admiral asked me again if I could assure him that none of the material would be made public. I told him that I was preparing a dossier for a man who was seeking closure for his grief. I had already figured out who had killed his son and the other young people. I would not be bound to secrecy on these matters. I also would suggest that the guilty parties had gone down on the _Indianapolis_. I would not hint at what I thought probable that the Navy had liquidated several of them. In short, I would advise against taking action on the grounds that there was no one left to be punished. I was confident but not absolutely certain that my client would follow this advice. Whatever I collected from him would be absolutely confidential.

He nodded his agreement.

You always have been a straight shooter, Ned, even though you're Irish!

Fortunately for him he was joking, more or less.

The two survivors were K, who was the head of security at the poison factory, and a yeoman named J. K had disappeared and might be presumed dead. J lived in Buffalo and worked as a skilled machinist.

I flew to New York City on a Dakota as we called the DC-3 in the Pacific, and on to Buffalo in a craft so old that it would not have been permitted in the Pacific theater in those days.

I found J in his machine shop, one he owns himself. I introduced myself as Captain Ryan. He welcomed me cordially and asked where I had served. Pacific theater, Pearl and Leyte. He raised an eyebrow. What kind of ship? I had my own destroyer escort in the gulf, I admitted. It was sunk. I was on one of the landing craft he said. You guys saved my life. A lot of others. Medal of Honor?

I don't normally play that game. The real heroes are dead. However in these circumstances, I inclined my head slightly. He shook my hand fervently. We sat down at his desk and he made a pot of coffee. What can I do for you, Captain, sir?

I told him.

He turned pale and lowered his head.

That night will haunt me as long as I live, sir. I didn't know what K was planning. He told the ensign and me that he merely intended to warn the kids that for the good of country they should forget what they had seen. We waited till they came out of the country club and got into the Packard. They were so young and so full of life. I dream of them it seems like almost every night. We pulled ahead of them on that street by the Forest Preserve . . .

"Thatcher Road?"

"Yeah, that's it. The lieutenant ordered me to stop the car. I did. He got out of the car with a can of the poison spray in his hand. I couldn't believe it. I kept thinking that I should do something, but in a couple of seconds he was next to the car. The driver rolled down the window. The lieutenant sprayed them all with the cyanide spray. He snuffed out those six lives in a few seconds. Then he rolled down the window so the spray would dissipate. It was very unstable, sir, so in a minute or two it was gone.

He came back to our car.

"Now hear this, men," he said, like he was a captain of a battleship. "This is war! Sometimes we have to take strong measures to protect the United States of America. Not a word of this to anyone or I'll have your asses. Understand?"

We both were terrified. He was crazy. He made the ensign drive the Packard to about fifty yards from where the tanker was stuck in the middle of the intersection. Then he jumped out and jumped in with us. We turned the car around and got out of there. The explosion hit us like the blast of a big gun. It almost drove us off Thatcher Road. Later that week the project was closed down. We were all ordered to the Western Pacific. I hear that K went down on the Indianapolis. *I feel terribly guilty, but I don't know what I could have done.*

Not much, I told him. It's hard to believe that your commanding officer is a homicidal maniac, as I well knew myself.

He gave me an affidavit which I append to this file.

Several days after I returned to Chicago I prepared a report, had it typed out and with the affidavit presented it to John and Mary Anne Burns. We all wept. Our own country killed them, John repeated over and over. I thought we fought a war to prevent these kind of things.

K is not dead. I don't know how we can find him. The Burnses do not want to do so. Yeoman J's affidavit is in my office file if the reader of this story wants to learn his name and K's name.

I gave my report to Dr. Burns. He read it in my presence, thanked me, and said that it didn't matter anymore.

Edward J. Ryan
Attorney-at-Law

211

Blackie

The Old Fella had not attached the affidavit to his story. It might or might not be in his office. The truth of the 1944 tragedy was worth uncovering. However, it did not shed any light on the incidents at St. Lucy's. I had permitted myself to be convinced that the story would help us. I should have known better.

And yet as events of the last several days whirled around in my head like a hurricane trying to find an eye around which to organize itself, an incongruity emerged which seemed very strange indeed. How had the Navy lieutenant known where the young people would be that night? How had he learned that they would emerge from the Club and drive down Thatcher Road to turn at North Avenue?

There could be only one answer. He knew who they were and where they were from. He was, if not from Austin, at least from Oak Park or River Forest or maybe Galesberg. He had recognized them at the poison factory and they had recognized him. It was a murder in the neighborhood and by the neighborhood. If he feared the disclosure of the insane plan in the woods near Delevan, he must have been certain that the young people would talk to families and friends about where he was doing his Navy service. This didn't excuse his brutality but it made it something more than random.

The only link between the snuffing out of young life sixty years ago and the St. Lucy mysteries was that Mikal Wolodyjowski had been present at both of them. Not that such a presence proved anything. Still . . .

I went through the newspaper clippings that he had inserted in his file, most of them about the victims' families. One of them, dated in 1955, said that Dr. John F. Burns and his wife Mary Anne had died in an auto accident. The funeral was at St. Lucy's Church. They were survived by their son Marshal, aged three.

So they had a little boy to replace their lost son, as if a dead child can ever be replaced. They hadn't lived long enough to raise him. Mary Anne was forty-eight at the time of her death. Marshal had come when she was forty-four and Jack had died when she was thirty-seven. She was a very young bride.

So much sadness.

Milord Cronin phoned from Rome. He still sounded like he was devastating the canary population of Italy. He would fly home tomorrow and expected that everything would be in order upon his return.

"Not likely. The situation gets murkier . . . Does the name John F. Burns mean anything to you?"

"Sure. I said his funeral Mass, just after I was ordained. He and his wife died in an auto accident."

"At St. Lucy's?"

"They lived on Race Avenue just across from West Suburban. Their son died in an auto accident, too."

"Jack Burns."

"I remember now . . . The scandal. Jack was blamed. They said he was drunk. I didn't believe that. Those kids didn't drink."

"He wasn't drunk," I said.

"Blackwood, how do you know that? What are you doing? . . . I ought to know better than to ask, right?"

"A full if confused report tomorrow."

He was silent.

"It was a long time ago . . . Yet it seems like only yesterday . . .

Annie Scanlon . . . She was so beautiful . . . every guy on the West Side was in love with her . . ."

"We all die," I said, "some sooner, some later."

"Right." He sighed. "Blackwood, clean all this up by tomorrow. I don't like sad memories. See to it."

The final instruction was delivered with less than its usual zest. The spring of 1944 was heavy on the hearts of all who remembered it.

I returned to the pictures of the six young people. Annie Scanlon was indeed radiant. No wonder Sean Cronin remembered her. What would her life have been if she had not died? College, a boyfriend dead in the Hurtgen Forest or Iwo Jima, love, marriage, children, disappointments, heartbreaks, sickness, beauty fading, tragedies perhaps . . . Would she be dead now anyway?

So great our hopes and dreams, so short our lives. Milord Cronin was well advised not to like bad memories.

When I finished in the office in the evening, I found an envelope in my box. I carried it carefully up to my study, slit it open, and shook the letter out of the envelope. More ogam script.

With the help of Nuala Anne's book I translated it.

Get ready asshole for the big explosion.

Camilla

"A real date!"

"As real as a date with me can be. I'll wear a tie."

"At Ambria!"

"I have a reservation . . . I'll pick you up at your house at eight if that's all right."

"That's a long ride."

"It is possible that you might be worth it."

I was scared.

That's silly, I told myself. Declan O'Donnell is not a scary man.

Yes, he is. When I hear his voice, I melt. He owns me already.

Well, not exactly. I can still get out. But I don't want to.

"You dress up pretty well," I said when the maître d' conducted us to what must have been the best table in that very special restaurant in the old Belmont Plaza Hotel. "Blue blazer, charcoal slacks, red-and-blue tie, freshly polished shoes—regular Yuppie financial services dude, not an undercover cop at all."

"Undercover cop on a date."

"Dragon Lady order you to take me out?"

He blushed, poor darling.

"You go take girl out, number one boy, you useless here now . . . You up shit creek anyway."

"She didn't say that!"

"No, she didn't, Camilla. She just said that I had been at the computer too long and I should escape for a while. I couldn't think of a better way to escape than to sit across the table from you."

I was wearing a black cocktail dress with spaghetti straps, a long way from naked. However, his eyes stripped me, consumed me, devoured me. I hate it when men do that to me. This time I enjoyed it. I wanted him to want me. It had been a long time since I had felt that way about a man. Never before quite like this. Then he took out his damn sketch pad and began to draw me.

I felt the flush creep up my body.

"What are you doing that for!" I demanded.

"Sorry, I'll stop . . ."

"No, don't stop!"

"I'm doing a series on you."

"What will you call it?"

"I'm thinking I'll call it *Girl of My Dreams*."

"Woman of your dreams!"

"Nope. Girl. I'm a boy in love with a girl."

"And we're both kids, Declan," I said sadly.

He nodded.

"Crazy in love."

"Crazy in love," I agreed.

We changed the subject to talk about our jobs. I told him that we arraigned the two perps from St. Lucy's. Held without bail. We wouldn't get anything out of them because they had nothing to give. He was vague about his work with the Unit, as he was supposed to be. They were struggling, he said, with a very tough computer problem.

"Hacking?" I asked.

"That's a very improper question, Ms. State's Attorney. You imply that the Chicago Police Department would invade the computers of suspects?"

"I warn you, Officer, that if you intend to use any evidence in court, you'd better get a search warrant from a judge."

"Search warrants? I've heard of those things!"

"You could hack into my computer and invade my personal life? Read my diary?"

"Easy . . . But don't worry about it."

Then he became serious, which he does a lot.

"I respect you, Camilla, even revere you. I'd never violate your privacy. Or anything else, as far as that goes."

"I know that, Declan."

"I promise," he said.

I wanted to cry.

"You'll just draw pictures of my boobs on that sketch pad of yours."

"Respectful pictures," he said with a laugh. "Well, moderately respectful."

He showed me the sketch as we left the restaurant. It was moderately respectful.

"I'm not that beautiful," I protested.

"Yes you are!"

"I look like a volcano ready to explode."

"Mt. Etna with smoke coming up."

"I do not!"

But I did.

On our way back to River Forest we had a stupid argument about love and desire. It was really a discussion, but I can't discuss without arguing and poor dumb Declan wants to reduce all arguments to discussion. Anyway, don't know what I said and I knew he was right, but I didn't admit it. All I could think about was the end-of-the-evening kiss. I hadn't done that since high school.

It was a kiss worth waiting for. He kissed my lips, my eyes, my chin, my neck, my shoulders, always gently, always respectfully but always with an implacable determination. I replied in kind without much restraint. We clung to each other in the warm summer night in front of my house, utterly alone in the world in the pleasant cocoon of our love.

"That wasn't bad," I said in an unsteady voice. "You're a pretty good kisser for South Side Irish."

He brushed my lips again.

"It would have been better, I think, if you were not a wild Saracen princess from the West Side."

I fumbled with my keys and managed finally to get the door open.

"Declan," I said as I stumbled into the house.

"Yes?"

"That argument we were having in the car? You were right."

"Discussion," he said.

My dreams were troubled but happy. In one of them I was a chalice he was kissing like a sacristan might kiss it, but a living chalice. I didn't mind being a chalice at all, even if I knew enough about Freud to know what that meant.

Declan

"You sleep with State's Attorney, Declan?" Captain Huong demanded when I returned to our fortress on Magnolia Street.

"That's an inappropriate question, Captain."

"You don't fool me, Declan. You old-fashioned like Dr. Huong."

Her husband may have had a first name. However, we never heard it. He was always "Doctor," spoken with great respect for his profession. I presume that he always referred to her as "Captain Huong."

In fact, he had better.

"What do you mean by that, Captain?"

"You screw woman only on her wedding night. I know your kind."

"Arguably," I said, quoting Bishop Ryan's favorite word.

"You better marry pretty soon. You go completely crazy otherwise."

"Did Dr. Huong go crazy otherwise?"

She laughed loudly, no giggle this time.

"He marry me pretty soon!"

"Good for him."

"He smart man. You smart man too, Declan. Now get to work. Be cautious. Our friend very clever."

Her point was well taken. If we were to marry, we'd better do it pretty soon. One encounter of forgiveness, one beach volleyball match, one movie, one dinner at Ambria, and I was thinking of marriage. Soon.

I was out of my mind. Now was the time to stop.

I blotted Camilla from my mind and concentrated on the computer tube. Our friend was very clever at covering his tracks. Perhaps he knew that his second invasion of the Combined Control system had been fire-walled. We must not let him discover that we were invading his own intricate system of protection. One misstep and we'd lose him.

After a couple hours of work with only Lieutenant King and Captain Huong in the war room I discovered something that might be important.

"His code name," I cried out, "is *Polacho*."

"That not good," Captain Huong exclaimed. "No damn good."

Blackie

Pan Mikal seemed relaxed when I entered his office on the first floor of St. Lucy's Rectory. He was wearing his Roman collar and clerical vest over a white shirt with Polish eagle cuff links. Like I say, Polish casual. As compared with my black tee shirt and Bears windbreaker.

"Blackie." He rose from the desk to shake hands. "It was good of the bishop to come out here. However, I am feeling very well for an old man."

"Milord Cronin returns from Rome this afternoon and will want an eyewitness report in preparation for his own visitation."

"That is hardly necessary."

"You know him well enough to understand that he will think otherwise."

"Will he be leaving us?"

"I hardly think so."

"You may want to show him this new drawing of our proposed school addition. I asked that it be delivered here so I could present it to the Cardinal."

"Before day is done," I agreed.

"Also the school board voted to postpone the opening for a week. I assented of course."

"Very wise."

"If we are forced to wait any longer, it will be a serious blow to the New Austin project. Yet I feel that it will continue, perhaps more slowly."

"We will solve it before then," I said with more confidence than I felt.

How dare this criminal mess with Blackie Ryan.

I put the envelope with the artist's drawing in my briefcase and removed the Old Fella's report.

"When you were in Mundelein, I believe a lawyer interviewed you about the events of Memorial Day 1944."

His eyes flickered momentarily, but his impassive Slavic face remained impassive.

"Yes. I remember, it was so long ago . . ."

"Do you remember the lawyer's name?"

"It was Irish . . . Let me think . . . Ryan I believe . . . Of course, he must have been your father . . . A remarkable man . . . some familiar family mannerisms . . . though he was more . . ."

"Sane?"

"Less inscrutable," he said with a brief grin.

Blackie Ryan with his broad Irish face inscrutable? How could this be?

"He is the only one who ever called me 'Johnny.' "

"He is no longer with us?"

"He is not . . . Though we Irish believe that those in the many-colored lands are always with us, kind of standing around and watching. So I must assume that he is present in this room."

His eyes moved around uneasily as if he feared Ned Ryan's spirit, the last spirit in the world anyone needed to fear.

I handed over a copy of the Old Fella's report.

"You may want to read this, Mickey. You will find it interesting I think."

"I think I will not want to read it, but I know that I will . . . They were extraordinarily attractive young people . . . Such a tragic accident . . ."

"My Old Fella didn't think it was an accident. They were murdered by the U.S. Navy."

He lifted the report like it might weigh a hundred pounds.

"Annie Scanlon," he mused. "She was their leader. Everyone adored her. That weekend I would have left the seminary for her. I felt that she found me attractive. Even now on Memorial Day I mourn her . . . We Poles are sentimentalists as the bishop well knows."

"Melancholy sentimentalists."

"Very *melancholy*." He smiled ruefully.

"Life is short, Pan Mikal, but it never ends. Maybe Annie Scanlon is with us in this office too."

"Perhaps."

"There is one aspect of the story that struck me. Will you read it while I wait?"

"Of course."

He closed the sacramental record book on which he was working and began to hear the voice of Ned Ryan from long ago. I looked around the room, not expecting to see the Old Fella, much less the radiant Annie Scanlon, but sensing—in my fantasy-driven imagination—that they might be around. An Irishman must not let his imagination run out of control. Yet in that old rectory office with its phalanx of monitors, there was an awareness of the sacred.

Tears were pouring down Prinz Mikal's face as he handed the dossier back to me.

"The world would be a different place if those children had lived," he said as he dabbed his eyes with a tissue. "It was evil."

"Perhaps we can say that it is a different and better place because they did live."

I didn't know quite what that meant, but I believed it to be true.

He looked at the newspaper clippings.

"Annie is as I remember. Perhaps the bishop is right. That beauty is a gift that can never die."

"Let me tell you what I think my Old Fella missed . . ."

"Why do you call him that?"

"It's what Irish in the old country call their fathers and husbands. It is normally a sign of great affection. My mother called him that when their first child was born."

"So?"

"It seems to me that the killer had to know where they would be that evening. Otherwise, why would he park in the lot of the Oak Park Country Club? And how would he have known that they would take Thatcher Road to North Avenue and drive towards Harlem?"

Monsignor Wolodyjowski pondered.

"That seems true."

"When you retreated back into the woods that day in Delevan you watched your friends talk to the security man."

He nodded.

"Did they seem to know him?"

He closed his eyes. His face contorted into a frown.

Then he sighed heavily and opened his eyes.

"It was indeed a long time ago, Blackie. But as I remember they seemed utterly relaxed, as if they did know him, more surprised to see him than afraid."

"So . . ."

"The killer was someone from the neighborhood!"

"So it would seem."

"There seemed . . ." He hesitated, trying to conjure up memories buried long ago. "I do not think I deceive myself . . . some tension between the young man to whom they talked and the beloved Annie . . . Perhaps she had once rejected him . . ."

"Arguably," I said.

If that was the case, there was even more ugliness in the crime.

Part of the old mystery was explained, though we did not know who the killer was. The current mystery remained insoluble. Yet in the occasional moment as I returned to downtown Chicago on the Green Line, I saw an improbable solution—as if the door of an elevator had opened, disclosed the solution, then slammed shut before I could see it.

This happens in some of my adventures. It does not guarantee immediate insight, however, in my befuddled mind. But I had the distinct, and perhaps superstitious impression, that my Old Fella and the wondrous Annie Scanlon were on the Lake Street L with me. They were shouting at me to wake up.

My mother might have been there too.

I had scarcely been in the rectory long enough to impose quiet on the Megans (a vain project) and to open my e-mail file when Sean Cronin, by the grace of God, etc., appeared at my door, luggage in hand.

He sank into my easy chair, which I had cleared of computer output in anticipation. He was clearly weary from his flight, but also satisfied with his accomplishments.

"I trust you left a few canaries in Italy," I observed.

"You been talking to Nora?" he said. "In truth, Blackwood, I managed to pick up all my markers. It was easy. Someone had made the decision which they should have made long ago that one does not fuck around with Sean Thomas Cronin."

"Indeed not," I observed.

"I stayed around until I collected all the signed documents." He patted a slender attaché case. "I didn't want some midlevel bureaucrat messing up the decisions, which they have been known to do on more than one occasion."

"Patently."

"Blackwood, I have consumed nothing but wine since I left here, no cognac, no Bailey's, nothing. Do you think you could pour me a small drop of your Bushmills Single Malt?"

"The laborer is worthy of his hire," I assured him and prepared something considerably more than a small drop.

He sipped it gently and affectionately, as one should.

"What do you have for me, Blackwood?"

"A story told by my Old Fella."

It was an impulsive decision. Somehow I knew that there was a path between St. Lucy's long ago and St. Lucy's today.

"By Ned?" he said, taking the file. "The one sane person in the whole crowd."

He read the document slowly and carefully. Halfway through, he put his Irish crystal tumbler on the carpet (there not being any other flat space). When he was finished reading, he placed the dossier next to the goblet and rubbed his face.

"What does it all mean, Blackie?"

Rarely does he call me by my real name. When he does it means that he's emotionally shattered.

"The story or life?" I asked cautiously.

"Life . . . Why do I waste my time fighting with those SOBs in the Curia when something like this can happen . . ."

"There are," I repeated my new mantra, "no big box stores available to solve the problem of evil."

He sighed, almost as loudly as I do routinely.

"Is her picture here?" He shuffled through the newspaper clippings. "Yeah, here it is . . . Just as beautiful as I remember her . . ."

"The fabled Annie Scanlon?"

"I don't blame Mickey because he fell for her. Everyone did. I often thought I'd leave the seminary for her, though I don't think my father would have let me. Paul was to be the senator and I the bishop . . . She was from St. Lucy's, you know."

"Indeed!"

"Her father was a big corporate lawyer type. Lived over on West End. He walked to the L every morning to ride down to work. Died a few years after her death. The tragedy dogged all the families down through the years. They never quite got over it."

"Now at least the truth is known."

"What difference does it make to most people? Only old-timers like Mickey and me care about it."

"Maybe the golden young people care too."

"Why should they?"

"Who is to know what the blessed care about? I had the impression all day that my Old Fella and Annie were shouting at me!"

"About what!"

Sean Cronin does not believe in the psychic, much less the mystical—though he acknowledges that Crystal Lane "has to be a saint." However, he is superstitious about ghosts.

"About why I haven't figured out the link between the two St. Lucy mysteries, past and present . . . You noted, by the way, the mistake the Old Fella made."

"Ned Ryan never made mistakes."

"So he claimed."

"You mean he didn't figure out that the killer was from the neighborhood? Of course he figured it out, Blackwood. He's protecting someone."

The elevator door opened again, then slammed shut on me.

He reclaimed his tumbler and began to sip it again.

"Tell me everything else."

I recited the events of the last several days.

"I knew I shouldn't have gone away."

"Patently."

"Will we open the school out there?"

"Not until we find who is behind the attacks. Currently Pan Wolodyjowski and his worthy school board are stalling for time."

"Not after that terrible school explosion in Russia."

"Precisely," I agreed.

My cell phone rang.

"The Dragon Lady told me to call you, Bishop Blackie. We have the code name of our adversary."

"Ah?"

"It's *Polacho*."

Indeed.

"She says it doesn't necessarily mean a thing."

"And the fair Camilla?"

"I think she's in love."

"Why does that not surprise me."

"We have to be very careful. The hacker apparently does not know we have hacked into his system. We're taking no chances."

"Understandably."

I told the Cardinal about the hacker.

"Mickey couldn't be raiding his own parish, could he?" he asked.

"Nor would he set up a raid on this own rectory, would he?"

"No," he said, shaking his head. "Your leprechaun has emptied my drink, Blackwood."

"He does things like that."

"Yet he's all over the story, past and present, isn't he?"

"That does not prove anything."

"Poor Mickey has been a target for love and hate all his life."

"So it would seem."

"That idiot Dogherty is capable of anything."

"Oh, yes," I replied. "I don't believe, however, that the distinguished former Notre Dame professor has the stamina for such elaborate plots at this stage in his life."

"Do you think that Mickey had an affair with his wife?"

"Surely not in the literal meaning of the word. An infatuation, perhaps only one-sided, or a flirtation maybe."

"You look at his file over in the secret archives?"

"Against the wishes of the archivist, who didn't realize till I told her that I was a moral person with you. There were a few letters, but nothing very credible."

He nodded as he drained the last of his Bushmills.

"Maybe I should have stayed in Rome. They offered me a very nice job . . ."

"With respect, I don't believe that you could survive more than a month beyond the Indiana state line."

He exploded in laughter.

"Touché, Blackwood, touché!"

"Mickey's problem is that somehow he exudes both sympathy and the need for sympathy," he went on. "I don't think he understands that. We got anonymous letters about him, but I threw those away. I refuse to take seriously a letter from anyone who won't sign his name. . . . Hell, Blackwood, as you know I have no right to be critical of anyone!"

"Would that everyone were that wise!"

"I can understand why Annie would want to take him under her wing. She always had her collection of strays, animal and human. And yet she seemed very vulnerable herself. Her father was a stern bastard."

"Indeed."

There was, I had begun to think, some danger in dwelling too long in the past—or listening too carefully to what the spirits of that era seemed to be whispering all around us.

"What's she like, Blackie?" he asked, his voice tinged with sadness.

"Who?"

"Annie Scanlon, if she's really haunting you."

I regretted telling him about my visitors from the many-colored lands in the West.

"I sense, feel, perceive dimly, intuit two presences—the Old Fella, wise, calm, always in control. The other . . . ?"

I paused to consider the other, whom to be honest I did not want hanging around my rectory.

"Well . . . there is a certain radiance, though I would expect that from all I have read about her, confident radiance, grace . . . and song."

"You heard her sing!"

"Not exactly singing . . . just a hint of something in the great distance that we would call for lack of a better word 'song.'"

I was acutely uncomfortable. It was a mistake to probe too deeply into these mysterious touches from the many-colored lands in the West. We didn't belong there.

"She had a beautiful voice, Blackwood! Wanted to be an opera singer! Her father wouldn't stand for it . . . Was it a particular song?"

"'Ave Maria,'" I said, the words springing to my lips unbidden.

Sean Cronin glanced at his empty glass.

"She sang that at weddings and funerals and graduations . . ."

He rose from his chair, unsteadily I thought.

"I had better unpack. Perhaps I ought to go out and visit Mickey tomorrow. Informal visit that you can leak to the media."

He had learned well how the game was played.

He returned to the office to snatch his attaché case.

"Can't have you peeking, can I, Blackwood! Spoil the fun!"

"What would be the point? I would still be bound by the secret of the Holy Office!"

He laughed again, apparently having left his ghosts, all his ghosts, behind.

I read carefully all the newspaper clippings the Old Fella had collected for his dossier. There was no mention that Anne Lourdes Scanlon had a lovely singing voice.

Look, I said to her presence, just in case she were around, grant that your reflection of God's saving light illumine all of us. Then I went back to work.

I slept long and well that night, unhassled by spirits, evil or good. When I woke I found that I was pondering the Cardinal's suggestion that the Old Fella had been protecting someone. Here was an important key, though I wasn't sure to what.

As I dressed, the ineffable Mary Alice Quinn appeared on Channel 3, paired with Abbey Kincaid.

"You're saying, Ms. Kincaid, that the Roman Catholic Archdiocese is responsible for the attacks on St. Lucy's."

"They are expelling the poor from Austin. I don't believe in violence," Ms. Kincaid said piously. "However, I can understand that the oppressed poor might want to take revolutionary action."

It was 1968 again.

"Didn't the Church insist that low-cost housing would be included in the New Austin project?"

"Only a small token and they don't really intend to do that. A source inside the Archdiocese has told me that the Catholic Church plans to drive all poor black people out of Austin."

"Can you name that source?"

"Certainly not! The Church would engage in reprisals."

"Well that's the story, Sherry. We'll have to see. Abbey Kincaid has alerted us to the possibility that the Church's plan for low-cost housing in Austin is a fraud. Now that Sean Cardinal Cronin has returned from Rome perhaps he will have a comment."

Perhaps he would.

I made the hospital calls with only a few mistakes and returned to preside over the Eucharist for our devout tourists. I prayed for all young lovers, living and dead, especially Declan and Camilla.

I was distracted by the thought that Anne Lourdes Scanlon was no longer a glamorous teen, nor yet an old woman like her admirers. She was perpetually young and yet possessed the wisdom of the very old.

"Lucky brat," I told her.

At the breakfast table, my peaceful reading of the papers, one of the few joys of the day, was interrupted by two phone calls and two visits.

Mike the Cop told me that a preliminary check of the Chicago police files could find no fingerprints which corresponded to the third person on the ogam notes.

A very weary Declan O'Donnell reported that they had found the location of the URL that had broken into the St. Lucy's alarm system.

"Wroclaw, Poland," he said. "I think that used to be Breslau in Germany. The captain says that does not necessarily mean anything."

"I'll try to get up there later. Go to bed Declan. You sound exhausted."

"I'm just about to do that."

"Pleasant dreams."

Maybe.

The first visit was from Crystal Lane, who knew better than to disturb me at the breakfast table.

"There's a loving presence hovering in the rectory, Bishop Blackie."

"And she's singing 'Ave Maria.' "

"Well, she does sometimes." Crystal drew back in surprise.

"Her name is Anne Lourdes Scanlon and she's dead."

"She's among the truly living."

"Fine, tell her to go home to heaven where she belongs."

"Oh, she won't do that."

Ms. Lane slipped away, doubtless puzzled by my seeming rejection of a good spirit.

You can stay as long as you want, I told her.

Then Milord Cronin appeared at the breakfast table in high dudgeon.

"You saw Channel 3 this morning?"

"I did," I said, looking up from the *Sun-Times* impatiently.

"Where did your good friend Mary Alice get that inside information?"

"Guess," I said returning to the plight of the Chicago Bears.

"Jeremiah Dillon."

"He likes to be called Jeremy now."

"You told him to shut up."

"With far more grace than that, as befits a mere auxiliary bishop."

I gave up on the sports page.

"Get Mary Alice over here. I want to make a statement."

"Better that we call a press conference. Invite everyone."

"OK. Where?"

"The weather is supposed to be nice today . . . In front of the Cathedral . . . Product placement."

"When?"

"One o'clock. Gives them plenty of time to get in on the early evening news."

"All right . . . see to it."

"Remember! Sound bites. Four points."

"Such as?"

"As follows:

1) Archdiocese supports quotas in all new projects of 20 percent affordable homes.
2) This quota has been agreed on in the New Austin project. If it should change, the Archdiocese withdraws support.
3) No one is being forced to sell their homes, save by the prices in the marketplace.
4) Anyone who purports to know of a change in policy is not telling the truth.

"You will likely be asked if you know who the source is. You will reply that you do and he is not part of policy making and is not telling the truth. You will be asked about a Polish pastor in a black neighborhood. You will dismiss the issue as a sign of bigotry and point to Msgr. Wolodyjowski's long record of service to the African-American community. You will assert that St. Lucy's School will be reopened as soon as the Chicago Police Department assures Msgr. Wolodyjowski and the parish school board that it is safe to do so. Then you will be asked whether you'll be in Chicago long enough to enforce the policy. You will laugh as one greatly amused and say you have no plans to leave. Then you may be asked about my fate in the Rockies. I leave it to your ingenuity how you cope with that one."

"Got it! See to it, Blackie!"

I sighed nosily and returned to the sports page.

He returned to the dining room.

"House robes?"

"As much crimson as possible. A warning call to Jeremy might be in order."

I gave up on the papers, finished my cup of tea, and went to work.

Keeping the record straight about St. Lucy's was of immediate importance. Maintaining Sean Cronin's media image was of permanent importance. However, neither would help solve the mysteries at St. Lucy's, that battered parish.

Andrew M. Greeley

Cardinal Cronin is, as I hope I have indicated, a very smart man, as well as a ruthless ecclesiastical politician (and withal a good priest and a loyal friend, perhaps too loyal). However, unlike many other powerful people, he is perfectly willing to put his fate in the hands of others more skilled than he. Thus he permitted Nora to take over his lifestyle and prescribe exercise, sleep, and relaxation and proscribe whiskey and coffee save in tiny amounts. She also checked each day about his consumption of the proper pills. He also permitted me to dictate the mechanics of public relations. Thus promptly at one-thirty, when I had given the signal, he emerged from the door of his Cathedral in crimson buttoned cassock, crimson cummerbund, crimson cape, and crimson zucchetto and walked down the steps with a broad smile. (He refused the crimson socks to which he was entitled.) With his white hair, trim body, and blue eyes, he looked like a Cardinal ought to look and few of them do.

There were a few cheers, which he acknowledged with a nod of his head. He stopped on the last step. We had not set up a podium. Sean T. Cronin does not need a podium to make a statement. Nor a text.

His invisible auxiliary had drifted around to the edge of the assembled media to watch the show.

"Good afternoon," he said pleasantly. "It's good to see you all again . . . I have a statement to make."

He ticked off my four talking points almost word for word, adding only another sentence of praise for Msgr. Wolodyjowski.

Then he answered the questions which arose, though not in the order I had predicted.

One sleeper question, from Mary Alice.

"Cardinal, do you know the identity of the person who leaked the story about low-income quotas?"

"False story, Mary Alice." Most charming smile. "It isn't true."

"All right, Cardinal, false story."

"Yes I do."

"Have you spoken to him?"

"Yes I have."

"Do you think he will continue to spread that story to people like Abbey Kincaid?"

"Not twice."

The final question was about my supposed translation to somewhere in the Rocky Mountains.

"Bishop Ryan is a wonderful priest, a brilliant bishop, and a loyal friend. But he does have this one fault. He could not survive for a half hour if he were forced to live west of the Chicago city limits. Therefore, thanks be to God, I expect he will be with us for a long time."

A big grin, a wave of the hand in dismissal, and he strode up the stairs to the Cathedral.

"I did OK?" he asked me uneasily as we walked back to the rectory. "I hate to admit it, but I'm beginning to enjoy those jousts."

"It could become addictive."

"Now I think I'll drive out to see Mickey. Call him and tell him I'm coming."

"Be careful. It can be a dangerous place."

He waved that away.

Sean Cronin was on a roll. There would be the stirring of many things in the Archdiocese.

"He's on his way out," I warned the pastor of St. Lucy's, "in full house robes. You may want to assemble a welcoming. Collect the kids from Mudhole Park . . . By the way, did you know that the fabled Annie Scanlon was also from St. Lucy's?"

"I think of her every time I drive by West End Street."

No small feat for a woman in her midteens, dead for six decades, still to be alive in so many memories.

I sat on the couch in my office parlor. It was quiet because school was not out yet and the Megans had yet to arrive to brighten the interface between Cathedral and world.

Despite my own hazy sense of her presence in the Cathedral rectory, I do not believe in such manifestations. I am a cynic, a skeptic, an agnostic about such matters. I believe very strongly that, as Père Teilhard put it, there is something afoot in the cosmos, something that looks like gestation and birth. I believe, to restate the matter, that creation is about implacably forgiving love. To believe that is to believe very little and to believe everything. All the rest is trivial. My own "dark" insights are merely a quick intuitive blink of my preconscious. So too for Declan O'Donnell's vision of the rifleman on the embankment. It was merely the natural suspicion in the circumstances of a young man with a very quick mind.

Nor was it unusual that after an intense reading of something that the Old Fella wrote long ago that my hyperactive imagination would picture him lurking at the edge of the meadow, so to speak, where the Celts on their dim and foggy days thought the denizens of the many-colored lands in the West might be watching—hopefully wearing cloaks to protect them from the rain. Similarly, so many had praised the radiance of Anne Lourdes Scanlon that it would not be unexpected that those images of her would transfer themselves to my imagination. As for Crystal Lane, sensitive and mystical young woman that she is, it was not at all unlikely that she would pick up my own images by some yet to be understood form of extrasensory perception—unintentional mind reading.

So that settled that.

As I left the parlor office and walked towards the elevator, I encountered the aforementioned Ms. Lane.

"Hi, Bishop Blackie! Here's the new Young Folks newsletter! I hope you like it!"

"I'm sure I will."

Crystal was magic. She had made the Cathedral the center again for the unmarried young by the power of her enthusiasm and goodness. Hiring her was a wise investment.

"Your friend won't stay here forever," she went on. "But it sure is nice having her around . . . What's her name?"

"Annie."

"Pretty name . . . She was especially happy when Cardinal Sean was talking to the media."

I fled to the elevator.

You should be going out there to your parish with him, I told the presence.

My eyes needed resting, but there would be no time for it. Instead I must think, something of which I had done very little in the last several days.

I pondered the mess on my desk—the Old Fella's story; the unopened envelope containing the new artist's projection of St. Lucy's with the O'Boyle and Sons card clipped to it, the ogam notes, the aged clippings from Chicago newspapers. These were not, strictly speaking, clues. They were a chaos of unconnected hints. Also perhaps the presence, which seemed to have left with the Cardinal's limo for the West Side and the very peculiar matter of the Old Fella's silence about the killer from the neighborhood.

It was most improbable that any of these individually, much less collectively, would provide a solution to the puzzle. Puzzles. Many people had reason to try to stop the New Austin project, but, as far as I could see, not the will nor the ability to use such drastic means. The West Lords certainly had the means and the resources. But would Pablo risk his own kids' lives? And what would he hope to gain? Perhaps there were people within his organization who were trying to take over.

I looked again at the *Trib*'s layout of the pictures of golden young people. They were handsome enough and Irish enough to step right out of the pages of one of Scotty's novels. Next to the sleekly handsome Jack Burns, Annie Scanlon—his date perhaps—seemed to leap off the page. There would have been many tears shed over her death by people who knew only her picture.

My heavy eyes demanded rest. I succumbed to those demands and drifted off. In the transitional state where one is not fully asleep and not fully awake, the elevator door swung open and stayed open. I ignored it. Then, when I awoke with a start—indeed I leaped out of my chair—the door was still open. I saw everything. Feverishly, I considered all the components of my insight. It was crazy, mad, unthinkable—a vision of good and evil so inextricably mixed that they seemed almost the same thing. There would be much suffering when the whole story was told, but told it must be. The dead should not be permitted to blight the present.

I moved the pieces of the puzzle around in my head. They all fit a second time, a third time. There were certain missing pieces, but I knew where I could find them.

The Old Fella might disapprove, but I thought not. His reasons had long since expired. As for Ms. Scanlon, who should have been out in St. Lucy's, she glowed brightly. There was no reason, in fact, why she could not be in the parish of her youth and in the Cathedral Rectory at the same time.

Why, I asked, does the Old Fella, the ultimate one that is, let you frolic around earth? Shouldn't you be somewhere else? Shouldn't you stay there? For someone that half believed in the nearness of the many-colored lands to our world, that was a pretty silly question.

Blackie

My first stop was at the Reilly Gallery for cinnamon herbal tea and oatmeal raisin cookies with Mike the Cop and his good wife Annie Reilly. They too were contemporaries—though from St. Angela farther north—of the Cardinal and the six golden young people.

I delivered the document to Mike with instructions. He accepted it with a quick nod. Then I sat back to relax for a few moments in the most peaceful place in my parish with two of the charter members of the North Wabash Avenue Irregulars. (In French *Les Irregulars d'Avenue Wabash du Nord*).

Mike seemed to think that CPD was at a dead end in its search for the St. Lucy's malefactors.

"I don't know what the crowd up on Magnolia is doing," he said. "They may crack it open."

"They impress you?" I asked.

"The Dragon Lady does. She's one of the best cops in the city. They're very good at keeping their doings secret. If that ever fails, their Unit will become a media sensation and die."

Mike was working on an impressionist painting of the new Millennium Lawn. He had captured perfectly the madcap wonder of that magical place, complete with the eager children waiting for the Crown Fountain to spit on them.

Much of the peace of the gallery was the warmth between

those two once-star-crossed lovers. I took the risk of recalling the past by giving them the Old Fella's story. Annie read the pages first (naturally) and passed them to her husband, caressing his hand in the exchange.

He gave me the text when he had finished and they both turned to the pictures. I sipped my tea and devoured my three oatmeal raisin cookies.

"Madam," I said, "is there a shortage of raisins in this house?"

"Blackie! You're impossible! And you never put on any weight!"

"Don't lose any either."

She darted into the small kitchen and returned with another plate of three cookies. It would be worth my life itself to ask for more.

"I remember this story like it was yesterday," Mike said. "I didn't move in the same circles they did, but I was as shaken as everyone else in the neighborhood. They had so much to live for . . ."

"I knew Annie Scanlon at Trinity," Annie Reilly said. "We joked about the same first names. She was amazing. So sweet that you just could not envy her beauty. In a way she was just too good to be true. You thought that something might come along and destroy her—the wrong husband maybe. Now it turns out that she was doomed, murdered by a nut."

"More likely by a hard-charging shavetail," Mike commented. "And probably someone from the neighborhood, someone who knew her and hated her . . ."

"With a good deal of joy in the act of killing," I added.

"Your dad missed that link, didn't he?"

"The Old Fella never missed a thing . . . He was hiding something that he thought he should hide."

"What?"

I told him, linking the past to the present.

Mike was silent for a moment.

"What is it that Sean says about you?"

"Sometimes in error, never in doubt?"

"No, his other mantra."

"Thank God, Blackwood, you are on our side."

"Yeah . . . You have to fill in some of the holes?"

"You can help with one of them."

I told him what I wanted.

"That makes sense. No problem. The CPD doesn't want to know about this yet . . ."

"No way."

"If I can find what you're looking for, Blackie, the case will be complete."

"There is one other thing you might want to check on. Review a previous estimate."

"You bet."

I took my leave, after many hugs from Ms. Reilly, with three more oatmeal raisin cookies in the pocket of my Chicago Bears windbreaker. As I waited for Mr. Woods's cab to come around the block, I considered the possibility that Anne Lourdes Scanlon had died precisely because of her perfection, a kind of womanly Billy Budd of the West Side—too flawless for her existence to be tolerated.

Why did God permit such a fate for one of his best creations?

Silly question.

Mr. Woods, my personal cabby, conveyed me to the Balmoral District on the North Side and to the Dragon Lady's lair, a great sprawling old house on a street corner. We turned down the alley behind the house and parked at a gate in the fence which protected a huge perennial garden. I pushed a bell on the gate.

"Who sent you?" an African-American woman's voice demanded.

"I know the code," I replied. "You don't want nobody that nobody sent."

"I want your name," she said.

"Father John Ryan from Holy Name Cathedral."

"You don't look like no priest, but the captain say you can come in."

"God bless the captain."

Captain Huong herself, dressed for the occasion in some kimono-like garment, met me at the door leading to the basement and bowed gracefully.

"Welcome to the house of Huong!"

"Jesus and Mary and Patrick be with this house and all who live in it."

"Jesus, Mary, Patrick, and Brigid be with those who come into this house," said Declan O'Donnell with a very straight face and impish eyes. It was patent to me what the fair Camilla had seen in him.

I was introduced to the group of young men and women who in shirtsleeves and tee shirts filled the war room, much like a group of commodity brokers trading on computers or listening on phone lines. A serious and competent police unit they did not appear to be, which was perhaps the reason they were so effective. I was also introduced to the Huong kids, who were serious and respectful. Their nanny took them back upstairs. Declan whispered in my ear that Dr. Huong was never seen in the nerve center but only from a distance walking through the garden.

Then Declan, a young African-American woman named Lieutenant King, and I entered the Dragon Lady's tiny office under the staircase. She poured tea for us in small cups with great ceremony.

On the wall there was a large sign in imitation Old English script which warned, "Dragons be here!"

"Hookay," she said, all trace of the phony accent disappearing. "Now we must make some tough decisions."

"The URL for *Polacho* is in Wroclaw, Poland," Declan O'Donnell said grimly. "The Polish connection in this matter is interesting."

"Moreover, Interpol," Captain Huong added, "tells us the Polish police are afraid to close in on him because he is an asset of a foreign power. You can guess which country that is."

"Why the G needs an asset in Poland is a mystery to me," Declan said. "It makes me even more suspicious of our government."

"The national security state," I said, "makes its own rules. It is not unlikely that *Polacho* has a link with our friends out in Brighton Lawn who were, and for all we know may still be, an asset—with some independent business on the side."

"They can do anything they want," Declan said, "so long as they can say they're fighting terrorists."

"We can of course," the Dragon Lady said as she renewed our teacups with foul-tasting green tea, "continue to probe *Polacho* gently so as not to alarm him. If we find a link between Wroclaw and Brighton Lawn, then there will be justification to ask for a police investigation regardless what the CIA might say."

"And if we don't get it," I observed, "we go to the media with our story. Our friends in Brighton Lawn will have to redeploy rather quickly."

"St. Lucy's gets lost in the confusion . . . We took a look at Father Wolodyjowski's computer," Declan said. "No sign of links between him and Wroclaw. Where is that anyway?"

"It's in western Poland," I informed him. "It used to be Germany, but, after the war, it was ceded to make up for the land they lost to Russia. Now of course Belarus and Ukraine occupy that land . . . Do you have access to the Brighton Lawn computer?"

"We haven't tried yet," Declan replied. "We're not sure what kind of security they might have in their machine, so we want to be careful before we try to enter it. We don't want to give ourselves away."

"And Chief Cragin of TacOne is very protective of Brighton Lawn. He thinks it belongs to him," the Dragon Lady added. "He kind of imagines himself as an extension of the CIA."

"Does *Polacho* know that we have breached his security?"

"He doesn't seem aware yet that we have a spy in his machine, but he must be hunting for us since he learned he couldn't turn off the alarms at St. Lucy's."

"Ah."

My poor battered brain was on overload. How did this information fit my theory? Then I saw it might.

Andrew M. Greeley

"What do you think we should do, Bishop?" Captain Huong asked with considerable respect.

"How should I know?"

I searched for a piece of paper I had brought with me. Alas, it was in none of my pockets. Then I looked in my wallet. Sure enough it was right where it ought to be.

"You might try to see what you can pick up on this computer. However, you'd better get a court order before you do so because it could eventually become evidence in a trial."

"What can we expect to find?" Declan asked.

"Perhaps Brighton Lawn's client."

"From him or her, we could get into them without much trouble and despite Chief Cragin?" Captain Huong said with her most sinister smile.

"Arguably," I agreed.

Upon leaving, I presented Sergeant O'Donnell with a coveted tee shirt of the Irregulars—Black with the entrance to the rectory (740 North Wabash) and the spire of the cathedral behind it etched in gold and on the back in cardinalatial crimson **North Wabash Avenue Irregulars.**

As Mr. Woods took me back to the Cathedral, I was uneasy. There were still too many ironies in the fire, Polacho or, as the case may be Polacha, did not make much difference if the solutions were all here in Cook County. I also worried about my friend Pablo and his playmates. They were criminals engaged in horrific business, though the American hunger for drugs and folly of American drug laws were the underlying context for their crimes. Yet Pablo was a family man worried about the safety of his children and his parish. There was no telling what he might do.

If the Old Fella and Annie Scanlon were continuing their occupation of my rectory, I sensed no evidence of their presence. However, Milord Cronin was sitting in my study, sipping a cup of green tea.

"Like some green tea, Blackwood? It's good for you."

"So it is alleged. So I am told is Guinness."

The Bishop *in the* Old Neighborhood

"What's happening?"

"I believe I have found explanations for both puzzles."

"They're related?" he asked, looking over his teacup at me.

"Arguably . . . However, the whole situation is unstable."

"And you're uneasy?"

"Yes."

"It could all blow up on us?"

"I would rather say that it all could go wrong. There are a number of different factors which are inherently unpredictable."

"Tell me all about it."

"No . . . You know my principle . . . I only talk about a solution when I have all the pieces in place . . . Besides, this time you may want what those in the G call deniability."

He looked at me intently, wondering what I meant and not really wanting to know.

"When will this stuff resolve itself?"

"With any good fortune quite soon. I have given Superintendent Casey, aka M. Flambeau, two missions. Both may require a day or two. Then all manner of things will be clear. Moreover a recent recruit to *Les Irregulars* is searching for some computer information. With the grace of God, we'll bring it all to a happy conclusion."

"See to it, Blackwood! . . . I told the brats downstairs that I'd say the five o'clock Mass . . . Do my part for the team . . . The little choir will sing Schubert's 'Ave Maria' even if the liturgists would object."

"So . . . Pan Wolodyjowski is recovering?"

Sean Cronin paused at the door.

"He looks a little worn, poor guy. However, he is determined as ever, as befits a member of the Polish nobility."

"Indeed a prince of same."

"Do you think his romantic flings—such as they might have been—could be responsible for the troubles out there?"

"Such flirtations could drive unhinged husbands like your good friend Brian Dogherty to such madness. Arguably there were others. However, I suspect there may be a different kind of fury at work."

247

Andrew M. Greeley

"I felt old, Blackwood, out there. Everything happened so long ago."

"A couple of days before the Allied invasion of Europe, you folks were remembering the last time you saw Paris and praising the white cliffs of Dover."

"And I was thinking of young women and wondering why I wanted to be a priest."

I said nothing to that. Sean Cronin had become a priest because his father had forced him to. There must be a president and a Cardinal in the family to beat his hated enemy Joe Kennedy at his own game. Young Father Cronin to his surprise liked being a priest and was good at it. He would, however, have left the priesthood in the terrible days of the 1960s if Paul VI had not named him Archbishop and Nora Cronin, his foster sister and sister-in-law, had not turned him down. Wise decisions in both cases.

"What did Mauriac say about the crooked lines of God?"

"Claudel."

"Whatever . . . Anyway clear this up, Blackwood! Now!"

I poured myself a tumbler of the water of life and continued to ponder.

A buzz from the office.

"Nuala Anne on the phone, Father Blackie."

" 'Tis yourself," I said.

" 'Tis."

"The last time you were Mrs. Coyne."

"Sure, am I not her too?"

"Indeed!"

"Those letters in ogam are *bad,* Blackie," she protested. "Almost Satanic!"

I had enough of mystics for one day.

"I quite agree."

"Don't I still feel the touch of them? He hates a lot of people and aren't you near the head of the list? He wants to show you that he's smarter than you are, which of course he isn't. Doesn't that infuriate him?"

"Why does he feel that?"

"Didn't I tell you that you're the one that's in his way? He has a lot of money, a terrible lot; but be wants more and he'll stop at nothing to get it. 'Tis terrible altogether!"

"Any recommendations, Nuala Anne?"

"Well, sure, shouldn't you be praying a lot and staying away from fire? There's a lot of fire around."

I thanked her and told her to pass on my blessing to himself and the small ones and dogs—two large affectionate Irish wolfhounds.

Then I said the Our Father with strong emphasis on the "Deliver us from evil" line.

Then I returned to what little remained of my drink after the resident leprechaun had consumed most of it.

A buzz again.

"Cardinal Sean is saying Mass, Blackie. Can we go over there?"

"How could I refuse you such a holy experience?"

"Good, I'll put the bells up."

Surely Crystal Lane would be there and directing the little five-thirty Mass choir that sang every night. She and the Cardinal would easily conjure up the ghost of Annie Scanlon.

Not even a pause for a thank you.

"Holy Name Cathedral Rectory, Father Ryan," I announced to the caller.

It was Mike Casey the Cop. He reported one finding which fit my paradigm and asked me a question I could not answer. It was stupid of me not to have realized that he would need an answer. I was not sure I could find it.

If it was anywhere, it would be in the Old Fella's files.

Blackie

Late August had become mid-October as it often does in Chicago when I emerged from the subway steps on Washington Street. The clouds were so low that one could not see the Sears Tower, if one really wanted to. A cool mist had drifted in from Lake Michigan. Having been behind the door when the deity passed out a sense of direction, I glanced around in an attempt to separate State from Washington. I was helped by a kind traffic officer whom I asked where the Conway Building was.

"It's 111 Washington now, sir. Right across from the Daley Center."

"Ah."

Nevertheless it would always be the Conway Building where the Old Fella kept his modest office.

"Hi, Uncle Punk," Eunice Ryan, Packy's youngest daughter greeted me as I walked into the minute outer office. "The Old Fella is in drinking his tea. I'll put on another pot for you."

Eunice looked just like her grandmother, but, so far in life, was innocent of that beloved person's fierce contentiousness. Patently I have inherited little of it either.

Packy's daughters, like those of the real Old Fella, worked in the offices in the summer, imposing enough order to last through the winter months. Ryan family lawyers rarely put anything in writing.

"Punk" is an affectionate diminutive which my siblings have passed on to their children, much to the scandal of those innocent faithful who cannot understand that it is affectionate.

Packy was seated in his office and engaged in his morning ritual of drinking a cup of tea—black in both senses of the word—and reading the papers—*Sun-Times*, *Tribune*, *New York Times*, *Wall Street Journal*, and the *Daily Southtown*—in that order.

I put the same used manila folder that he had sent over to me on his desk.

"Anything in it?" he asked, looking up from the *Journal*.

"Good stuff. Read it."

"I will." He nodded and put it under the pile of papers.

Packy would read the papers, make some phone calls, answer other phone calls, and go out for lunch—always a meeting with someone. He then would return to the office, answer any calls that Eunice or the answering service provided, then take the two-fifteen or, worst case, two-forty-five Rock Island on the twenty-five-minute ride back to our old neighborhood. Depending on the weather he would play golf and swim at the Club (or run in the winter) and spend the rest of the day with his family, in which context his personality changed completely and the silent lawyer became the master of the revels.

No one ever said we were an ordinary family.

"He keep any affidavits?" I said, nodding towards the storeroom.

"Lots."

"Mind if I have a look?"

"Help yourself."

So saying he flipped the *Journal* away and picked up the *Southtown*—the neighborhood daily.

I entered the storeroom, which smelled like a library of fading old manuscripts and searched among the ancient wooden file cabinets. All the cabinets had reasonably new labels, the work of Eunice or her predecessors. None however said "affidavits." It was of the highest importance that I find the document. Without it my carefully built house of cards would collapse.

Then, at the very end of the cabinets I came about one in which there was no label. So I opened it to discover a large folder with *sealed* scrawled on it in very faded black ink. Patently it wasn't sealed, so I opened it. Inside, jammed together, were thick sheaves of paper, some stapled together, some with thick clips and some bound by rubber bands.

Given my own habits of bookkeeping—even with the help of computers—I could hardly afford to be critical of the Old Fella. I worked my way through as carefully as I could. I then opened the second folder in the cabinet and found another folder stuffed even more densely with aging papers. As I pushed aside reams of income tax returns (on which the statute of limitations had vanished several decades ago) I noted an edge of a document with "Affidavit" just barely visible. I pulled it out carefully and found that it was the testimony of one Milos Nowak taken by hand in Buffalo, New York, in 1949. Milos had signed and a notary had certified it. Evidence, despite the faded black handwriting!

I read it carefully. It was indeed the basis for the account in the Old Fella's story. I hesitated. Would Ned Ryan want this document to be used in a court after all these years? Why had he not made it public himself? Was he protecting someone?

I looked back in the cabinet and found, also buried in the tax returns, an additional note.

I presented my report to Dr. Burns without the name of the killer to give him the opportunity to make the decision about revealing it. I offered him an opportunity to read this affidavit. He looked at me sadly and asked if it was someone we know. I said it was. He sighed. What good would it do? Justice, I replied. Justice will not bring them back, Ned, will it? It might open all the wounds again? It might. He thought about it. Ned, I may be a fool. I hired you to track him down because I wanted revenge. Now I know that won't bring us any more peace. Revenge, I replied, is like eating popcorn. You never get enough of it though you're sick of the taste. Forget about it, he said.

So with some uncertainty I have placed this document in my file. If anyone goes through the effort to find it, they must make the decision as to whether it should be revealed, even against the will of my client.

EJR

I knew who the killer was. My father knew too. He had made the decision to accept John Burns's verdict. Was it because he felt the client had the right to forgiveness of some sort? Or that subsequent events had displayed contrition for the murder. I knew of course what had happened after he had written the story and after the Burnses themselves had died. Had that influenced his continued secrecy?

Did I have the right to reverse his decision? Had not the Lord said that we should let the dead bury the dead? The answer was simple enough. The miasma of evil from that spring evening on Thatcher Road was still with us. The crimes at St. Lucy's were directly linked to it. Sometimes contrition isn't enough to turn off a storm surge of evil.

"Are you dying in there, Uncle Punk? It's horrible. I tell Dad we ought to clean it all out."

Seeing for a brief moment my mother's face, I knew what Ned and Catherine Ryan would have said.

"Go get 'em!"

"Find it?" my brother asked.

"Yes."

"Took long enough."

"Shall I take it downstairs and make a copy?"

"Keep it."

"You read the story?"

"Yeah."

"And?"

"The Old Fella would say 'go get 'em.'"

So I did.

I flagged down a cab, went up to the Reilly Gallery and delivered the document into the hands of Michael Patrick Vincent Casey.

The lovely Annie Reilly served me once again my ration of oatmeal raisin cookies and cinnamon herbal tea, even though I had already consumed my weekly allotment.

Mike glanced at the documents I had retrieved.

"Incredible, Blackie! You've got 'em cold."

"Let me confirm that for a moment."

I dialed the valiant Declan O'Donnell.

"Bishop Blackie, your tip provided an absolute gold mine. It's all on his computer, communications with both *Polacho* and our friends out in the suburbs."

"We got them!"

"Pretty much. Right now I'm infiltrating the friends very carefully. They are potentially dangerous people."

"Indeed."

"In a day or two we will have all we need."

"Proceed carefully, we're in no rush. The school hasn't opened yet."

"Our Unit is always careful . . . Can I ask a personal question . . . I'm in a secure place."

"Naturally."

"If one has known someone since grammar school would it be rushing too quickly to propose marriage?"

"How long has this one known this other one as an adult?"

"Is that relevant?"

"Arguably."

"I was afraid so."

He sounded like the air had been exploded from his balloon.

"But then again arguably not."

"OK."

He still sounded like he had sunk into a morass of dejection.

I was not Lloyds of London. I was not about to provide reinsurance for his love.

But neither was I about to reject it out of hand, especially since I was reasonably certain what would happen in any event, even without my practically worthless endorsement.

The mist had lifted when I emerged on Oak Street. Not only was the John Hancock Center visible, but even the Sears Tower had slipped into view. The promise of clearing in the afternoon might well prove accurate. However, I felt almost as sad as the noble Declan. There was trouble ahead.

I knew that it would be big trouble when the good witch of Connemara called me at seven o'clock.

"Blackie, something terrible is going to happen."

She didn't seem very happy.

"What?"

"There's going to be a big explosion."

Declan

Camilla haunted my work that afternoon. I admitted to myself that my emotions were irrational. I hardly knew the woman. All right, she was beautiful and intelligent and sensitive and personable and strong and witty and Catholic. Fine. But there were thousands of young women in Chicago like her, many of whom might be better suited to my personality. No, our personalities might be better suited to someone else's personalities. Marry in haste, repent at leisure, my mother would say. My father would accuse me of "knocking up the Sicilian bitch." Should I not proceed cautiously? Should we not have an extended courtship to get to know each other better?

On the other hand, some of my friends who had extended courtships with their partners and even lived with one another for some time, had divorced after only a few years. Yet on the average and statistically was it not true that fools rush in, to quote my mother again, where angels fear to tread?

Besides, Camilla was an exuberant extrovert and I am an inhibited introvert. Would not that be like mixing oil and water?

Besides, she might turn me down. Probably she would turn me down. I'd look and feel like a fool.

So after I had sought advice from Bishop Blackie and received his "arguably . . . arguably not" which I might have expected, I called Camilla to propose supper at the Everest the day after the beach volleyball finals. She wasn't in the office. I didn't have the nerve to call her cell phone.

Still, Bishop Blackie had not strongly suggested that I should wait, which a sensible priest might have done . . . should have done. He did not say marry in haste, repent at leisure. Maybe he approved. Maybe he thought that we were well matched. Or maybe he thought we would dash into marriage anyway, then murmur, as my mother does when a marriage falls apart, that the Lord made them and the devil matched them.

I concentrated once again on the Brighton Lawn computer. It had some firewalls built in that were superior to the ordinary commercial software protection, but they were not too sophisticated. I would have expected more of experienced mercenaries if that was what these guys were. It would take only a couple of hours, very careful hours, to break through. Our adversaries had been careless, very careless. But that is the way of it with crooks who think they're smarter than anyone else.

After about an hour and a half of very tedious plugging along, my cell phone rang. Fearing the Dragon Lady's disapproving frown I flipped it open immediately.

"Hi, Declan, you called? You can always call me on my cell phone. If I'm busy, I'll tell you. What's happening?"

Captain Huong obviously had picked up the goofy look on my face. She rolled her eyes.

"We're making good progress here. I wonder if I could take you to dinner the day after you win the volleyball championship."

"Sure . . . Where?"

"Everest?"

"My treat, Declan," she said firmly. "You paid for Ambria."

"Only a tip. The dinner was complimentary. They see Declan come in with a beautiful woman. It's on the house. Might be the same way at Everest."

"You have great clout, Declan O'Donnell . . . Do we have to win for the invitation to be valid?"

"Certainly not!"

"Hey, great! Now get back to work. I don't want Captain Huong bawling me out. Bye, love."

"You marry girl, then she not distract you so much."

"If I marry her, Captain, and I probably won't, she'll distract me for the rest of my life."

The captain giggled.

"Lucille, you help number one boy. No mistakes."

She walked away.

"Do you mind, Lieutenant?" I asked. "I think I'm getting in there, but I need someone to watch what I'm doing. It's too important . . ."

"I've been hoping you would ask . . . even peeking over your shoulder."

We carefully went through my moves.

"Number one boy didn't make any mistake," Lucille King informed the boss.

The response was not so much a giggle as a snort.

"You want me to peer over your shoulder?" Lucille asked me.

"Please do. These are dangerous people. I don't want to blow it."

The hours slipped by. The rest of the team left to go home. Lucille called her husband to say she'd be home late. He was a cop too. He understood. Someone said that the weather had cleared up and it would be a lovely evening. Not much use to us.

About eight o'clock we finally slipped into their files. Many messages to *Polacho,* all in English. We dumped them into our disk. There were also messages to Blackie's subject. Not surprising because the subject had provided us with the access to the gang. We dumped those too. No matter what they might do to their computer, we now had a record. Since we had a search warrant for the subject, it would include any correspondence the subject had with other subjects.

The last message to Blackie's subject said, "We blow St. Lucy's tonight."

Then a bunch of cops, dressed in gray body armor and helmets and carrying automatic weapons forced their way into the room.

"I'm Chief Cragin, TacOne." A fat man, looking even fatter in the armor, with a ridiculous red face, looking even more ridiculous in his helmet with a single gold star on it. "I'm in charge here now."

"Who the fuck do you think you are, Clifford?" the Dragon Lady shouted.

"I'm authorized by the deputy superintendent to take charge of this Unit, Annamaria. You will obey my orders. You may make one call before I shut down the phones in this place. Call your boss and tell him."

"They're not coming here, Chief," I said respectfully as I had been trained to do. "They're going to blow St. Lucy's Church to-night."

"Who the fuck are you?"

"O'Donnell."

"Yeah, punk. I know who you are. They all say you will never be the stand-up cop your father and uncles are."

"Don't leave out my grandfather."

At this point I fear that I was losing my respect. How did an ass-hole like this get to be a chief?

"Look at my computer screen, sir. We have penetrated their computer. They say they're blowing St. Lucy's tonight."

"I don't give a goddamn fuck what your fucking computer says, you understand you fucking prick!"

"How do you know they're coming after this Unit?" Captain Huong hung up, obviously dissatisfied with her conversation.

"One of my men infiltrated them," he said. "He ratted them out. They're coming here because they know you've been messing with their computer."

"We just got into it a couple hours ago!" I fired back.

"I said that you should shut the fuck up."

The Dragon Lady, in jeans and tee shirt, managed to look like an offended Ming Dynasty empress.

"You talk to me in that language, Clifford, and I'll have you up on charges. I may do so anyway . . . Now what are you planning?"

"First thing you tell your husband and kids to evacuate this house. We don't want any civilian casualties when the fighting starts."

"Are you going to evacuate the neighborhood?"

"That will attract notice to TacOne's presence. We're going to take out these mercenaries with surgical precision. They have two Chicago police cars . . . We'll have our sharpshooters hidden in the front and backyards . . . They'll probably come the back way . . . We'll cut them down as they come out of the cars . . . A few careful shots with silencer-controlled weapons will cut them down. It will be all over. And we're out of here. And, Dragon Lady, you're out of business."

"That's what it's really all about, isn't it, Clifford? I hope you're prepared to swear that your man told you that we were the target."

"I don't need to swear to anything tonight, bitch."

"Hookay. I'll file charges."

Somehow she had managed to throw the switch which recorded everything that was said in the war room.

"They'll come with rocket grenades," I said, falling back on my intuition, "and they'll blow up the house and half the neighborhood before your snipers can fire a shot. These are real commandos, Chief."

"I thought I told you to shut the fuck up."

"And," I added, "you'd better get your cars out of the alley before they show up."

"Officer, I ordered you to shut the fuck up."

"Sergeant," I said for the tape recorder.

"Quinn, get the fucking cars out of the fucking alley. Davis, you take One Squad and deploy them in front of the house. Jones, you take Two and Three Squads and deploy them in the backyard. Captain Huong, I order you to redeploy your husband and children out of this house. Meehan, you and headquarters team stay here and set up our equipment. Break out the gas masks. Riordan, you go upstairs with Captain Huong and make sure she does not use the phone. The rest of HQ team stays here."

"The man is crazy," Lieutenant King whispered to me. "Off the wall."

"That's what happens when you give a stand-up cop a crowd of would-be commandos."

"I warn you, Clifford, you will be responsible for damage to my house, and my garden and the inconvenience to my family."

"You're finished, Huong," he shouted.

The Dragon Lady wandered over to my screen, looked at it, and rolled her eyes.

"I said redeploy your family out of the house."

She went up the stairs followed by the hapless Riordan.

I slipped my cell phone to Lucille.

"When he goes outside to check his forces, you go into the bathroom, press 9 on the phone, hopefully Bishop Ryan will answer, you tell him we are occupied by TacOne and that he should call Superintendent Casey and tell him there will probably be an attack on St. Lucy's tonight."

She nodded.

"What the fuck's the matter with you guys? Didn't I tell you get fucking moving? Deploy outside. HQ team set up the television cameras outside and the monitors in here. Get the communications in operation. I want to be in instant contact with our air assets. I'm going outside to make sure the assholes are all in the right places."

He strode out the back door like he was General George Smith Patton Jr. save for the pearl-handled weapons.

All in all TacOne consisted of about twenty-four men bumbling around in their armor and helmets and lugging their heavy weapons. I suspected they felt foolish and that most of them knew the chief was an asshole.

While they were moving the equipment into place, Lucille King slipped towards the john.

"Hey, where you going, bitch?" a very young cop asked.

"To the john, punk. And it's 'Lieutenant,' if you don't mind?"

"Sorry, Lieutenant." The kid blushed and apologized.

"Come in Copter One, this is Tac One? Do you read me Copter One?"

A burst of static.

"Come in Copter One, this is Tac One? Do you read me Copter One?"

More static.

In the midst of many such exchanges, Lucille slipped out of the bathroom and joined me.

She winked and smiled.

Good enough, I thought. Blackie Ryan was on the case.

I felt better. St. Lucy's would indeed be ready when the mercenaries arrived. Maybe they would come here afterwards. I didn't think so, but it was possible.

Lucille nudged me. And pointed at the screen.

There was an e-mail message on the screen to Blackie's subject.

"Leave at 2100. Blow church at 21:40. Will withdraw then."

It was 8:35. Twenty-five minutes to go. An hour before they tried to fire a rocket into St. Lucy's. Captain Huong, lips thin with anger, walked down the stairs to the war room.

One of the cops whispered to me as he passed by with a sawed-off shotgun under his arm. "You stood up to him, Sarge. Good on you."

A stand-up cop after all, though not the kind my family had in mind. I hoped that Mike Casey was raising hell with his successor. I motioned the captain over and showed her the screen. She inclined her head slightly. I dumped the message into our hard drive. I prayed that Bishop Blackie had found Superintendent Casey.

Chief Cragin returned in a towering rage. The focking motherfockers didn't have the equipment working yet. He became apocalyptic at the inability to pick up Copter One.

"Could I ask a question, Chief Cragin, sir?" The Dragon Lady flashed her best inscrutable Asian smile.

"Yeah?" he said impatiently as he shoved a hapless black kid away from the controls on the communication equipment.

"Why didn't you raid the mercenaries out at Brighton Lawn instead of risking a dangerous shoot-out here?"

"It won't be dangerous. We'll take them out with surgical precision. Besides, Brighton Lawn is out of our jurisdiction."

"Their cops would certainly have cooperated."

"We need to catch them in the act."

"Couldn't you have gotten a court order to search their house and arrest them on weapons charges?"

If he had done that, there would be no glorious shoot-out.

"Too dangerous for my men. They're safer here."

"But is not the neighborhood at risk?"

"How many times do I have to tell you, we'll take them out with fucking precision?"

Captain Huong smiled again.

"Chief, we got the monitors up."

"Fucking time you made something work!"

He strode over, now Douglas MacArthur returning to the Philippines, to the control panel they had established.

"Davis," he screamed into this communicator, "get that fucking motherfucker of a camera out from behind that tree."

"Chief Cragin," the Dragon Lady said sweetly, "I invite you to look at the message on this computer screen."

She pointed at my screen.

"It says that they are attacking St. Lucy's at nine-forty. Don't you think you ought to warn the police out there in Austin?"

"It's fake! They're coming here!"

He strode away.

Why was he so convinced? Was his informant deliberately lying? Was he just telling the chief what he wanted to hear? Had the mercenaries set him up? Or had the chief jumped to a conclusion he wanted to jump to and misheard the warning?

I wondered if we would ever know.

And I prayed fervently that Blackie Ryan would protect St. Lucy's. My sense of a rocket being fired kept coming back.

I thought of Camilla. I wished I could call her. If the real commandos came by here, the amateurs deployed outside the house would not be able to stop them. We could all go up in an explosion of exploding grenades. A lot of quiet citizens here in the peaceful Lakeview Balmoral District would be terrified, some of them might be dead.

Dear God, please protect us all!

I was taught that when I really wanted something from God that I would make a vow to give up something that I liked. I don't believe that one can bargain that way with God. Still I might as well try to make a deal. After all, I was a Chicagoan.

If we all make it alive, I proposed, then I almost said I won't marry Camilla.

God wouldn't like that deal at all. So I said, I'll give up my fear of marriage. I figured God would like that.

"Copter One to Tac One, where the hell are you?" a voice boomed.

"Where the fuck have you been?" Chief Cragin yelled back.

"Where we've been for the last half hour? We're southwest of Midway Airport, out of all landing vectors."

"You're still in our jurisdiction?"

"Just as you ordered, Chief."

"Stay in touch from now on, you hear!"

"We've been trying to get through for the last half hour."

"I never hear excuses . . . Now what can you see from where you are?"

"There's some haze but we can see the object under surveillance. It is an isolated home near the railroad embankment, a half block away there are more houses. They look pretty old from up here. There are two cars parked in a driveway next to the object under surveillance. There appear to be lights in the house."

"What kind of cars?"

"Cars."

"Put your binoculars on them and see if they're police cars," he barked impatiently.

"Roger."

Then a moment later.

"They appear to be, Chief. It's a long distance away."

"Now listen to me. There's no room for errors or excuses on this one. As soon as those cars leave, I want to know. They you follow them at an altitude where they can't see you but you can see them."

"That'll be tough, Chief."

"That's not tough, that's an order."

I put my Timex in front of me on the desk next to my computer. I watched the minutes slip away. Five to nine.

Lucille whispered to me.

"The bishop was outraged. He said he would see to it. I'm sure they're ready at St. Lucy's."

"I hope so."

I was afraid for St. Lucy's and for myself. I was convinced, more or less, that we were not the gang's primary target. Why should we be? It was the fantasy of this half-mad cop. Still, there might well be a shoot-out here on Magnolia. I doubted that the make-believe commandos could cope with real-live commandos, especially with this overweight John Wayne in command. I had my weapon in the desk in front of me. I had passed my last marksman test at the highest level. But with two sets of gangbangers shooting at one another, marksmanship wasn't worth much.

I did not want to die without telling Camilla again how much I loved her.

You must understand, I told God, that is pure Irish romanticism. But I do love her.

Nine o'clock! What would happen?

Nothing it seemed.

Then I saw a huge explosion—in the back of my head but

somehow in front of my eyes. I shook my head to drive away the image; slowly it faded. The screen in front of me was dead. I pushed a few keys. My computer was still working. Brighton Lawn was not working . . . No, it was dead. Even if it had been turned off, we still would have been inside it. Something had destroyed their computer.

"They're not coming!" I announced brightly. "Something destroyed their computer and I suspect them, too."

"Fucking bullshit, punk! I don't trust computers!"

"Copter One to Tac One . . ."

The copter operator was shaken, his voice hoarse.

"Yeah?"

A burst of static, then a voice inside the static.

"We got a situation here, Chief . . ."

"What kind of a situation . . ."

Silence, then more static, then a voice lost in static like it was caught in a thunderstorm.

"What are your issues, Copter One," Chief Cragin demand. "What's going on out here?"

"The issue is . . ."

The voice went out again.

"You want to keep your job, you answer my questions!"

"The issue is that the surveillance object just blew up!"

That was the explosion I had seen before and the one I had just seen.

"Blew up!"

The chief took this as a personal affront to his authority and dignity.

"Yes, Chief . . . It rocked us back and forth . . . I was afraid we were going in . . . One of the Southwest flights was badly shaken . . . I think they're going to close Midway down . . . the explosions are still going on."

I turned on a police radio band and hunted for the Brighton Lawn frequency.

"What are you talking about! What explosions!"

"There were three at first, the first two right after each other, small but powerful . . . then the house blew up . . . It's still blowing up . . ."

The Tac guys in the room were edgy. They had not been all that excited by the shoot-out at Magnolia Corral. Now they sensed that something terrible had gone wrong and they might be up the creek along with their chief.

"Whadya mean blowing up?"

"Chief, it must have an arsenal . . . We're getting out of here before one of those rockets hit us . . . Copter One out."

"Where you going, you fucking asshole!"

I found the Brighton Lawn police band and turned up the volume.

"Car Five . . . Car Five . . . Do you read me, Car Five? What's going on out there Car Five . . . This is Dispatch calling Car Five . . ."

"Brighton Lawn police," I announced.

"Are you still alive, Car Five . . . Come in Car Five . . . This is Dispatch calling Car Five . . ."

"I'm still alive, Dispatch, just barely. A house out here by the tracks just blew up. It's still blowing up . . . There's ammo and rockets exploding all over the place. A lot of smoke and fire . . ."

"I'll get fire out there right away."

"They'll need help from Chicago . . . and it will be dangerous . . . there must have been a lot of ordnance in the house . . ."

Captain Huong turned on our large-screen television.

"We interrupt the nine o'clock news to follow a breaking story."

A clearly worried black male announcer.

Channel 8 has learned that there has been a massive explosion on the southwest fringe of Chicago, perhaps in the suburb of Brighton Lawn. Midway Airport has been closed till further notice. We learned that a Southwest Airline flight for Phoenix was forced to ascend very quickly to avoid the sudden fire that is raging out of control. Copter Eight is on the way out there as is a camera crew . . . We have on the line Lu Campenella who lives in Brighton Lawn . . . Mr. Campenella, can you tell us what is happening out there . . .

Mr. Campenella is Hispanic and badly frightened.

At first I thought it was the end of the world. I fell on my knees and prayed to the Madonna to spare my life. My poor dog went crazy. There are still bullets flying round down there. The fire is so bright you think the sun has come up . . . the sky itself is burning . . .

Could you describe to us what is happening, Lu?

This house is at the very end of the street, right next to the tracks. There's a half block of vacant land between them and my house, thanks be to God. I take my dog out every night and walk down to the tracks and come back. There's usually nothing in there, no lights or nothing. Tonight I notice two cop cars in the driveway and lights in the house. I don't pay no attention. Then we walk back and I get to my house and I see a flash of light and I turn around. I see one car blow up and then the car behind it, then the whole house, then I hear the explosion and the blast knocks me down. Inside the house my wife and kids are hysterical. Every window blown out. All down the street, too. No one hurt, thanks be to God . . . it was terrible . . .

Thank you, Lu.

Channel 8 has learned that the chief of police in Brighton Lawn has said that he believes the house was the headquarters for an Al-Quaida group or some other Islamic terrorist organization.

Copter 8 is now on the scene. You can see the explosion site in Brighton Lawn. The fire is burning fiercely. It's hard to believe anyone can still be alive in that inferno. Jaime, there are no fire department units on the scene yet, are there?

Jaime is a breathless woman.

We've been told, Roger, that the fire units from Brighton Lawn and from Chicago are standing down till the explosions stop. As you can see there are still explosions erupting out of the flames. I don't think that by the time the fire units can approach the scene of the blast there will be anything left but a dark hole in the ground.

Captain Huong turned off the TV.

"I don't think, Clifford, that you're going to have any firefight here on Magnolia Street tonight."

"I'm staying right here," he said stubbornly.

Bemused by the scene on television, he sat slumped in a chair, head down.

The defenders of St. Lucy's had taken matters into their own hands. I didn't want to know who they were.

The Dragon Lady picked up a phone and called, presumably, her boss. She was far more creative in her use of obscenity, scatology, and blasphemy than Chief Cragin. The burden of the message was that she wanted Cragin and his storm troopers out of her headquarters. And now.

She apparently had made her point. A few minutes later, Cragin's cell phone rang.

"But, sir," he said politely, "I am not convinced that there will not be an attack here tonight too . . ."

"But sir . . ."

"Yes sir, right away, sir."

"Don't stomp on my flowers as you leave, Clifford," she said with her usual giggle.

"All right, you motherfuckers, we're out of there."

They were out of there very quickly.

The Dragon Lady lighted her votive candles and incense pods.

I called Camilla.

"Declan . . . Are you involved in this explosion on TV?"

"No," I said, "not really. We can talk about it over dinner at Everest."

"OK. Are you all right?"

"I'm fine except I'm hopelessly in love."

"Silly!" she said, not however rejecting the sentiment. She has it as bad as I do.

Chief Cragin was leaving the war room, lugging the last of their equipment with him.

"Oh, Chief," I shouted after him, "be sure you tell my dad and my uncles that I stood up to you."

Blackie

"You involved?"

Sean Cardinal Cronin, in shirtsleeves and slippers (not crimson be it noted), appeared at my door, breviary in hand, finger marking the page, and gestured at the TV screen.

"Certainly not."

He seemed dubious.

"I presume that St. Lucy's is safe now."

"Arguably."

"You didn't know this was coming?"

"Certainly not."

"You're not surprised?"

"Certainly not."

"People rising to the defense of their parish?"

"Arguably."

"A bit extreme, isn't it?"

"There was, I believe, a threat to blow up the school with the children in it."

"You approve of what they did?"

"Certainly not."

"You know who's behind it all?"

"Oh, yes."

"You can tell me who?"

"In a day or two when all legal matters are resolved."

"Mickey can open his school next week?"

"I don't see why not."

"Will the cops come asking us questions?"

"I think not. They will not want to take too close a look at who wired the stolen police cars with explosives. They'll be content to cite spontaneous combustion set off by the ordnance in the house. They did not act all that wisely in this matter, not at the highest levels."

"Feds?"

"They will not risk exposure of the truth that some of their 'assets' were involved in a little side business in Chicago while waiting for their next overseas assignment."

"Their security must have been pretty bad if they let some guys wire bombs to their cars."

"Criminals are often lacking in intelligence. I suspect that the bombers were quick and discreet."

"You have it all figured out, Blackie, don't you?"

"I try."

"Like I say, I'm glad you are on my side."

"Patently," I said, as he left the room.

He did not ask about Don Pablo and his merry men. He did not want to know. Nor did I want to know. But, in fact, I did. However, I couldn't prove anything and could not add anything to the meager evidence that the police had. Doubtless they would talk to Pablo about rumors, but rumors cannot provide grounds for arrest. There would hardly be enough evidence when the fire subsided to establish that the two cars had been wired with bombs. Since they were police cars that exploded, it would not pay the CPD to investigate too closely. The file would remain open.

When an arrest revealed who was behind the attacks on St. Lucy's, some enterprising reporter might wonder why the police had not been more active in pursuing the subject of the clandestine group before they were blown up. The truth probably was that the

G warned them off, not realizing exactly what was going down. There might even be some happiness in certain quarters on the police force that someone else might have put down the mercenaries.

Alas for their fate. I asked the Lord to deal kindly with them and their families such as these may have been. Presumably they once had been very brave American soldiers in various special forces. Then they began to cut corners and subsequently cut more corners. The Lord still loved them and I could commit them to his mercy and forgiveness. Also Pablo, who in some quarters, not mine, would be considered a hero.

Mike Casey called just as I was contemplating the wisdom of turning off the tube, consuming what the leprechaun had left of my splasheen of Bushmills, and retiring for a sleep, which would be troubled by violent dreams.

"You saw it all on television?"

"Assuredly."

"St. Lucy's is safe now."

"Keep your people on it a while longer."

"Cragin is toast, you'll be happy to hear, roadkill, history. The Dragon Lady recorded his whole performance at her Unit. He'll be given a paper shuffling reassignment. Huong will be promoted to chief and her Unit will continue to be operational. Young Declan was impressive too. He probably will become an acting lieutenant."

"All of these things have already been decided?"

"My successor is busy covering his ass. Cragin was some kind of cousin. He should have taken out the mercenaries earlier. He didn't because someone in the G told him not to. So my successor is smoothing everything over. The arrests of your friends will be handled by Austin Precinct."

"So my other friend goes untouched?"

"Who has anything on him? Other than rumors?"

I assumed as much.

"Cops figure that his own will put him down unless he retires, which he ought to."

Camilla

"*Timothy Patrick O'Boyle, I arrest you* on the charge of the murder of John Francis Burns, James Edward Reilly, Burke Thomas Boland, Mary Elizabeth Dwyer, Anne Lourdes Scanlon, and Elena Maria Martinelli on May 30, 1944, on Thatcher Road in the village of River Forest in the County of Cook. You may remain silent, you may contact a lawyer. Anything you say, however, may be written down and used against you."

We—Dawn Collins and I—had invaded the Sears Tower offices of O'Boyle and Sons along with a dozen or so cops from the Austin Police Station. Several of the cops were seizing all the computers in the offices.

"You can't touch those computers, bitch," Marshal O'Boyle had snarled at me. "They have priceless designs in them."

"We have a court order to seize them as evidence. Once we ascertain there is no evidence we will return them to you."

"With the architectural plans ruined."

"We will exercise great care to assure that nothing is done to harm the designs. Once we determine there is no evidence on a computer we will return it to you."

"I'm calling my lawyer," Marshal shouted. "This is not a police state. You cannot enter our offices and remove our property."

"You certainly are within your rights, sir, in calling your lawyers."

I was a nervous wreck. This was a big deal. The boss should have sent over someone more senior. I also was a bundle of aches and pains from the volleyball champion match the day before. I had to do all of this right. There might be very big and important lawyers facing me if the cases came to trial. I also had to keep in mind the psychological reactions I was likely to encounter. There were many twisted, tangled, sick emotions that might explode. Six decades was only yesterday.

"I didn't kill them," Timothy O'Boyle shouted, his pale skin turning red, "this is a pack of lies."

"You killed them," I recited my lines, "in the name of protecting the security of the United States. You abused your status as an officer in the United States Navy to murder them. However, you hated them personally and took great pleasure in snuffing out their lives."

We had no proof of that, not that we needed any. However, we were aiming at a confession.

"You're full of shit. You can't prove it."

"Mr. O'Boyle, we have two affidavits from your yeoman on that day, Milos Nowak, describing your activities, one from a time close to the accident, the other from last week. We have no doubt about the validity of the charges."

"It was a long time ago," he pleaded. "I was serving my country."

"Did you take particular joy in snuffing out the life of Annie Scanlon, who had turned down your advances? Did you rejoice when you saw her life vanish in a spasm of pain?"

That was a guess.

Timothy O'Boyle collapsed into his chair and began to sob.

"I'll never forget the look on her face," he said. "Never."

"You don't have to answer any more questions, Mr. O'Boyle," I warned him before he incriminated himself. Our video camera was grinding away.

"We were at war," he pleaded. "There were enemy agents all

around. We were warned often that loose lips sink ships. We were doing important secret work which could end the war early. That's what we thought anyway. These spoiled kids wandered into our station. I was afraid they might babble. My superior officer told me to get rid of them. This is war, he said . . ."

His sobbing by then was almost hysterical.

"You killed my brother, you bastard," Marshal sneered. "And then you ruined my life too!"

"You talked your superior officer into ordering the execution because you were angry at the young people and envious of them," I pushed ahead, struggling to keep my own conflicting emotions under control.

"I don't know, I don't know . . ."

"Mr. O'Boyle," I said, "I remind you that you need not answer my questions. I urge you to call a lawyer and to remain silent till he meets you at Fourteenth and Michigan."

"I don't need a lawyer . . . I'm glad it's over . . . I hated them but I loved them too . . . I wept for them the next day . . . I was only a kid myself . . . I didn't know what I was doing . . . They've haunted me ever since . . . Now maybe they'll leave me alone . . . Maybe I'll have some peace."

I was close to tears myself. So much evil, so much pain.

"He's a mean old son of a bitch," Marshal O'Boyle said, "but you can't prosecute him for something that happened sixty years ago."

"There is no statute of limitations on murder, sir."

"When Doc Burns died, they found he didn't have a penny left. So I adopted this piece of shit to kind of make up for what I had done. He's been a pain in the ass since the day he walked into the house . . ."

I repeated my warning about a lawyer. Timothy O'Boyle dismissed it with a wave of his hand.

"I don't want a lawyer," he cried. "Don't you understand, I want to confess! I want to get her off my conscience . . . She was so beautiful . . . I loved her so much . . ."

He lost complete control then. I tried not to feel sorry for him.

"Mr. O'Boyle, Detective Grogan will escort you to the police station at Fourteenth and Michigan, where you will be booked on the charge of first-degree murder. You really should call a lawyer at that time."

I glanced at Skip Grogan, who had been standing next to me. I was the arresting officer because the crime had been committed outside the city and I was a county official, indeed a deputy sheriff for the day. I was now turning the subject over to the Chicago police. Skip nodded.

"Cuff him," he ordered.

The two cops helped O'Boyle on with his jacket, put on the handcuffs, and led him out of his office.

"I'll take care of the firm," Marshal O'Boyle growled. "You'll never set foot in these offices again! It's mine now! All mine!"

He was a piece of work, a nasty son of a bitch.

"Nice going, Cami," Skip said. "You did good."

"I kind of felt sorry for him."

"I know what you mean."

We watched as the cops led him out of his office, a big, pathetic wreck of a man, still sobbing bitterly.

"I loved her . . . I loved her . . . I didn't mean to kill her . . . I loved her . . ."

I wondered if somehow in the world to come he would be able to find Annie Scanlon and seek her forgiveness. She would surely grant it, poor kid.

"Now if you officers will leave," Marshal O'Boyle said briskly, "I have a firm to settle down."

"I'm afraid you'll have to come along too," Dawn Collins said, dry ice in her voice. "I am arresting you on charges of conspiracy to commit murder, accessory after the fact in murder, conspiracy to destroy property, and other crimes which will be detailed when you are arraigned tomorrow morning!"

"What are you talking about?"

She read him his rights.

"Damn sure I want a lawyer. You have nothing on me."

"Quite the contrary, Mr. Marshal O'Boyle. We have the records of your e-mail to a computer hacker in Poland and to a gang of criminals in Brighton Lawn. Apparently you wanted to delay the New Austin project long enough so that your father would run out of money and you could buy the firm."

"You can't use my e-mail against me."

"On the contrary, Mr. O'Boyle, we had a court order . . . Cuff him, Officers."

So the two O'Boyles, criminals linked by a crime long ago and now destroyed by their link to a recent crime, were led out of Sears Tower and delivered, in separate police cars, to Fourteenth and Michigan. They would be booked, fingerprinted, and questioned with lawyers present. I would be present for the interrogation of the elder O'Boyle, an event to which I was not looking forward.

We drove over in Skip's car because I had come in on the L. Declan would drive me home tonight. Declan existed at that point in another and distant world. I did not want to see him.

"I hear you're dating young Declan O'Donnell," Skip began.

"That overstates the intimacy of the relationship," I replied.

"Yeah? Well, I just want to say he's a hell of a good guy, a great, stand-up cop, and a wonderful human being."

Dammit, I knew all that. I just didn't want to hear it right then.

"I gather his family doesn't think he's a stand-up cop."

"Well he sure stood up to Chief Cliffy Cragin the other night. The whole department is talking about it. His family are just dumb. Everyone knows that."

"Really."

"He's a bright, tough man."

"Is that compatible with his being a wonderful human being?"

"OK, Cami, OK. I won't embarrass you. I just wanted to say you're a very lucky woman."

"That," I said coldly, "remains to be seen."

" 'Course, he's a very lucky guy."

I didn't dignify that remark with a reply.

Deep down, in the most secret recesses of my womanhood, I knew I was a very lucky woman. Yet I really didn't want to have dinner with him tonight. I would probably fight with him, push him away for a while till I had a chance to think about where we were going.

That might be really stupid. You don't do that to a lover.

He's not a lover, not in any sense of that word.

Don't drive him away, Cami. You'll never find a better man.

Who says so? Besides, if I want to have a fight with him, I will.

The rest of the day was a queasy nightmare.

Tim O'Boyle had pains in his chest. A doctor did an electrocardiogram and said his heart seemed OK. The suspect wanted nothing more than to confess. We made him wait till his lawyer showed up. The lawyer, a dapper little Irishman in his midsixties dashed into the interrogation room and announced that his client had nothing to say and that he would fight us in court every inch of the way. The suspect said he wanted to confess. The lawyer forbade him to confess. He insisted. The lawyer told us that his client was in no condition to confess to a crime that was committed so long ago.

"Counselor," I said finally, "despite our repeated warnings, your client admitted his guilt repeatedly. We are not prepared to go to court on the basis of these admissions. We want to take a statement from him. He wants to give it. I think the decision is up to him."

"I want to confess . . . get it all off my chest before I die."

"I will argue in court that any confession today was given under duress."

"That is your right, sir."

"Who the fuck are you anyway?"

"I'm an Assistant State's Attorney."

"What's your name?"

"Camilla Datillo."

"Never heard of you."

"I am suitably put in my place . . . Now I think Detective Grogan has some questions."

Amid sobs and warnings that he didn't have to answer, Timothy

O'Boyle told the story of how he destroyed six lives because of a noxious mix of love and hate which twisted his soul. The horror of those quick deaths sickened me as I listened, despite my sympathy for the poor old man who had paid for it by six decades of guilt.

Murder one, I decided, we'll have to ask for murder one.

The lawyer resisted us to the bitter end. As the suspect signed his confession, the counselor warned me, "I will have you up before the Bar Association, young woman. Your inexperience and lack of knowledge of the law is deplorable. You should not be permitted to work as a prosecutor."

"That's your privilege, sir. We have recorded on video this whole interview. I would imagine that the Bar Association would find your behavior interesting."

Skip suppressed a laugh.

"I demand that my client be given the medical care he needs."

"We'll see that he has a full exam to complement the EKG he has already received," Skip promised.

The suspect was weeping now in relief.

"I finally got it all off my chest."

In the corridor, the counselor changed his manner completely.

"What will be the charge?"

"I will have to consult with my boss. Murder one, I presume."

"You can't put that poor old man on trial for something that happened sixty years ago."

"My knowledge of the law may indeed be deplorable, Counselor, but I somehow seem to remember that there's no statute of limitations on murder."

Later my boss came down to my office as I was typing up my notes. He does that sort of thing often. It's a compliment. You see him in his office only when you're in trouble.

"Wrenching day, Cami?"

"Good participle, sir."

"Tell me the story . . . I don't mean legally just yet . . . Just the story."

So I told him.

He listened solemnly.

"And he still loves the girl he killed?"

"Love of his life."

He sighed, not as loudly as Bishop Blackie, however.

"What are we going to do with him, Cami?"

"We have to arraign him on murder one."

"He'll plead guilty?"

"Over his lawyer's objections."

"He'll want a hearing on whether the defendant is capable of pleading, won't he?"

I thought about it.

"Probably, sir, and the judge will grant it."

"What does the lawyer want?"

"Manslaughter, I suspect."

"What's his health like?"

"Not too good. His blood pressure was high today and his EKG was erratic. He's in his early eighties. He's in Mercy Hospital now under observation."

"He won't last long in jail, will he?"

"I doubt it . . . for reasons of health we might have him confined to a hospital."

"What do you think, Cami?"

"It's your call, sir."

"Buck stops here, huh?"

"Yes, sir."

"Manslaughter with maximum sentence, in a hospital?"

"I agree, sir."

"Do you think he'll care?"

"I think that he would welcome the death penalty. He wants to see Annie Scanlon again and ask forgiveness."

Blackie

Mulier Fortis *that she is, the* virtuous Camilla Datillo nonetheless was worn out when she called me to report the events of the day, as all good members of *Les Irregulars,* even brand-new ones, should do.

"It went just the way you said it would, Bishop Blackie. He wants to die so he can ask Annie's forgiveness."

"Which will be graciously given as another woman I know has done recently."

"Different story, Bishop."

"Arguably."

"It will be all over the papers tomorrow. We'll arraign him and charge murder one. We'll let his lawyer plead him on manslaughter. Jail in a prison hospital."

"He will not live long enough to serve, Camilla?"

"Suicide?"

"I hardly think so. He wants to die and he will."

"You think so?"

"Oh yes. And he will see Annie waiting for him in the hospital room to take him home."

"He's at Mercy Hospital . . . Maybe he should see a priest."

"Bishop."

"Of course . . . I'm having dinner with Declan tonight at Everest."

"Another nondate?"

"What else . . . I'm so bummed out I'll probably fight with him."

"Is that wise?"

"Patently it is not," she replied.

All would be well.

I called Mr. Woods and asked him to take me to Mercy Hospital.

Camilla

Not wise, patently. But I was still in a terrible mood. I was determined to fight with my wonderful human being/smart, tough guy.

Until I saw him at the table waiting for me with that beautiful, innocent smile on his wonderful face and his eyes drinking me in. I melted completely. He stood up and kissed me lightly, but not too lightly.

"Counselor, you look like you had a difficult day."

"So difficult that I came here to take it out on you," I said as a shiver of delight raced through my body. "I just can't do it."

"Hooray for me . . . You do need a drink. I'm driving, you may remember."

"Red wine is about all we Saracens do."

"Barolo?"

"Too expensive!"

"I'm an acting lieutenant now, my love, I can afford it."

He filled the wineglass almost to the top.

"Besides, this bottle is on the house."

He put a little bit in his own glass.

"To the champion in her beach volleyball league!"

He smile and raised his glass.

"Salud!" he said.

"Slainte!" I replied, showing off that I knew the Irish word.

I didn't even need the sip of wine to feel good about being with him. Patently unwise to feel any other way.

"Your behavior at the match was disgraceful," I said without much conviction. "Drawing those pictures which pretended that my clothes were on."

"No such thing! Your parents thought they were adorable."

"And your eyes stripping me every time you looked at me . . . Just like they did when I came into this restaurant. I was so embarrassed."

I really wasn't and he knew it.

"A man's eyes in the presence of such a beautiful woman are not responsible agents . . . When do I get to drive the Fulvia?"

"You don't! That's final."

"I'm a responsible driver."

"I don't care. I love that car."

"More than you love me?"

"I'll plead the Fifth on that question."

We bantered back and forth for a while, enjoying each other's company and the food.

"I really am a Saracen, by the way. Our family is from Agrigento on the south coast where all the Arabs landed."

"And the Greeks before them. That's why you have the face of a Greek goddess . . . As well as the body."

"You are outrageous, Declan Patrick O'Donnell. You have a one-track mind."

My face became very warm and not from the wine either. I must be careful.

"So tell me about your day."

So I told him.

We were both silent at the end of the story. I drank more wine than I had planned. To hell with it. Declan wouldn't try to rape me. Not that night. Not ever.

"Bishop Blackie thinks he's going to die soon. He went over to Mercy Hospital this afternoon to see him. He says that he wants to go to heaven to ask Annie Scanlon's forgiveness, only that she will be in the room with him when he dies."

"I guess those things happen . . . I'm glad I asked for your forgiveness before my deathbed."

My eyes filled with tears and I reached over and touched his hand.

"Don't be silly, Declan dear . . . Now tell me your story. I've been dying to hear it. Skip Grogan told me you really stood up to some Chief Cliffie Something or the other."

"Cragin."

So he told me the story in crisp cop narrative. The Irish are great storytellers, even when they're trying to be humble over their own roles.

"You were wonderful, Declan." I sighed like an adoring teenager.

"I was showing off . . . He was such a jerk . . . My father was on the phone this morning. He blamed me for what happened to Chief Cragin, who is not a chief anymore. He said the whole family was ashamed of me. They were thinking of disowning me."

"And you said?"

"That was fine with me."

"Nothing more?"

"No point in arguing about Cragin. He was their ideal of a stand-up cop."

"Poor Declan." I touched his hand again.

"Well, the Unit is still functioning and Captain Huong is now Chief Huong and TacOne has a new boss and the bad guys are all dead."

"And you're a lieutenant."

"Acting lieutenant until I've been a sergeant long enough and take the test."

"Tough test?"

"A lot easier than the bar exam."

We had raspberry torte and cream for dessert, despite my

protests. I noted that they didn't give him a bill and that he left four twenties under the plate. A good and wonderful man. And I loved him.

As we drove home I wished that the evening could have gone on forever. I also wondered what the good-night kiss at the door of my house would be like.

It was more than I had bargained for. The kiss itself was typically Declan, very gentle yet so intense that it took my breath away.

"Wow," I said softly.

He studied me very carefully, like he was peering into my soul. It would be difficult to fool this man, I thought. So I'd better not try.

Then he began very slowly and very delicately to unbutton my blouse, push aside my bra, and kiss my breasts.

If a woman has boobies like mine, she gets used to guys trying to grope her. They disgust me. But his was different. I remembered again seeing a sacristan nun reverently kissing a chalice when I was a kid. I was a chalice. I liked being kissed. His tongue touched, ah so briefly, a nipple. I sighed or groaned or did something, because he laughed, then just as slowly and delicately rearranged me and buttoned up my blouse.

I leaned against him, filled with warmth and joy.

"What's happening, Declan? Where are we going?"

"Where?" He laughed. "To the altar, where else?"

"For what?" I wasn't thinking too clearly. I needed a long, cold shower.

"Why do a man and a woman normally go to an altar together?"

"For a wedding?"

"What else?"

"When?" I asked, immediately the practical Sicilian woman.

"Soon."

"Easter?"

"Christmas."

"Christmas next year?"

Outrageous practical questions, but someone has to be practical, don't they?

"Christmas this year."

"That's only a few months away!"

"Four, more or less . . . Call Blackie and have him pencil in a date."

Now who was being practical?

"OK, you're the boss."

I leaned against him, not sure I could stand up. My body was still resonating to the electric shock which had raced through me when his tongue touched my nipple.

"Camilla Maria, I'll never be the boss, except on rare occasions like this."

"Declan, I never expected you to be so masterful in seducing a woman."

"I didn't think so either, Camilla. I'll be looking forward to a lifetime of being masterful in my seduction of you."

Another electric shock coursed through me. I'd better get in the house. I reached in my purse, fumbled for my keys, and dropped them.

"Stupid," I said.

"You don't become engaged every day of your life, Camilla Maria," he said, picking up the key while he still supported me with one arm. "You have every right to be flustered."

"Engaged? Is that what I am?"

"I think so."

He touched a breast, as if to lay claim to me permanently. Even through a blouse, the touch exploded through me. I must really be turned on.

"You have to ask my parents for permission."

I would tell them tonight, but they would feign surprise.

"I'll look forward to doing that."

He opened the door and gave me the key back.

"Pleasant dreams, my beloved."

"You too," I breathed. "You too."

I closed the door. Then I opened it. He was way down the walk.

"Declan . . ."

"Yes, ma'am."

"You can drive Fulvia anytime you want."

"That's good news!"

How could he be so damned calm when he had just captured me?

I leaned against the inside of the door. The arousal slowly ebbed from my body.

Why had it been so easy for him? A kiss, a little minor foreplay, and he owned me? And I had known him for only a week or so.

It wasn't a tongue touching my nipple, it was this particular man's tongue. I sighed.

Well, I owned him too.

Then I raced up to the family room to tell my parents the good news.

Blackie

"Annie Scanlon was there when he died?" Milord Cronin asked as we sipped our preprandial drink of the Creature in the unnatural quiet of my study.

"He certainly thought she had come to take him home."

"And what did you think, Blackwood?"

"I think that for someone who patently lives in the many-colored lands she does get around."

I would concede no more than this. However, I would certainly not deny that grace had flowed into the room and powerful grace at that.

"So you go in the room at Mercy Hospital and he's having a little trouble breathing and you administer the Sacraments to him which makes him very happy?"

"He averred that he was now ready to go home. His breathing became more difficult, so I summoned the nurse."

"Who incidentally offers proof that you did not smother the poor man?"

"A thought. In any case, I also asked the cop who was acting as guard, a certain Jose Maria Velasquez, to enter the room and we began to pray. He died very quickly and very peacefully."

"And this Jose Maria whatever saw Annie."

"He thought she was Our Lady of Guadalupe with blond hair."

"OK, I want a complete explanation of how you figured all these things out."

"In the matter of the incidents at St. Lucy's I realized that all the people who would like to destroy the New Austin project and/or get rid of Pan Mikal, lacked the resources and the will to do it. And those who had the resources—Pablo and the O'Boyles—lacked the motives. So I began to reexamine the motives they may have had. It would appear that there was considerable antipathy between the senior O'Boyle and the younger one, especially perhaps because the younger one was adopted. He wanted the company as a base to showcase his presumed talent. Though he had more than enough money to establish his own firm, something in the chemistry between father and son forced him to want *that* firm. There was certainly enough money in the company to continue the New Austin but if there were a serious slowdown, they would have to fall back on money that belonged to Marshal O'Boyle. Thus the firm as such had no motives for a slowdown, but Marshal O'Boyle did. He seems to have been crazed on the subject. Witness also his bizarre letters to me in ogam script. I suspected him because he had studied in Ireland. But I knew he was the one when we were able to compare his fingerprints, taken from his reworking of the artist's perspective on the St. Lucy's School."

"Why would anyone want to do anything that risky?"

"He knew I was poking around. It has been suggested that he wanted to prove he was smarter than I am."

"But that's crazy!"

"A man who was adopted at four by an irascible parent who suffered from guilt for having killed the boy's brother and ruined his father's life may well be driven to manifest his superiority to his father—which one gathers he was trying to do all his life . . . In any event I turned his e-mail address over to Declan O'Donnell, who is alleged to be the number one boy for your good friend Chief Annamaria Huong. He quickly uncovered links between Marshal O'Boyle and the gang in Brighton Lawn as well as to the hacker in Poland who disarmed the security at St. Lucy's."

"This Marshal O'Boyle must be around the bend, Blackwood."

"Let us say he suffers from seriously complicated emotional problems and delusions of grandeur such that he drove away his wife and children and has entertained a long series of mistresses from foreign countries. He didn't murder anyone, however."

"He could have been responsible for the murder of Mickey Wolodyjowski."

"When you hire thugs and goons, you don't have complete control of what they do."

"Is this the way your reasoning went?"

"Hardly. I came at it from the perspective of 1942. I had picked up from family folklore that my Old Fella had dealt with some sort of scandal from that era. Fortunately, there was a record of such a case in his files. He had discovered how the young people had died, though he seemed not to have noticed that the killer had to be someone who knew them—as you yourself observed, the late Admiral Edward J. Ryan, USNR would not have missed that."

"No way."

"So he was covering up for someone with what he took to be good reason. Then I noted when considering the pictures of the golden youths, as I thought of them . . ."

"Recently on the front page of the *Tribune* again."

"Indeed. I noted that Jack Burns looked much like Marshal O'Boyle. I also remembered that Marshal O'Boyle did not look at all like his father. My Old Fella had left a note in the file saying that when Dr. Burns died, Marshal had been adopted by a friend of the family. Thus I concluded tentatively that Tim O'Boyle had adopted Marshal Burns and that the Old Fella was silent about the deaths of the young people because he figured that some sort of amends were being made."

"Which I suppose it was."

"It has developed that it was never a happy family relationship. Marshal was a brilliant young man who wanted his own architectural and development firm because he believed he was in the class of Frank Gerry. He also had made a substantial amount of money in various successful speculations. Why would he not then establish his own firm? However, he wanted his putative father's firm, to show that he had trumped his father. He is, it develops a seriously warped person. He did not need the money. He wanted fame and in some fashion fame at the cost of his father's failure."

"Weird."

"Patently . . . I later learned through the offices of Mike Casey . . ."

"Your Flambeau?"

"Some would say Captain Hastings, I think quite unjustly. I learned that the younger O'Boyle had a very large amount of money and had made many offers to buy the firm, but the older man would have none of it. However, after further exploration Mike the Cop learned that the New Austin project, while developing nicely, was not on as solid a financial footing as one would have hoped. Thus Tim O'Boyle might have been forced to take money from his son to finish it successfully, enough money to give Marshal a controlling interest. The result of this crooked reasoning was, at considerable saving to the taxpayers, the authorities were able to arrest father and son at the same time."

"The project will continue?"

"It has to. The firm has too many commitments to back out of it now. Fortunately, several of the junior partners are not without talent."

"Will the young guy do time?"

"Doubtless. He may not have been directly involved in the two raids at St. Lucy's but he certainly conspired with the commandos in both, at least as the conspiracy laws are interpreted. Moreover, he knew they were coming after St. Lucy's again the night they met their fates. He might also be considered an accessory to murder, though we don't know who killed the people whose bodies were placed in the sanctuary of the church. So that charge will be hard to prove."

"He's a weird duck, Blackwood. Why bother with all that stuff?"

"It may well emerge in court that he enjoyed conspiracies."

"What would they have done that night if parties unknown had not wired their cars?"

"I consider it likely that a number of them would have found their way to the L tracks and fired four rockets into the school, which would have been enough to destroy the whole building. That, alas, cannot be proven in a conspiracy charge, but then it need not."

"How much do these mercenaries charge for such services?"

"Mercenaries who were assets of the G . . . One would think a lot of money. The State's Attorney is searching amid Marshal O'Boyle's records to discover evidence of any transfer of funds to accounts in the Caymans. If the G finds out that's going on, they won't like it."

"Anything more?"

"I was also struck when I was in the O'Boyle office, by the younger O'Boyle's claim that they were receiving threats from Islamic terrorists. I saw no reason to believe that, so I was skeptical even then. Why should Al-Quaida waste time and effort on St. Lucy's?"

"It's almost"—he frowned thoughtfully—"as if the whole thing were designed with the happy death of Timothy O'Boyle in mind."

At times Sean Cronin's wisdom surprises me.

"Arguably."

"I noticed on the wedding schedule that the O'Donnell kid is going to marry that gorgeous Sicilian woman in three months. He didn't waste much time, did he?"

"Would anyone?"

"A good point . . . Well, Blackwood, you do the ceremony and tell your strawberry story. I'll preside from the throne."

"They will be delighted. However, I must note for the record that it would be equally perspicacious to say that the virtuous Camilla didn't waste much time either."

"Not bad, Blackwood, not bad at all . . . You were lucky in some ways . . . Of course your father was a big help to you."

"For which I offer thanks every day."

"Also that the criminals were both so stupid."

"Yet they almost got away with it."

Blackie

Six in the morning this time around.

The ineffable Mary Alice with her usual greeting.

"Blackie, what the hell's going on over there?"

"To my knowledge, nothing."

"There's something on the line from DC. It says you have been appointed Archbishop of Chicago."

"Patently absurd."

"Let me read it to you. 'The Papal Nunciature announced this morning that His Excellency the Most Reverend John B. Ryan, Auxiliary to the Cardinal Archbishop of Chicago, has been elevated to the rank of Coadjutor Archbishop' . . . What's a Coadjutor?"

"A helper, just like an auxiliary. As our German friends would say, *mach nichts*."

"Oh," she said, disappointed it would seem. "But, hey, it also says with right to succession . . . What's that mean?"

"Does it say anything more?"

"Nope, it has a bio of you and of Cardinal Sean; yours is shorter."

"Utterly appropriate."

So I was not to be Apostolic Administrator. I breathed a very loud sigh of relief. However, that had always seemed unlikely. Sean

Cronin would never have made the deal if that were to be the case. What would be the point?

"Does right to succession mean you'll succeed him someday?"

"Only if Cardinal Cronin sees fit to resign, which I take it we both agree is most unlikely. Or if he should die before I did, which, given his health and mine, also seems most unlikely."

"Do you have a comment for the record?"

I had been prepared for the event. Why else had Milord Cronin gone to Rome save to cut such a deal? I had not, however, an appropriate comment.

Then it came to me.

"I am very happy that I do not have to face the prospect of living west of the Fox River."

Then I rolled over in my bed and went back to the sleep to which the just man, if only marginally just, is entitled.